SAPPHIRE
OF
PREJUDICE

Forbidden Conflicts
~~ Book Four ~~

ANN M PRATLEY

BY ANN M PRATLEY

Forbidden Conflicts Series
Amethyst of Youth
Ruby of Law
Diamond of War
Sapphire of Prejudice

Power Moore Investigation Tales
Hoonigan
Resolution of Happiness
Home by the Sea

Freedom of Flight Series
Christian
Brandon

Painful Deliverance Series
Painful Deliverance
Darkness of Heart
Friendship of Desire

Golden Desires Series
The Golden Desires
The Golden Supremacy
The Golden Unity

Chisholm Manor Series
Alessandra

CHAPTER 1

As Greg Leadbetter used his well-defined and well-tattooed arm muscles to smoothly slice through the piece of wood in front of him, his mind was active. Months had passed since the night of the gala event that had gone so wrong. On that night, the Leadbetter gang had planned to steal diamonds. In charge of the night had been Pete Leadbetter - at that time, the head of the Leadbetter gang. Greg didn't know who was now in charge of the family, but he knew it wasn't Pete. It couldn't be since he'd been shot and instantly killed that night.

Greg moved forward to place another length of log on the chopping block. It was hard work, living the way he was, but since he'd left town, he hadn't looked back. He was out in nature. That was good for his soul. He was living off the grid and away from everything and everyone. Even the home he'd been living in until that night, he didn't miss. He knew he didn't have to worry about that. He'd left his cousin's son, Phillip Leadbetter, living in it. Even if Phillip went and moved in with his girlfriend, Phillip would still make sure the house was alright. Phillip was a Leadbetter, but he was a good man. Not all Leadbetters were. Phillip was.

Slicing through yet another length of log, Greg wasn't surprised by his thinking and memories flowing over him. Although he had no desire to return to the populated town or the Leadbetter lifestyle, he did still miss a few good people from his life. His cousin, Mark Leadbetter, had always been more than a cousin. They'd been friends. Greg hadn't contacted Mark to tell him where he was, or even tell him that he was okay. That would eventually change. Even if Mark's daughter,

Sasha, had remembered to pass on the message that Greg had given her shortly after the gala, saying that Greg was okay and going dark for a while, Mark deserved better. Greg wasn't ready to make contact yet, but he would.

Yes, he missed Mark, and Mark's wife, Stacey. They'd grown up close together. It still didn't feel normal to not see or talk to them. It equally didn't feel normal not to have Rhett around. Rhett wasn't a Leadbetter but had been pulled into the Leadbetter gang by Mark's mother and father when Rhett, Mark, and Greg had been teenagers. There had always been a close bond between Mark, Greg, and Rhett. That bond had lasted right through to their current ages. At the golden age of fifty, Greg had to concede that he didn't generally feel as old as the number sounded. He'd always kept fit, as had been the way of the family - not in a gym-goer kind of way, but more of a naturally rugged lift-and-cart-heavy-items kind of way, and a punch-up kind of way. Violence wasn't something that Greg liked, but it went hand in hand with how the family lived. It had been exciting in his youth. As he'd grown older, the excitement had worn off. He didn't want to hurt anyone. He equally didn't want to see anyone he cared about get hurt - or worse.

Assessing the amount of wood he'd chopped, Greg looked up at the sky. The sun was high. He knew it must be about noon. That meant it was about time to quit with the wood chopping and knock off for the rest of the day. He'd never been one to sit around for too long. Since arriving at the cabin that he'd inherited from his mother's family, he'd begun to appreciate the peace of it. His cabin was remote, with no other home nearby. All around him were trees. From the cabin's small veranda was a view he'd grown to love. It was just open enough for him to be able to see the blue water of the lake below, but also enclosed enough by trees so that anyone glancing upward from down below wouldn't necessarily see the cabin. It was a perfect spot for him to be.

After taking time to stack his freshly chopped wood against the small area of wall that got a few hours of sun each afternoon, he walked indoors. Before truly relaxing each day, he liked to make sure he was prepared for the night to come. In the city, he hadn't taken as much notice of when the sun disappeared, or how the temperature changed when it did. In his city home, he'd had electrical heating of one sort or another. There was no electricity at the cabin. No electricity and no bills. He'd left much of modern-day living behind when he'd decided to walk away from the life he'd been living.

Filling a large basket with some of the oldest and driest chopped wood, he thought about his departure from his city life and his gang-like family. He'd planned to escape all of that straight after the gala job. He'd not been sure how the theft of the jewels would go that night. Pete Leadbetter had been a criminal of the natural kind. Although Leadbetters had always survived off theft, they tried to avoid hurting anyone. It had been a consensus that no piece of jewelry was worth going to prison for. For the most part, it was a peaceful type of crime - pickpocketing or small scale theft. The job that had been attempted the night of the gala hadn't been intelligent or well-planned. Pete had heard about something he'd wanted to grab for himself, and that had turned out to be his entire plan - smash and grab.

Greg shook his head as he once again considered the stupidity of Pete over that night. There was no possible way that the Leadbetters could have walked away with those jewels. Greg suspected that Pete might not have been missed by many in the gang following his death. Pete had formed a pretty solid reputation for violence and murder. He'd never been caught, but he'd equally never hidden from his own people and family that he'd done the horrific things he'd done. He'd used his tales of horror to intimidate and control others. That had been his way since they'd been kids. It had been years since Leadbetters had stopped having large social family gatherings, but Greg could remember them from his childhood. He could clearly remember how Pete would torture any dog unfortunate to have been taken along to a gathering. For his ways of hurting people and animals, Pete had always ended up getting hurt by one adult or another on those days. He'd been a kid. That had never been a valid excuse to any of the grownup Leadbetters. He'd caused pain. They'd made sure he felt it as a consequence.

Carrying in and unloading the second basket of firewood, Greg felt the familiar conflicting emotions about Pete's death. It hadn't come as any surprise. Pete had been a vicious person all his life. In that regard, some would say that he deserved to be killed. Regardless, family was family. Greg wanted to be free from the Leadbetter name and lifestyle, but one of their own being killed was something that made him consider the value of his own life.

Preparation for the evening to come completed, he grabbed a can of beer from the large bucket of cold water he always kept handy in the kitchen. The cabin wasn't subjected to external heat for much of the day, but it had been built to take advantage of a freshwater spring that flowed nearby. It had taken a while for Greg to get used to washing in the coldness of it, but he'd persisted in doing that rather than waste firewood to run a fire and boil water early in the day. He'd never have thought to take cold showers in the city. He'd grown to like them at the cabin.

On the veranda, he sat on his favorite wooden chair. He knew his mother's grandfather had hand-crafted it from wood that grew near the cabin. It was just one of many items that had been made rather than bought. Inside the cabin were many remnants that told the story of what his great-grandfather had been like as a person, and what he'd been like as a husband and father.

As he took a well-appreciated sip of his cold beer, Greg subconsciously glanced to his left. There sat the matching chair that had been crafted with the same level of care and love as the one he sat in. Two chairs that had stood the test of time - that was what Greg believed anything with strength and heart should be like.

Weeks earlier, Rhett had sat in that other chair. Greg felt wistful about that. They'd known each other for much of their lives, seeing each other almost every day for one reason or another. They'd been friends. The two of them, along with Mark, had formed an unbreakable bond early on that had served each of them well in however they'd needed it. Greg had never anticipated the three of them would ever grow apart.

Thinking about Mark, he knew he missed him. Greg knew there was no reason why he couldn't go home. He'd escaped to the cabin purely out of a desire to get away. He could call Mark at any time, but he hadn't. Mark would know he was okay, thanks to Sasha passing on Greg's message. The time would come when Greg would feel the need to be around people again. Until then, he would stay where he was.

Glancing down toward the lake, he felt tears threaten. He missed Mark. He missed Rhett. He missed Stacey. He even missed all of Mark's kids - each of them now a young adult that he'd watched grow up from birth. He had no kids of his own that he knew of. Being a part of Mark's kids' lives had always been something he'd enjoyed. Phillip, David, Sasha, Rex, and Anya were all good kids, even though they got into trouble. That wasn't their fault. That was the way of the Leadbetter family. Greg knew he was fortunate to have them in his life. If anything happened to any of them, he suspected he'd be as devastated as Mark and Stacey would be.

He took a deep breath as he felt the tears subside. He'd go home when it felt right. It didn't feel right yet. Alone in the cabin that had been left to him was right where he was meant to be. He'd needed the solitude before the night of the gala. He'd needed it even more since. There was a part of him that wished he'd taken women more seriously throughout his life. Every time he'd gotten involved with someone, he'd tried to make it work. It had never been a long time before what had seemed like happiness in love leaned more toward unhappiness. He hadn't worried about the high turnover of women when he'd been younger. Having reached the ripe old age of fifty, he did have some regrets in that department. He currently wanted to be alone. He didn't think he wanted to be alone forever. The unknown was, who was he supposed to be with?

That question was one that had plagued him for some time. He'd always been drawn to naturally select women for partners and lovers. His heart, however - that told him it was quite possible that his soulmate wasn't a woman at all. Not only was it a man, but it was a man he'd grown up with and had known for almost his entire life.

He could still remember the moment that Rhett had kissed him. The gala night had been crazy in more ways than one. Rhett had kissed him, and he'd kissed Rhett back. It was something they'd never done before, but it hadn't felt wrong. It had felt like something they should have taken some time to explore. They hadn't. As soon as they'd reached the cabin, whatever had pushed Rhett to be so bold had then pushed him to retreat. It had seemed like the kiss had never even happened. That saddened Greg. He was confused about his feelings for a man, but he still would have preferred to have explored them. For Rhett, the only option appeared to have been to turn away and leave. Whether that was because of embarrassment or regret, Greg had no idea.

CHAPTER 2

Rhett woke sharply from the nudge the body beside him delivered. Turning, he took a moment to look at the shape in the sunlight filtering through a drawn curtain. He didn't know who the woman was that lay next to him. He remembered meeting a few the night before. Which one had taken him back to their place, he had no idea.

Sitting up with as much subtlety as he could muster, he hoped he'd be able to slip out of the bed and out of the room without notice. He didn't get far with that desire as he realized the nudge hadn't been accidental. A hand wrapping around his lack of erection made the idea of leaving not so important.

As he felt the hand begin to stroke up and down along the length of him, he eased back till he was lying down again. He didn't want to have anything to do with the woman, whoever she was. Regardless, if she was going to help him with more escaping from thoughts about someone else, Rhett knew he might as well lie back and let her.

He quickly grew aroused, just as he always had when he was with any woman. He'd only ever been with women. He knew with full honesty that he'd never looked at a guy and desired him sexually. Why, then, did that moment when he and Greg had kissed remain so vivid in his head? Time had passed since that night, and he'd gotten out of there as soon as he could. Greg had been his friend forever, so of course he would miss his company and his conversation. The problem was that it wasn't just the company and conversation that he thought about. It was that kiss.

Annoyed that his thoughts had yet again returned to a moment that he didn't want them to, he pushed the woman onto her back and worked his way down her body. Not only was he attracted to women, but he gained true enjoyment from using his talents to please them.

Feeling the hips under him begin to move as he worked his tongue, he smiled to himself without stopping his effort. He loved women's bodies. They were beautiful, soft, and incredibly sexy, no matter their age, size, or shape. He'd never desired anything different - *never*.

Straight after hearing and feeling the woman reach orgasm, Rhett moved upwards and plunged into her. If one thing could turn his mind off from thinking about having kissed his best friend - a man - it was hard-out thrusting into the moist warmth of a woman.

After toppling over the peak of pleasure, he rested on the woman, not bothering to kiss her or tell her he wanted to see her again. Those formalities, he had no time for. Whoever she was, she'd served the purpose of providing Rhett with a bed for the night and taking his mind off someone else. The night before, it had been the same thing but with a different woman.

The pattern had repeated since he'd walked away from Greg. Night after night, he'd been drifting. He hadn't stayed with Greg at the cabin. He didn't want to be there with so much confusion in his head. He equally didn't want to face Mark or any other person from the Leadbetter gang. He'd kissed a man. That was something that he knew certain people in the Leadbetter family held the highest level of prejudice about. Rhett was confused about his feelings, but he'd never had any strong feelings about the sexuality of other people. He'd quietly hated hearing the prejudicial slurs of the people who had taken him in when he'd been a teenager. He didn't feel the same way they did. That didn't mean he wanted them to know how he felt about Greg or the kisses they'd shared.

CHAPTER 3

As Mark Leadbetter looked around the small family gathering in his home, he felt a mix of emotions. At the table with him was his wife, Stacey - the only woman he'd ever loved, desired, and wanted to have as his lover. Also at the table were three of their children. Sasha, Anya, and Phillip were all alive and healthy. For that, Mark was grateful. Two of his other sons weren't there. One, he knew might or might not turn up anytime. David had gone on the run after the gala night had gone bad. Nobody had heard from him since. The other son missing from the table was Rex. Having been shot and killed at the gala event, Rex would never again attend any event held by the family or anyone else.

As his thoughts briefly pondered Rex, Mark quickly refocused. He still had plenty of moments when he had to sit and let the tears flow as he thought about the son he would never see again. He suspected the sadness would never go away, but every day he tried to focus on the positive things in his life.

"You want me to be your bridesmaid?" Sasha asked after hearing the question Phillip's bride-to-be, Daisy had asked.

Daisy grinned at Phillip and then turned back to face Sasha again.

"Phillip and I both want you to be my bridesmaid, Sasha," she said. "And you, too, Miss Anya," she continued, looking at the youngest Leadbetter at the table. "If you'd like to."

Anya smiled and clapped her hands excitedly, inspiring everyone to laugh at her enthusiasm.

"Yeah, of *course*, I want to!" she exclaimed. "Wedding now, and little baby flowers on their way too?"

Phillip looked at Daisy and saw her knowing smile. They'd already planned when they wanted to begin their family, but that plan wouldn't kick in until they were wed.

"Not yet, baby sister," he said, teasing Anya and knowing exactly how she'd respond.

"I'm not a baby!" Anya said on cue, laughing with her oldest brother.

Mark looked at Stacey and saw her smile. It was good to see her happy again. He knew it wasn't a secure happiness. She had her moments of intense grief, just as he did. Regardless, they both knew they had things to be grateful for.

"If your wedding is only a couple of weeks away, what can we help you with to get ready for it?" Stacey asked as she turned toward the young couple. Seeing her oldest son so much in love was something that provided her with not only a sliver of happiness but also hope.

Although she hadn't been born as part of the Leadbetter family, when she'd fallen in love with Mark, she had accepted their ways. She'd followed their direction about raising kids to become pickpockets and thieves, but she'd always worried about it. The flow-on had resulted in the death of one of her boys and the disappearance of another. Some days, that was more than she thought she could bear. With Mark to lean on, she pushed through each day, focusing on one day at a time.

As she listened to the reply from her oldest son, she felt Mark's hand reach under the table and seize hers. It was his way of providing her with strength and reassurance. Strength to keep going, no matter how hard it felt at times. Reassurance that he was there with her, no matter what they had to go through.

"Nothing," Phillip said. "It's only our two immediate families, so the number of people is small. It's being held at the beach - just a small ceremony. The only thing we've had to pay for is the celebrant, and that's already done."

"But afterward?" Stacey asked. "You can invite people here, and we'll put on food and drinks for everyone?"

Phillip looked at Daisy and smiled. They'd already agreed that they wouldn't ask his parents for anything, given their ongoing grief. They'd equally decided that if his mother and father offered anything, they would accept.

"We would love that," Daisy said as she grinned at Stacey and Mark. "If you're sure."

Stacey smiled. She'd lost two sons, at least for the moment. She needed to feel needed by someone else to fill the gap that had been left.

"We're sure," she said. "Let me know the numbers and any particular foods to avoid, and we can do that for you. It'll be nice to meet your family, Daisy."

Daisy felt happy. She'd met the man of her dreams, and they were on track to begin a long and happy life together. Part of that was her dream of becoming a mother. She was glad that Phillip was equally happy to be a parent. He came from a family who'd gotten in a lot of trouble with the law, but he was a good man with a good heart. She didn't doubt that.

"Can we bring guests?" Sasha asked, still surprising everyone in her family with how much she'd changed. She'd spent so many years as an angry child and then an angry young woman. To see her flourish and open up was a constant source of astonishment to all around her.

Daisy grinned at her and nodded.

"If you're asking if you can bring that handsome man of yours, then yes, you sure can," she said, delivering a wink that made Sasha blush.

"Of course, he's welcome, Sasha," Phillip added.

Sasha was pleased. She'd been spending time with James Stonewarden for a while. There had been some challenges between them, but they seemed to get past them. A small part of her still wondered what he wanted from her, but she was slowly accepting that maybe he liked her. Perhaps it was just that simple.

"Thank you," she said to Phillip and Daisy.

As Stacey looked around the table, she smiled to herself. She'd recently experienced a loss like she had never felt before and hoped she'd never feel again. Around that loss, other things had happened that could only produce joy. Seeing Phillip and Sasha so happy with the people they'd each met was something to see.

For so long, Stacey had wished her oldest child would find love. Now he had. That was evident to anyone who saw Phillip and Daisy together. In some ways, they were an unlikely couple, with her being a lawyer and him being a Leadbetter. At the same time, the two of them together made perfect sense. The same was true for Sasha and the young man who'd begun to get to know her.

It was early days for them, but Stacey was just as confident about that relationship. James had worked some kind of magic in helping Sasha to be less angry and more open to people getting to know her. How he'd done that, Stacey wasn't sure, but in doing so, he'd done something nobody else had been able to. The process of change had started in Sasha after she'd saved a young mother and her daughter one night in the local park. Sasha had connected with young Nicky in a surprising way. James seemed to have then joined in to contribute to the progression of Sasha's self-growth. It was something that Stacey and Mark both took great pleasure in watching. Their always-angry daughter was hardly ever angry anymore. Nobody from the legal system or the mental health system had been able to facilitate any change in her. What it had taken was a ten-year-old girl with no self-esteem, and a pretty boy who appeared to be from a well-off family. Stacey still shook her head at that.

CHAPTER 4

James Stonewarden loved his part-time work as a bartender in one of the local nightclubs. As far as work went, it was pretty good meeting new people every night that he was there. For a long time, he'd loved it because it provided him with the opportunity to meet new chicks. If there was one thing that always made him smile, it was women. He'd loved them for as long as he could remember. The nightclub had always provided quite an array of women to meet. At times, he'd likened it to a luxurious breakfast buffet.

His days of bartending weren't over, but his enthusiasm for meeting new women was. It surprised even him, but he was happy. He'd met someone who was in no way like him, but her uniqueness and rawness had lured him in and made him want to only spend time with her. It wasn't his usual way to take time to get to know a woman before anything sexual happened, but he wasn't missing it. It had proven kind of cool to have a woman want to spend time with him but not have sex with him. It was a new experience, but he liked it.

Sasha Leadbetter. If he'd known her last name from the moment they'd met, he wondered if he would have continued to want to know her. Her brother had shot at the supermarket. It had been her brother's bullet that had hit Max and left him in a coma. That connection between Sasha and James still freaked James out on occasion. The odds of everything having happened as it had, and the two of them finding each other, seemed weirdly remote. But they had, and she seemed into it as much as he was. It was weird, but it was pretty cool at the same time.

Hearing his alarm go off, James turned over and

looked at the curtains in his apartment bedroom. He didn't need to set his alarm for work since his shifts usually started around eight or nine at night. He always got up at the same time, regardless. Sunshine helped him feel good. He never wanted to miss it.

Seeing the familiar and welcome glow of orange seeping through the curtain fabric, he lay back and looked at the ceiling. He never had trouble finding things to do during the daylight hours, but he'd woken with a strong desire to see family. That left him options. He could go home to the Stonewarden house and see who was there. At most, it would likely be his dad, Mitchell, and his brother, Max. His other younger brothers, Fitz and Regan, were hardly ever there anymore. James got on well with Regan. With Fitz, not so much. Their youngest brother was an oddball. James had always thought it, even though he was his brother and he had amazing skills with technology.

James took a moment to think about the previous year or two. Things had changed a lot in the Stonewarden family. His sister - the youngest of the siblings - had fallen in love, gotten married, and was now a mother. How she'd done all of that so easily was beyond James's comprehension, but he was happy for her. James had wondered why anyone would want a relationship, until that day when Max had been shot. That had been a timely reminder that life could be short. It hadn't changed James completely, but it had made him begin to appreciate that it might not be so bad to love someone and be loved in return.

He scoffed at where his thoughts had gone.

"Enough of *that* thinking!" he said to himself before throwing back the bedcovers and jumping out of bed. "Get on with the day, James!" he went on to instruct himself, grinning as he dropped to the floor and did his standard fifty sit-ups and fifty press-ups. When they were complete, he finally left the confine of his bedroom.

Standing under the hot water, he pondered options for the day. The feeling of needing to see family was strong. He wouldn't deny that. He'd go over to his family home and see if anyone was about. Whether they were or weren't, he'd then head out to the ranch and see how Charlie was getting on. He briefly wondered if Sasha would like to go to the ranch. She'd met Charlie at the hospital when little Caroline had been born. She hadn't seen any of James's family since. When they hung out, they tended to do it alone, either out in public or at his apartment. To many, it would have seemed like a brand new thing, whatever it was that he had with Sasha. To James, it already felt like a lifetime. He'd never spent as much time with any woman as he had with her.

Sasha. She was an individual, alright. He'd once seen her dressed up with makeup and all the effort other women indulged in day after day. She'd looked sexy that night, but he had to admit that he preferred how she looked naturally. She emanated a very strong 'take me as I am or fuck off' vibe, and he loved that. He didn't want her to change anything about who she was or what she looked like. She was raw, and that was incredible.

For a moment, James thought about soaping up and enjoying himself to another degree in the shower. He dismissed the idea. Even in that, he knew he'd changed a lot. Instead of self-indulging in pleasure, he climbed out, dressed, and got ready for the day ahead.

Before walking out, he again considered inviting Sasha to go to the ranch with him. He let the idea slide away. He knew her family was dealing with all sorts of things going on. He didn't ask her for details, but she'd hinted at a few things. She didn't need to be bothered at that moment.

Driving over to the Stonewarden home, he hoped Max would be there. James didn't know if he would. He kept getting hints that Max was involved with someone, even though nobody seemed to know who the woman was. All of his brothers kept their love lives private to a degree. None of them ever brought their girlfriends to any family-related events, so James was never sure who was in a relationship and who wasn't. He'd never expected Max to be. Max was like him - a player.

He chuckled to himself. He used to call himself a player. He couldn't do that anymore. He was enjoying getting to know one woman at a slow pace and actually liked the idea of keeping getting to know her. Maybe they'd go somewhere as far as romance went. Then again, maybe they wouldn't. With her fear of sex, it was difficult to gauge what could happen at any time with Sasha, but James was prepared to wait it out and see what happened there. He wasn't missing sex. He wasn't missing the entire lifestyle he'd had. He'd changed. There was no denying that.

"Anyone home?" he called out when he entered the large Stonewarden home.

"Yep!" he heard Max's voice reply from the upstairs level.

James bounded up the staircase, unexpectedly keen to see his younger brother. When he reached the landing, Max was standing half in and half out of his bedroom door.

"Hey, what's up?" Max asked, partly in a panic. "Has something happened?"

"No!" James exclaimed. "I just wanted to see who was here."

"Oh, okay," Max said, retreating into his bedroom. "Just me! I think Dad's out, but I don't know where."

Before the bedroom door closed, James moved forward.

"Hey, are you seeing someone?" he asked his younger brother. "Like, *seriously* seeing someone?"

Max turned in surprise, grinning.

"Whoa! We don't have talks like that, big brother," he said, teasing James. "Perhaps what's going on with *you* should be the real question!"

He watched James's face as it grew slightly annoyed at the question having been thrown back at him.

"Nothing!" James retorted.

Max laughed out loud.

"Yeah, sure, James," he said. "If you want to talk about it, let me know. I'm happy to listen."

James looked at his brother. It had been difficult seeing Max in the coma after the supermarket shooting. That period had highlighted to James just how important his family was to him.

"Nah, I'm going to go and see Charlie," he said. "Do you want to come along?"

Max shook his head.

"No," he replied. "Thanks, but I've got plans today. Tell Charlie I'll go and see her tomorrow, though."

"You got plans?" James asked, seizing the moment to grin and tease his brother. "Yeah? Who with?"

"Forget it," Max said as he grabbed his jacket and nudged James toward the door. "You ain't getting nothing out of me."

James let himself be guided out of the bedroom and down the staircase. Once outside, he turned to Max.

"Are we going to meet this mystery woman?" he asked.

Max smiled as he unlocked his Mustang.

"Who knows," he said. "Maybe."

James watched as his brother jumped into the driver seat, started the grunty engine, and then eased away, giving a grin and a wave as he did so.

For a third time, James considered asking Sasha if she'd like to go to see Charlie at the ranch. He pulled out his phone and was about to send a message before he put it away again. That could happen another day.

~~~~~

"Hey, Ash," James greeted his brother-in-law at the ranch. "Is Charlie around?"

Ash smiled at his wife's older brother. He was still skeptical about any of the Stonewarden men, but he'd taught himself how to keep quiet about that. It wasn't Charlie's fault that her family were thieves. She'd been born into it and intended for it, but she'd walked away from it. That was the only degree to which he ever wanted to give thought to what the Stonewardens were.

"Yeah, she'll be down soon," Ash replied. "Come through."

James followed Ash into one of the small living rooms in the vast building. On entering the room, his eyes fell to the tiny human nestled in the arms of Molly Stonewarden - the great aunt of James and Charlie.

"Aww, now see, little Caroline, that your Uncle James is here to see you and give you a cuddle," Molly said to the little one in her arms before giving a cheeky smile to Ash.

James quickly held up both of his hands as if to surrender.

"Whoa, I'm happy for her to stay in *your* arms," he said. "I don't know anything about holding babies."

Ash chuckled as he reached out and took Caroline from Molly.

"Your niece really isn't as scary as you think, James," he teased.

"Is my big brother afraid of a little baby?" James heard Charlie call out as she approached the room. He kept quiet as she moved to him and hugged him. "What's up to bring you out here?"

James watched Molly leave the room and close the door behind her. Although he'd been at the ranch a fair few times, it still didn't feel right for him to be there. It was a large home made up of weird areas of very old
~~~~~

and very new. He wasn't sure what it was about it, but in some ways, it gave him the creeps.

"Nothing," he replied as he studied his sister's face. Since the shooting, he'd watched her mature at an incredible pace. She'd gone from being an insecure and timid teenage girl to a confident wife and mother. The transformation continued to leave him in awe of her, even with her being eight years younger than him. "I just felt like being around some of my family today."

Charlie raised an eyebrow, she was so surprised by his words. James was always nice to her. He wasn't always so open about how he was feeling.

"Is everything alright with you?" she asked.

"Oh, yeah, I'm just … in a weird … kind of mood, I guess," James replied. "How are you going?"

On noticing Caroline had fallen asleep, Ash stood up with her in his arms.

"I'm going to put her down, and then I need to go out and give Tom a hand in the stable," he said in almost a whisper.

Charlie smiled at him. She knew his tactics in politely extracting himself so she could have one on one time with whichever of her siblings visited. He loved her and wanted her to be happy. He didn't want to know too much about any other Stonewardens in case he heard something he wished he hadn't. She respected that.

Once James and Charlie were left alone, Charlie began to apply her friendly, sisterly pressure.

"Now, tell me what's really up with you," she said. When she saw his face change to indicate he was going to try and say there was nothing wrong, she cut his effort short. "Don't even think about denying it. Is it something to do with that girl you met, who came to the hospital?"

James smiled. He didn't particularly like sharing too much about his private life with any of his siblings, but about love, he couldn't help but respect his youngest.

She'd done the whole love thing so easily, it was almost sickening.

"Nah, I don't think so," he said, not sure why he was feeling how he was.

"Are you still seeing her?" Charlie asked, curious. She'd known about the playboy antics of Max and James since she'd been old enough to understand about boys liking girls. It had been a surprise to see James with a woman by his side the day that Caroline had been born. Time had passed since then. James seeing someone for an ongoing period of time was previously unheard of. "Are you in *lurrve*?" she teased.

James grinned at her.

"You can't be serious with that question," he said, tactfully not answering what had been asked.

Charlie chuckled. "It's really not that scary, you know. I recommend it to anyone."

James laughed out loud. "That's because you found the right one for you straight away! Did you even *date* anyone before Ash? You defied the rules of gravity!"

"Come on now, James, that's a bit of an exaggeration," Charlie replied, laughing with him. "I don't think any gravity-defying was done! Come on. Out with it. I hardly hear anything anymore. What's happening with the chicky babe that you brought for all of us to meet at the hospital that day?"

"I didn't bring her to meet you all," James said, still smiling. "We were hanging out together when I got the text saying you were in labor, that's all."

"*And?*" Charlie pushed.

"*And* … you're a really annoying sister, do you know that?" James teased her. "But, yeah, she's cool. I like spending time with her. It's … different … from what I've had with other girls. I don't know if it'll lead to anything, but I'm enjoying her company."

"You mean you're enjoying shagging her,"

Charlie said, being her often blunt self.

"Charlie!" James mock-scolded. "Actually, she and I have never crossed that line." When he saw the look of surprise on his sister's face, he found it easier to speak with sincerity. "It's not something she's … ready for, and I respect that. I like her company without anything physical."

"Just a friend, then?" Charlie asked.

"No," James replied, shaking his head. "I do feel … *romantic* about her. We kiss. We just don't move past it." He took a moment to understand what had just happened. "How did we get to this point where I - your 27-year-old brother - am talking about my lack of sex life with you?!"

Charlie grinned. "Because I have superpowers in persuasion," she replied.

"Uhuh, and how are things in your marriage?" James boldly asked, mostly because he wanted to do to her what she'd just done to him. "All good?"

"Yeah, I don't have anything to grumble about," said Charlie. "Ash is good to me, and he loves being a dad - so far, anyway."

"You don't think that will change, do you?" asked James, curious.

"No," Charlie replied. "But then, none of us know what's ahead, do we? Anything can happen at any time. But no, all I see in Ash is happiness."

"Planning another baby then?" James asked.

Charlie nodded. "We have been talking about it. He's leaving that decision entirely to me, which is kind of cool. I'm not ready yet, but it's nice to know that I can decide whenever I feel like I could handle another one."

"You are happy, though, aren't you, Charlie?"

"I am," Charlie said in full honesty. "I love my husband, I love my daughter, and I love living and working here. Really, I do genuinely just love my life, James. I'm fortunate. I know that."

"I'm envious of you," James said. "You have such strength in you, knowing what you want and going after it. I don't know if I've ever had that kind of strength."

"I think you might be one step closer to finding a new kind of happiness too, don't you think?" Charlie asked. "You're spending time with a woman you don't even shag. That's saying a lot."

"We'll see," replied James. "I still keep getting hints that Max is involved with someone, but he won't give me any details. Do you know?"

Charlie smiled knowingly. "Maybe."

"You *know?* What the *hell?*" James asked in exasperation. When he saw Charlie chuckle, he smiled. "I guess it's your turn to give the goss, then."

"No!" Charlie exclaimed. "Don't even try to get anything out of me about Max's love life. I don't tell him about yours, and I'm not gonna tell you about his!"

James laughed but nodded.

"Alright," he said. "He probably isn't seeing someone anyway."

Charlie didn't respond. She hadn't yet met the intrigue of Max's love life, but he'd mentioned her a few times. It was always enjoyable teasing her brothers when she could, though, especially making James think she knew more than she did.

"Time's a ticking, big brother," she said to tease him further. "Time for you to settle down soon, I'm thinking."

To that, James could only chuckle and shake his head.

CHAPTER 5

Rhett spent another night with another random woman. The scenery changed, but the feelings never did. He met someone, he charmed them, he encouraged them to invite him to their place, and then he had sex with them. There was nothing wrong with the sex. There was nothing wrong with the women. While he was intent on staying away from Greg and the Leadbetter family, what he was doing was working great. He just didn't feel great *about* it.

Two weeks on, and he had to accept that he couldn't go on forever as he had been. He'd been pleasantly surprised by how many women - young and old - had responded to his charm, despite his age. It had been a boost to his ego, as well as a way to hide his true feelings. He suspected there could be more opportunities with new women, but in his heart, he knew he'd reached his limit of running away. It was time to get back to real life.

He had two options. He could get back to the cabin that he'd known Greg was going to remain in. At least there they could be mates again without anyone else looking at them and seeing anything. They could both continue to pretend that the kisses had never happened. In his analysis of that scenario, he wondered if Greg would do the same, or if he'd want to talk about it and explore more.

Rhett felt his body shudder. Although he'd initiated that first kiss, something about being sexual with a guy just did not appeal to him. It was a weird place for him to be. He wanted to explore, but he equally wanted to fight the idea of it. He wished he could talk to someone about it, but for most of his life, he'd only been close to Greg and Mark.

He considered his other option. He could go back to normal life. That would entail going to see Mark and the two of them getting on with their lifelong friendship. As he thought about that possibility, he considered the questions that could be asked. Mark might want to know what had happened that night, as far as the gala and the getaway went. He'd want to know where Greg and Rhett had gone. Then he'd want to know why they'd separated. That would be the crunch question that Rhett was unsure about having to answer.

Why had they separated? It was his doing. Greg had offered him a place to stay for as long as he wanted to. When he'd sensed that Rhett was a bit freaked out about their kisses, he'd said straight out that they didn't have to talk about it. Rhett hadn't given the option of staying a chance. He'd wanted to get the hell away from the cabin, from Greg, and from the memory of those fucking kisses.

He knew he had to make a choice. He had to see Greg, see Mark, or keep doing what he was doing. None of those options particularly appealed more than another, but something had to be done.

Sitting in an ocean-side park of whatever small town he'd ended up in, he sat on a bench and looked out over the water. He sat like that for hours with things churning over in his mind. After weighing up all of his options, over and over, he finally reached a decision.

He was going home.

CHAPTER 6

Stacey Leadbetter stood in her kitchen, looking out toward where her family was setting up a small marquee. It was going to be the first wedding of any of her children. She couldn't help but be excited. Added to the excitement was the humor at watching Mark, Phillip, Anya, and Daisy attempting to put the temporary shelter up. She'd purposely held back, leaving it to those who swore it was an easy thing to do. She liked the mess they were making. It was real, and it provided something for her to laugh at. She knew she hadn't had enough laughter in recent times. It felt good to be able to indulge in it.

When she heard a knock on the door, she was surprised. The only person she might have expected could turn up was Sasha. If it was, she had a key. Whoever it was, they were insistent. The knocking continued to get louder as Stacey moved closer to the door.

"I'm coming!" she called out in a brief moment of annoyance at whoever it was.

Opening the door, she was surprised, but pleasantly so. Without a word, she pulled Rhett into a hug. The two of them hadn't been as close as she was to Greg, or Mark was to Rhett, but she knew him well enough to have been worried about him for what seemed like a long time.

"Where have you been?" she asked as she pulled away, then looked behind him. "Greg? David? Are they with you?"

Rhett wasn't surprised that she asked about Greg. Hearing David's name, however, was a surprise.

"David?" he asked. "I haven't seen David since the night of the gala."

Stacey felt like her heart dropped in her chest. Although she hadn't expected David to have gone with Rhett or Greg, there had been a sliver of hope that the three of them might have been together. Rhett showing up alone and not having seen David meant her boy was still out there somewhere.

"Come in," she said, dismissing her worries for the moment. "Mark's attempting to set up a tent for Phillip's after-wedding feast..."

"Phillip's getting married?" Rhett asked in surprise.

Stacey stopped walking and turned to face him.

"A lot's happened since you were last here," she said, smiling. "I won't ask where you've been or what's happened with you, but *here*, things have been changing!"

Rhett didn't question what she meant. He was more Mark's friend than Stacey's, even though they'd known each other for decades. He followed her through to the kitchen and watched as she opened the door and called her husband inside.

On seeing the seriousness on her face when she called out to him, Mark dropped his piece of the marquee and moved quickly to her. Whatever was going on, an annoyingly difficult tent wasn't going to get in the way of it.

As he walked into the kitchen, he moved toward her out of concern until he sensed another person approach. When he turned, he said nothing. He made no attempt to stop himself from moving forwards and wrapping his arms around Rhett.

"Rhett! Oh, thank God," he said as they did their manly hug and then pulled apart. "Where..." he started to ask before seeing the expression on Rhett's face. "Let's go to my office."

Mark turned and looked at Stacey.

"Go!" she said. "I'll do better than you with that

fucking tent anyway."

Mark smiled at her and kissed her before guiding Rhett away. Once inside with the door closed, he couldn't hold back the questions any longer.

"Where've you been? Is Greg with you?" he asked. "I got a message from Sasha saying that Greg had gone away and was taking time out. She didn't mention you."

Rhett sat and formulated words in his head before he replied. He'd known the questions would come. He only had to skirt around one aspect of anything that had happened. There was no reason why Mark would even guess that Rhett and Greg had kissed and were confused by it.

"I was only with Greg right after the gala," he said. "After that, I took off. I've been drifting since, just needing to take some time out by myself. To be honest, I wasn't sure I was gonna come back."

Mark studied his friend's face. There was something serious behind his expression, but Mark wouldn't pry too much. It was enough to know one of his close friends was home again.

"Are you all good now?" he dared to push just a little bit.

"Yeah," Rhett said, nodding. "Greg was okay when I left him, too. I think he was feeling the same - just needed some time in solitude. That gala night job was fucked up. I wish I'd never agreed to do it. Still, Pete got what was coming to him, I guess."

For a moment, Mark wondered if Rhett thought Rex had got what was coming to him, too. He then considered another possibility.

"You do know that Rex died that night, too…" he began to say, initially with strength before tears began again.

Rhett was stunned. He'd seen Pete get shot and then heard that he'd died. Nothing had reached him about

Rex.

"What?" he asked to make sure he'd heard correctly. "I saw Rex as I was leaving…" he started to say and then paused. "What happened?"

"The cops … the cops saw him pull out a gun and start shooting into the crowd, just like Pete had…"

Rhett took a moment to process what he was hearing.

"Rex had a gun?" he asked and saw Mark nod. "Where the fuck did he *get* it? Don't tell me that Pete gave…"

"No," Mark replied, cutting his question short. "We think Rex took it from David's room. We haven't seen David since that night, so there's no way to know for sure, but Sasha saw him the next day. She's pretty sure he had a gun in his room, and Rex took it and used it that night."

Rhett sat in disbelief. All the time that he'd been taking time out to process his own stupid feelings, one of his closest friends had been dealing with the death of his son. He was disappointed in himself. He'd dwelled on his stupidity for too long. Nothing he'd been thinking about or feeling could possibly compare to losing a child.

"How have you guys been dealing with that?" he asked quietly. "I'm so sorry that I haven't been here…" he began to say before he felt tears threaten.

Crying wasn't something he'd done for decades. It wasn't seen as acceptable in the land of Leadbetter. Since Mark's parents had taken him in as a teenager, he'd taught himself how to hold back from feeling anything. Hearing the news about what Mark and Stacey must have been going through was enough to undo almost a lifetime of emotion suppression.

Mark was surprised by Rhett's reaction but also appreciative of it. He knew as well as anyone how much his parents had drummed into all of them that they mustn't cry. Leadbetters were tough. If they felt anything weak, they were strictly told to harden up. He'd had it drummed into him by his parents, as had Rhett.

"We're doing okay," Mark replied. "It's not easy. As trying as that kid was, he was my son. I'm not too proud to say that I loved him, just as I love all my kids." He paused as he watched Rhett attempt to hide his sadness. "It'll be a long, hard road, dealing with that, but we've got some happy things happening too. Phillip's getting married, and Sasha's got herself a guy…"

Rhett couldn't help but burst out laughing.

"Sorry, can you repeat that?" he asked, knowing it was cheeky.

Mark grinned. It felt refreshing after the seriousness of the previous few minutes.

"Yeah, you heard right," he said. "My daughter has a man in her life."

"What…?" Rhett started to ask. "What kind of … guy … is he?"

"A surprising one," Mark replied. "He's clean-cut, well-spoken, polite … looks like a bit of a pretty boy, to be honest."

"So, not like us…"

Mark chuckled as he shook his head.

"He's definitely not like us, but he's okay. From the couple of times I've met him, he really seems to care for Sasha, which is all I care about," he said. "She's changed since we lost Rex. I think this guy has something to do with that."

Rhett smiled. He'd missed a lot in a short amount of time. He felt some regret about that.

"And Stace?" he asked quietly. "How's she been with everything?"

"She's a strong woman," Mark replied. "It hasn't been easy, knowing Rex is gone forever, and David hasn't shown himself or even let us know he's okay, but she is happy about Phillip getting married. That's something that's provided some sunshine in what seems like a year of grey."

"But David? What's the story there? He was in the gala when I was there. He was…" he began to say before coaxing the memory of that night into the forefront of his thoughts. "Oh, was he still there when I left? I don't know now if he was or not. I remember seeing Rex. When I walked out, I thought he was heading toward the door, so I didn't hang around. I didn't see him with a gun or anything … shit, I can't believe…"

As tears began again, he didn't stop them. He'd been on a rollercoaster of emotion for a long time. The tears had to be set free, as did all his held-back emotion.

"Whatever happened that night, it's over with now," said Mark. "I hope David reappears somewhere or comes home sometime. I don't know if he will, but he knows we're always here, as is his home."

"But why would he have taken off?" asked Rhett. "You think he needed time out like me and Greg did?"

"No," Mark said, shaking his head. "What we think happened - but can't know for sure until we speak to him - is that David might have had a gun and used it in the supermarket shooting last year."

"David?" Rhett asked. "That makes no sense!"

"I know it's surprising, but it's looking more and more like that's what happened," said Mark. "He had a gun, he used it in the supermarket shooting, and then he hid it in his room. The night of the gala, Rex took the gun and used it. The cops took him down, and then took the gun, which was found to be the same as what had been used in the supermarket shoot-up that day."

"So the cops are looking for David?"

"No, I think they've assumed that the gun was Rex's, so Rex was the one who shot up the supermarket," Mark replied. "I think David might have run, thinking the cops would be after him, and not even know that they think it was Rex anyway."

"No need for him to be on the run then?" Rhett asked.

"Correct," replied Mark. "Well, that is only what we think, though. There's no way to know unless we can talk to him."

Rhett thought about all that he'd learned in the previous few minutes. He'd made a mistake when he'd run away that night. He'd made that mistake and not been there for his friend when he would have needed as many people around him to provide support as possible.

"I'll find him," he said, his mind working quickly.

"What?" asked Mark.

"I'll find David," Rhett replied. "You guys have all this good stuff going on. I haven't been here for you during the bad stuff, Mark. I'm your friend. I should've…"

"Rhett, nobody blames you for anything," Mark said, surprised by his friend's reaction. "You didn't know about Rex…"

"But I should have!" exclaimed Rhett. "I should have been here for you and Stacey and the kids…" he said before breaking down again. "I can't undo that, but this - *this* is something I can do. Nobody needs to know I'm doing it, and it's probably best that Stacey doesn't know since I can't guarantee success."

Mark nodded but remained silent.

"I'll go and try to find him," Rhett continued. "I've been drifting around anyway. It'll be no different."

"Stacey knows you're back," said Mark. "She'll want you around for the wedding."

"Okay," Rhett said, nodding. "When is it?"

"Tomorrow," said Mark.

"I'll be here if you want me to be. After that, I'll take off quietly," said Rhett.

"Just don't disappear again, Rhett," Mark said in almost a whisper. "Whatever's really been going on with you, I'm here for you. If you go off and search for David,

I appreciate that, but you make it a point to contact me at least every couple of days to let me know you're okay!"

Rhett smiled. Mark sounded far more sincere than any Leadbetter ever should, but it was nice. Mark's parents had shown no sincerity, even though they had invited Rhett to live with them. It had always felt like a bittersweet thing to Rhett, being welcomed into a family but then realizing that the family was more like a gang.

"I promise I'll keep in touch," he said. "But, right now, what do you need a hand with? I've been wallowing in self-pity for too long. Give me something to work on."

Mark didn't question what the self-pity remark was about. He knew that Rhett would speak up if and when he felt he needed to talk to someone.

"We have to set up an entire marquee with tables and chairs," said Mark. "Then … how's your cooking skills these days?"

Rhett burst out laughing. His culinary skill level was zero, and Mark knew it.

"Unless you want to poison your guests, I'll steer clear of the kitchen, thank you very much," he said as Mark stood.

Mark moved around the desk and hugged his friend once more. It didn't matter that he hadn't been around during the toughest times. What mattered was that he'd returned. Not only had he returned, but he also appeared set on going out to find David. Mark didn't fool himself about that. There was a high probability that Rhett wouldn't find David. That didn't matter. Rhett was willing to look, and Mark knew Rhett had contacts all over the place. He wouldn't mention the search to Stacey, but inwardly, Mark was very happy to have his good friend back.

CHAPTER 7

The day of the wedding had arrived. While Phillip spent the morning with his family, Daisy indulged in getting ready with friends at a hotel overlooking the beach. As she looked from the high window, she could see where the small number of seats were being assembled. It wouldn't be a huge wedding, but it would be exactly as she and Phillip wanted.

"Another hour and a half from now, and you'll be Mrs. Daisy…" her friend, Emma, began to say before remembering what she'd been told. "Oh, no, wait. You'll still be Daisy Leefton! What a great man he is, to take your last name. You're so lucky with that one, Daisy!"

"Hell, yes!" her friend, Vinnie, chimed in. "He's hot as. *I'd* definitely do him!"

"I concur!" added Nicola.

Daisy chuckled at her friends. She was glad her three closest friends had all been able to attend her special day. During her time studying to be a lawyer and then working in the legal industry, she'd met a lot of people and formed some great acquaintances. No matter how many she met, she only considered Nicola, Emma, and Vinnie her true friends.

"This is a nice suite for you guys to have your honeymoon in, too," Emma said as she walked to where Daisy stood.

"It is," Daisy agreed, nodding. "After we have the ceremony down there, we'll go to Phillip's family's place to hang out for a few hours, then come back here."

"Is there anything we should know about his family or their home?" Vinnie asked. "I mean, I know Phillip must be normal. Are his family? Do prepare us, Daisy!"

Daisy considered all that she knew about the Leadbetters. She'd known about them even before she'd met Phillip's family. There was nothing that she knew, that she would *ever* share with her friends.

"They're just a normal family," she said, grinning. "You'll meet his two sisters and his mother and father. I have no idea who else from their side is going to be there, but it's only small, so you guys will survive okay. Just don't embarrass me!"

"As if we ever could!" Vinnie said, making the friends laugh.

"And!" Daisy added for good measure. "His sister's bringing her boyfriend, who is just your type, so don't go getting any ideas, *you!*" she said as she pointed at Vinnie. "He's *taken!*"

Vinnie grinned at her.

"Worry not, my fair flower, I am very happy with my new lad," he said. "And even if I wasn't, you know very well that I don't go near anyone who knows anyone I know!"

Daisy grinned at him. She knew she didn't need to worry about any of her friends doing anything that could be unwelcome. As boisterous as they could get sometimes, they were all respectful people.

"I'm so nervous," she said, resuming her stare out the window. "Why am I so nervous? I'm marrying the man that I love and want to be with for the rest of my life."

"Every bride is nervous, Daisy," Emma said.

"Yeah, but *why?* I get why it was the case when people didn't know what was going to happen in the wedding bed that night, but now…"

"*Now*, you've already shagged the living daylights out of that boy, so there's not going to be any surprises at all," Vinnie added in true Vinnie style.

Daisy laughed with him before moving to hug all three of her friends.

"Thanks for being here, all of you. I love you all!"

~~~~~

Walking to his designated place to wait for his bride, Phillip couldn't help but think about his brothers. It was his wedding day, but neither would attend. He hadn't been overly close to Rex or David, but their absence was particularly obvious that day.

While waiting for his bride-to-be to appear, he wondered again if David was alright. As a family, they'd still not heard anything. Did that mean he was successful in whatever plan he might have had to hide? Was there a chance that Rex wasn't the only one of the family who was now dead?

Glancing at his father and mother, he was pleased to see them at least trying to smile. He wanted them to be happy. He and Daisy both hoped that the wedding would provide them with some joyful relief from the sadness they emanated. He was also hopeful that if Daisy got her way and was pregnant soon after their wedding, his parents could then focus on being grandparents to the new generation.

When he saw his father smile at him, he wondered if he truly was as happy for Phillip to have decided to take Daisy's surname rather than make her a Leadbetter. His father had expressed he was fine with the idea. Phillip was hopeful that his father did understand why Phillip didn't want his wife or any future children to take the Leadbetter name.

Deep in thought about the seriousness of things surrounding his family, it took him a long moment to realize that his bride was walking onto the sand from the hotel beachside exit. Even from the distance they were apart, she looked stunning. Phillip could see her blond tresses were loose and curled, creating an exceptional frame that displayed the smile she exhibited. From that moment, Phillip couldn't think about anything else.
~~~~~

CHAPTER 8

Mark watched his son move into position at the head of the small makeshift walkway set up on the sand. The last wedding he'd attended had been his own. None of his close friends had bothered with the whole marriage thing, thinking it was a waste of time. When he tried to imagine life without Stacey as his wife for all of the years they'd been married, he couldn't. She'd been his rock, his support, the most amazing mother of his children, and the sexiest woman to have as a lover. His life couldn't have been anywhere near as fulfilling if he'd never married her.

Now his firstborn was getting married. As he looked at Phillip, Mark remembered the day he'd been born. He and Stacey had both felt blessed that day as they'd held such a tiny being in their arms. Now that tiny being was a man. He'd expressed that he wanted his own family, and he and Daisy would be starting one as soon as they were married and fully settled.

There would be another generation of his family. It was a funny but welcome thing for Mark to think about. For Stacey, in particular, he thought it would be nice to have grandkids. They'd lost two sons in one night. That loss would never be forgotten, but it would be nice to have a little one or two to occupy their thoughts.

Hearing the familiar wedding march music begin on someone's phone, he turned. He couldn't deny that Phillip had chosen well for his bride. It wasn't what Daisy looked like that made Mark think that, but rather, the way that she looked at Phillip. They were in love. There was nothing fake about it on either side. That made Mark happy. He knew what a difference a happy marriage made. He wanted all of his kids to experience that.

All of his kids. He no longer *had* all of his kids. One of them would never marry or even experience love. The thought made Mark force himself to stop thinking such things. It was a day of happiness, not of sadness. Regardless, since Rhett had said he'd try and find David, that had played on Mark's mind. It had always been an unpleasant challenge to keep things from Stacey, but he knew he had to about that. He didn't want her grieving all over again if she thought Rhett would find their missing son, and then he didn't.

He watched as Daisy walked past him and joined Phillip. The words that followed between Phillip, Daisy, and the celebrant, he concentrated on to make sure that his mind was at rest.

Soon after, the ceremony was complete. His oldest son was no longer a Leadbetter. Phillip had changed his surname so that he was Phillip Leefton. Mark held no concern or resentment about that. His son wanted a life away from the Leadbetter family and the Leadbetter name. His children would never be expected to join the Leadbetter gang. That was a great thing.

Glancing around, he saw Sasha sitting with James. That was still taking some getting used to, but he liked the way that the pretty boy seemed to provide support to Sasha. The few times that Mark had seen him, James had seemed to be watching her and anticipating how she'd best need him next. It had been something to see, but it made Mark feel positive about the connection. Even if it went nowhere, the young man had contributed to the dramatic change in Sasha. That was something to be thankful for.

"Shall we?" he heard Stacey ask as she stood and reached out her hand to him.

He didn't hesitate in standing, pulling her into his arms, and kissing her like she deserved to be kissed.

~~~~~

From behind a large white pillar at the hotel's beachside entrance, Pete Brandon stood and watched the ceremony. When he'd first heard through a long grapevine of friends that Daisy was marrying the lowlife Pete had seen her with on a short getaway, he hadn't wanted to believe it. Sure, she hadn't contacted him since they'd seen each other that weekend, but he'd maintained hope that as soon as she'd moved on from the rough guy she'd been with, she'd seek Pete out and beg him to take her back. He'd waited and waited, his confidence never wavering in his belief that she was still meant to be his forevermore.

Although he'd expected her to, Daisy had never contacted him after that weekend. She'd never made contact, and she'd never ditched the tattooed idiot she'd been with. Then Pete had received the devastating news that she was going to marry the lowlife. What the hell was she thinking? The guy she was with looked like a common criminal. Why would someone like her want to be with someone like that?

He didn't know the answer to those questions. All he knew was that he'd been the one to end their relationship, and he'd been the one who'd grown to regret their split.

When he saw Daisy pass through the hotel doorway and make her way down the makeshift path on the sand, he felt a broad mix of emotions. He was angry at her for making such a stupid choice. He was angry at the criminal-looking guy for thinking he was good enough for Daisy. It didn't even occur to Pete to be angry at himself for throwing her away - the very action that had provided her with the opportunity to start over with someone new.

He remained where he was as he watched her walk to her husband-to-be and give him the kind of smile that made Pete's heart skip a beat. It could have
~~~~~

been him up there. It could have been him saying the vows to her and hearing her say vows back to him. Not that he'd have allowed them to get married on a beach. That only showed how cheap the guy was that she'd chosen. If she'd returned to Pete, he would have given her the dream wedding any woman would have wanted.

He conveniently forgot the few times she'd mentioned a possible future together, with a wedding and kids. He conveniently forgot all the bad things he'd done and said that had made it so easy for her to walk away when he'd split up with her.

Watching her deliver her vows and then kiss the man she'd married, Pete felt fury growing inside of him. All reasoning left him as he vowed to not let that be the end for them. Even if she was a married woman, he didn't mind the thought of edging himself back into her life. He wouldn't care if he was the other man. He deserved only the best, and she was it. She wasn't meant to be with the asshole she'd just shared vows with.

He stayed out of general view for as long as possible without there being any chance of being seen. When he saw the married couple begin their walk back down the aisle together, he turned and walked away. There would be no confrontation of any kind that day. He would make a plan to seek her out when she was alone, and he would remind her of who he was and what they'd had. She would want him back, and she would break that asshole's heart in facilitating it.

Pete smiled as he made his way back to his car and sat inside. He'd followed her around for a long time since seeing her that weekend. He'd begun to know her routines, the places she went, and even where her in-laws lived. He knew far more about her current life than she'd even imagine he would. That was his advantage. He'd have the element of surprise.

He'd leave the happy couple to their brief honeymoon at the hotel. After that, she'd be his again.

CHAPTER 9

It wasn't often that James Stonewarden felt out of place, but at the Leadbetter home, he did. He'd driven Sasha and Anya both back to the house. Personally, he'd have preferred to have Sasha alone, but he was glad to help however he could.

As he stood inside the marquee, he looked around. He couldn't help but notice the diverse range of people. Sasha's family definitely had one kind of look about them. In almost direct contrast, the bride and her friends had a very different look about them. It puzzled him until he felt someone's hand sink into his.

Turning and seeing Sasha had changed into different clothing, thoughts about the different groups of people faded. Sasha wasn't like anyone he'd ever met, but he loved being around her. She wouldn't be considered someone who could easily fit into any mold in society, but he loved that about her.

"Are you alright?" Sasha asked him.

James turned so that they were almost chest to chest. Seeing she'd taken off the bridesmaid's dress and replaced it with clothing of her own, and she'd removed all shred of makeup she'd had on for the wedding and photos, he felt drawn to her. For some time, he'd felt a deeper connection to her than he had to anyone else previously. It equally thrilled him and scared him.

"I am," he said, smiling at her. He then boldly moved forward a little more, raised both hands, and lightly stroked her arms. The move wouldn't have meant anything to anyone else. To him, it meant a lot. It had taken time for Sasha to let him touch her skin in any way. They hadn't moved past that physically, but that she continued to let him do it, and she seemed to enjoy it, was incredible to him.

Sasha reveled in the feelings. She was warming up to touch. She knew it, and she didn't hide it. The whole time she'd known James, he had respected her initial declaration that she'd never have sex. He'd never tried to convince her to try it. One time, she'd tried to lure him into it. Even then, he'd respected her wish and not let it happen. She loved that about him, but she equally knew that things were changing in her to another level. She'd changed in her levels of anger and her social skills.

There was also another change happening. Although she hadn't told anyone about it, she could feel it. She wasn't only growing receptive to touch. She was also growing in her body's response to how he touched her. She'd had sex once before. She'd walked away from that with the resolution to never let any asshole do that to her again. With James, her body was waking up, and she liked it.

"This won't go for too long," she said to him. "Are you working tonight?"

"Not tonight," James replied, enjoying the look on her face. "I'm thinking that Sassy Girl has something on her mind," he went on to tease her.

Sasha tried unsuccessfully to hold back a chuckle.

"Maybe," she said suggestively as she grinned at him, moved closer, and wrapped her arms around him.

"I think you are trying to lure me into kissing you," James said in almost a whisper. "At your brother's wedding! I'm not sure that's the right thing to do, Sasha Leadbetter."

Sasha pulled her head back far enough so that she could look at his lips. She wanted to kiss him. There was no denying that. She raised her eyes to his to distract herself.

"I can't help it," she said, making James laugh out loud. She enjoyed his laugh. It was carefree and happy.

That was something she hadn't felt for most of her life.

"Sasha!" both heard a young voice call out. Turning, they saw Nicky running toward them with her mother, Susan, behind.

"Hey, hey, Nicky-kid!" Sasha said, holding out her hand for their unique hand greeting. "I'm so glad you guys could come!"

"Well, thank you for inviting us," Susan said as she reached them. "We wouldn't have expected to be invited to your brother's wedding reception, Sasha."

"You are very welcome here, Susan," Stacey added in from behind them. "As are you, Miss Nicky," she continued, bending down and giving Nicky a hug.

From a distance, Phillip saw the interaction and made his way over.

"Susan, thanks for coming," he said, still grateful for her having helped Sasha not be charged with something she'd been accused of the year before.

"Oh, Phillip!" Susan said as she wrapped her arms around him. "I'm so happy for you! But where is your bride? I haven't met her yet."

Phillip led her away to meet Daisy, leaving Nicky with James and Sasha.

"Are you gonna marry her?" Nicky asked James, a smile wide across her face.

"Who? Sasparilla here?" James asked, pointing at Sasha and making Nicky giggle.

"You know her name!" Nicky said.

"Hmm, I just don't know if I could marry someone called Sasquatch, Nicky," James continued. "Imagine the wedding invitations reading 'Sasquatch and James'. Yeah, I just don't know if that works."

Nicky, knowing his teasing wouldn't end, rolled her eyes at him, making James and Sasha both grin.

"You're just a funny guy, aren't you," she teased him back.

"Yeah, but you know as well as I do, Nicky, that

whoever marries this sassy girl will be a very lucky man indeed," James said, glancing from one to the other. "But who do *you* want to marry, huh?"

"I'm only eleven, silly!" Nicky replied, giggling.

"Oh, right. Hmm…" James said, not knowing where to take the conversation from there.

"Nicky, come and meet Phillip's bride, Daisy," Susan said in a timely manner as she approached and reached out for Nicky's hand.

Sasha and James watched as Nicky waved and walked away, leaving them alone in their corner again.

"She's such a cool kid," James said, grinning. "Cheeky little monkey, though."

Sasha smiled and nodded in agreement.

"So, about later," she said, making James smile even more.

"Yes, Sassy Girl?" he asked, teasing her. "What would you like to do? Your wish is my command."

In response to his suggestive tone, Sasha moved close and put her arms around him once more before placing her lips on his.

James loved the feeling that flowed through his body when she kissed him. It had been something new for her, and she'd taken her time to experiment as she'd explored his lips with her own. She'd since practiced enough to have perfected how their lips fitted together. He wasn't usually one to even think about whether a woman was initiating a kiss or he was, but with Sasha, he always let her set the pace.

"Beach," Sasha mumbled against his lips as she pulled away. It was never easy breaking their kissing moments, but she did agree with him. Her brother's wedding feast wasn't the time for it.

"I'm into that," James said as he smiled and nodded. "See how your evening goes, though. We have plenty of days for that if you need to stay here for more bridesmaid duties."

As Sasha looked at him and heard his words, she felt a familiar sadness. It was easy to imagine that there were plenty of days ahead. Rex having been killed while only a teenager proved otherwise. There were no guarantees. Whatever life she had left to live, she wanted to do exactly that - *live*.

James watched her face. She had the same look that she'd had many times before. On those occasions, she'd shared with him her feelings and thoughts. It was something more that he loved about her. It had taken a long time for her to open up and relax around him. Since she had, she'd proven she had an incredible ability to talk about things that were real inside her. It was just one more way that she set herself apart from the many women who had crossed James's path previously.

"Hey," he said as he pulled her even closer. "I'm right here, however you need me."

Sasha nodded against his shoulder. He'd told her that many times. It had taken a while, but over time, she'd grown to believe him.

"I know," she said as she pulled back from him. "Thank you for coming to this. It's not much fun…"

"Not much fun?" James asked, grinning to encourage her to do the same. "All weddings are fun to attend. Good food, good people, good conversation, and…" he said as he held out his hand. "Good … dancing?"

"I'm not a dancer," Sasha said, embarrassed.

"And that guy is?" James asked as he redirected her attention to someone on the dance floor.

Sasha couldn't help but chuckle. She didn't know who the guy on the dance floor was, but she had to agree that James had a point. The guy did *not* look good.

"Come on. You know you want to see me shake my booty," James said, glad to see her laugh in response.

"Okay," Sasha said. "I have no idea what I'm doing, but yeah, let's see that booty shake, Pretty Boy."

CHAPTER 10

As Rhett circulated among the people attending the after-wedding feast, he did his bit and smiled when he should. Mark's immediate family were his only real interest there. He didn't desire to meet any new people, even though he did his best to pretend to, especially with Phillip's bride. It was a short time before he finally moved to stand with Mark and Stacey.

As he stood with them, Stacey was aware that something might be a bit off with Rhett. She'd not asked Mark any questions about his conversation with Rhett the day before. Whatever was causing the tenseness, she just hoped it had nothing to do with another job. Since the night of the gala, no mention of combined-effort theft had reached her. She trusted that Mark would tell her if something was happening that could prove dangerous. If there was any chance that he was going to do anything that could put his life in danger, she didn't know if she'd be able to forgive him. The last great Leadbetter effort had resulted in them losing two sons. She knew she'd reached a point where she would stand up and say a very firm 'no' if anyone even tried to lure Mark or any of her kids into anything like that again.

To stop herself from focusing too hard on something that might only be in her imagination, she left the men to walk around and talk to other people. There was something they obviously wanted to talk about, and not in front of her. She was well used to that. As long as it didn't put any more of her kids in danger, she was happy to leave them to it.

As soon as Stacey had left, Mark turned to Rhett.

"Are you still thinking about what you said yesterday?" he asked. "About searching for David?"

"Yeah, I'm going to head off soon," Rhett replied. "I'll keep you in the loop. Who else has looked for him?"

"Phillip had a look in places he remembered David mentioning over the years, but he could be anywhere," said Mark. "I didn't make it a priority to go and search for him…"

"Mark, you couldn't go and search for him. You and Stacey have had something tragic happen, and you needed to support each other in that. Especially with me and Greg having done runners…"

"Stop that," Mark said. When Rhett looked at him, he continued. "Stop thinking that you somehow let us down. Whatever made you take off and stay away for so long, you had to do it. Don't apologize for that."

"Yeah," Rhett replied, nodding. "But I'll give my best effort to find your son, Mark. He's got to be out there somewhere."

The two men sat silently for a long while, pretending to look at all the happy people surrounding them. Eventually, Rhett moved.

"Okay, I'm gonna get going," he said. "I'll contact you in a few days to give you an update."

Mark pulled him into a hug.

"You better," he said. "And I don't mean just about David. You let me know you're okay, no matter what's happening in your search!"

"Yes, dad," Rhett teased him, relaxing the moment. "Yeah, I will. You take care of your family and that wife of yours. You're lucky to have her."

"Don't I know it," Mark replied, grinning.

From where he remained, Mark watched Rhett go shake Phillip's hand, say something brief to the bride, and then walk away. For a moment, he wondered if he'd ever see Rhett again. A moment later, he was glad that at least he knew Rhett was going. That was more than he'd had to work with the previous time Rhett had disappeared.

CHAPTER 11

After packing up his meager possessions to hit the road again early the next morning, Rhett drove to the nearest beach to take some time to assemble his plan and his thoughts. Sitting on the bonnet of his car, he watched the sun begin its ascent in the sky.

He felt dissatisfied with everything. It wasn't a good way to feel, and he knew it. He'd never been a bubbly person, but how he was feeling was something he really didn't like. He was determined to make it up to Mark and Stacey for having been absent during their time of need for support. It was something that might prove pointless. He suspected even Mark knew that the reason David might not have made contact might be because something had happened to him. It wasn't a good thought, but it was realistic. Rhett wouldn't accept that as the ultimate result of David being missing until he had explored as far and as wide as he could. He had contacts all over the place. He would at least go and investigate some possibilities before he would go home again.

Seeing Mark again had been good, but it had been brief. They hadn't spoken about anything personal to do with Rhett. That was how Rhett had wanted it to be. He wasn't ready to share thoughts in his head with anyone, especially a Leadbetter, but he did need to get things out of his mind. They were clouding his thoughts. That could impact his success in finding David, and he couldn't bear that.

Finishing off his cigarette and tossing the butt aside, he got back in his car, took another minute to enjoy the warmth reaching him from the sun, and then started the engine. His thoughts had been focused on

Greg for too long. They weren't going away. They needed to be dealt with. He didn't know what kind of reception he would get if he went to the cabin. Greg had been his friend for most of his life, but Rhett had turned away when they could have confronted their discomfort together.

It wasn't something he felt comfortable doing, but the decision was made. He would go to Greg. If for no other reason, Greg wouldn't know about Rex's death, and he would want to. They had personal things to discuss, but Rhett would make sure that piece of news was at the forefront of what he wanted to share.

As he hit the open road, he looked at the time. It would take him a couple of hours to reach the cabin. He hoped that his friend was still there. Greg had indicated that he planned to stay there for as long as he needed to, and that might be a while. Rhett assumed he was still there. If he wasn't, he would have made his way back to see Mark. They were more than friends - they were cousins.

All the way to the cabin, he thought about what he wanted to say. It wasn't easy. He had feelings for Greg, but he didn't want to. What could he say about that? What could happen between them? It felt like an impossible situation to be in. He didn't even know why he was in it. He'd known Greg forever. He'd only ever looked at him as one of his best mates. He'd never looked at any guy and been attracted to him. The thought of any guy on guy stuff grossed him out. He loved women.

He recited the same arguments to himself for the entire two hours of the drive. His heart told him one thing. His head told him another. As he drove up the final approach to the cabin, he wasn't any clearer in his plan or even his desire for what he wanted to happen.

After parking in front of the cabin, he remained still for a long time.

CHAPTER 12

Greg heard the car long before it appeared in view. He knew the sound of it. There was no doubting it was Rhett's vehicle that was approaching. When he realized that, he felt his heart begin to pound. He'd accepted that he might not ever see his close friend again after the way Rhett had left. While it had saddened him, he had understood and accepted it. Hearing the car drive up to the cabin and then stop with the engine idling, he prepared himself for anything.

The car continued to idle for a long while. Greg didn't move to go out onto the veranda. He wouldn't pressure Rhett to stay. If Rhett had traveled that far and then decided he wanted to go away again, Greg respected that. He remained where he was, just inside the cabin door, and waited.

When the car engine was shut off, he waited further. He knew the sound of Rhett's driver door opening and closing. It was a long wait before he heard that. When he finally did, he held his breath in anticipation of what was going to happen. It was only when he heard Rhett's footsteps on the veranda that he realized they were finally going to face each other.

"You here?" Rhett called out, not sure if Greg would be inside the cabin or somewhere outside in the vast wooded area.

Greg pushed away the excitement he immediately felt upon hearing Rhett's voice. Taking a deep breath, he opened the cabin door, determined to force something resembling normality.

"Where the fuck else would I be, Idiot?" he greeted his long-time friend.

Rhett couldn't help but smile. He was confused,

but he'd missed his friend. It was only natural that they'd both move forward and share their manly hug and then pull apart quickly. That was what they'd always done. Neither thought to stop it from happening.

"Got a beer?" Rhett asked. "I need to tell you something that ain't good."

"Yeah," Greg said, moving to grab two cans.

When they'd settled into the two seats on the veranda, Greg waited for the news. He suspected something was coming about the kisses they'd shared. He thought he was prepared for anything that Rhett might say. He was wrong.

"Rex is dead," Rhett said, turning to face him.

"What?" Greg asked, sure he couldn't have heard correctly. On no point of the what-might-be-said spectrum had something like that been an option.

"He was killed by the cops the night of the gala," Rhett continued.

Greg took time to process the news. He'd been responsible for taking Rex to the gala event that night. He'd equally been responsible for getting Rex home.

"We should have waited..." he started to say before seeing Rhett shake his head. "You told me to drive without waiting for him. Did you *see* him get shot?"

At that moment, Rhett felt tears threaten. He'd forgotten he'd told Greg to drive as soon as he'd jumped in the car that night. Why had he said that? Why hadn't he said to wait for Rex?

"No," he replied, shaking his head. "No, when I left, I saw he was with one of the others. I thought he was leaving..."

"If you thought he was leaving, why did you tell me to drive before he reached us?" Greg asked, confused. What his friend was saying made no sense.

Rhett shook his head. Everything was mixed up. He thought he knew the order of things that had happened in the gala event building. The more he considered it, the more he couldn't get things straight in his mind. Had he seen Rex move toward the door? Or had he seen him move toward the diamonds that were on display?

"I don't know!" he said. "I don't know what happened. He was alive when I last saw him. I'm sure of that. He and David were both there, and they were both okay."

"David? What's he got to do with it?" Greg asked, not understanding anything that was being said. It reminded him of the night of the gala. Rhett had been the same then, not giving any details about what might or might not have happened inside the building before they'd left. He'd been flustered and confused then, and he looked and sounded like he was still in that state.

Rhett raised his eyes and looked at Greg. It seemed like so much time had passed since the two of them had last sat in Mark's office, having a laugh about something or other. One night had changed so much for each of them.

"He's missing," he finally said. "Mark said Sasha saw David at their home the day after, but he hasn't been seen since. I've told Mark that I'm going to go and search for him."

"Nobody's already done that?" Greg asked.

"He said Phillip went out for a while to have a look around, but they were dealing with Rex's death. They've had enough to deal with," Rhett replied. "I'm going to search for him. I have the time, and I know people. Someone might have seen him…"

"Or the Valiant," Greg added, remembering how distinctive David's classic black car was.

"Yeah, although that's possibly been put into hiding," Rhett said.

Greg nodded as he took time to think about Mark's sons. They'd been raised the Leadbetter way, taught to steal whenever and whatever they could. Rex had enjoyed the lifestyle a little too much, resulting in him spending a bit more time with the cops than any older Leadbetter appreciated. If there was a way to get in trouble, Rex had been pretty good at finding it. As Greg gave thought to the sadness of his death, he couldn't help but also smile even as he felt tears begin.

"What?" Rhett asked, seeing the odd grin on his friend's face.

"Rex," Greg scoffed as he smiled more and wiped his eyes. "He was such a little shit."

Rhett smiled. It was the first smile he'd experienced in a long while.

"Fuck, yes!" he said. "That kid didn't deserve what he got, but he had the craziest knack of getting caught for almost everything he tried to do."

Through the smiles, Greg felt the heaviness of the loss his friends must have experienced. He was equally close to Mark and Stacey. The thought of their loss was incredibly hard to digest. He tried to stop the tears. After a few minutes, he gave up and wept. He wept for his friends and their losses, he wept for a teenage boy who had lost his life far too soon, and he wept for an entire lifestyle that just didn't work, even though it continued generation after generation.

Rhett respectfully remained quiet while he watched his friend go through the same level of emotion he'd experienced on hearing the same news. They lived a lifestyle that resulted in people leaving either by going to prison or by being killed. It was a horrible fact, but it was a fact, regardless. That didn't make it any easier when something happened to someone close to them.

Getting his feelings under control, Greg turned to face Rhett straight on. There were a lot of things he wanted to ask, but whatever the two of them had to work through, it could wait.

"Where do we start?" he asked. He instantly saw a

look of confusion on Rhett's face. "Where do we start in trying to find David?"

"You wanna come with?" Rhett asked, surprised.

"Why would you even question that?" Greg asked. "Of *course*, I want to fucking help find him!"

"Okay," replied Rhett. "Well, I'm heading up to see a mate a little up the coast. He knows everyone and everything that happens in that town. If David's passed through there at any time, he'll know. It's not much, but it's a start."

"Let's go then," Greg said as he stood, continuing to rub his eyes. "I'll just…"

"Hey," Rhett said, standing and cutting Greg's words short. When Greg turned to face him, he knew he had to speak. He had to say *something*. "I left because I was confused. I'm *still* confused."

Although he didn't expand or provide context, Greg knew what he was referring to. It had been a nice moment, them kissing. It had been nice to know that Greg's feelings hadn't been one-sided. It hadn't been enough to lose an entire lifetime of friendship over.

"We don't have to talk about…" he began to say. His words were cut short again.

Rhett had been honest about his level of confusion. He'd never felt so conflicted about anything in his life. Regardless, it felt good to be with his friend again, and while he could have pretended, he wasn't sure he wanted to. Standing close to Greg, he decided instead to seize the moment.

Moving closer with a swiftness that declared his eagerness to confront the situation straight-on, he raised a hand to Greg's cheek. One quick check to make sure he wasn't going to get punched, and then he kissed him.

On the previous occasion, there hadn't been time to focus on the moment. They'd had to drive to get away from the cops that had gathered at the gala. The kiss had happened, mixed up with adrenaline that flowed from the scene. The current situation was different.

Greg felt the incredible level of passion flow through him. He remained still for a moment, letting Rhett set their pace, before wrapping his arms around him. It was different, feeling a bulky man against him instead of the women's bodies he had a lifetime of holding. It didn't matter. The feelings that Rhett's kisses produced in him were too strong. He was aroused, and he didn't know what to do about that, but as long as that kiss was on offer, he was happy to stand and accept it.

With his thoughts turned off, Rhett indulged in the kissing. They quickly moved past lips-only action. Arms wrapped around one another, it was exciting for him. He and Greg had hugged enough times for that to not be anything odd to him. When he felt Greg's erection pressing against his own, however, that was a different story. It was like a bucket of cold water had been thrown over him. That was the stark reminder that he was holding and kissing a man, and he was aroused from it. His lifetime of having had it drummed into him that guys shouldn't be with guys pushed him to naturally pull away.

"I can't..." he started to say.

Greg fully understood the conflict. He'd been raised the same way. Internally, he'd never accepted the level of prejudice the Leadbetter family had openly shared their views on about different aspects of humanity. He'd never regarded himself as having any desire to be with a man, but he'd never seen anything wrong with it either. He knew that Rhett had been more affected by the Leadbetter form of brainwashing than he had.

"Rhett, you're my mate," he said quietly, keeping the distance his friend had set between them. "I don't understand this either, but I get why it feels so wrong. I'm not going to push you in anything, and we can avoid talking about this or ever kissing again, but just know that, as far as I'm concerned, *that* was one fucking incredible kiss!"

Rhett couldn't help but smile. He didn't want to, but it was natural. What Greg had said was only the truth, not only for Greg but for Rhett as well. It *had* been an incredible kiss.

"I'm so confused by this," he said, looking Greg directly in the eyes.

Greg tentatively took a step closer and nodded.

"I know," he said. "So am I. I'm not willing to give up on our friendship over it. Are you?"

"No," Rhett replied. "I feel like … I feel like I don't know what to *do* with this."

"Then let's not do anything with it," said Greg. "You want to find David, so let's go together and search for him. For the moment, let's just focus on that. Mark and Stace must be going through hell."

"Yeah," said Rhett. "They were happy when I was there, with Phillip getting married…"

"What?"

"Yeah, there was actually some good news that I was bringing to you," Rhett said. "Phillip's married. Did the deed yesterday."

"Fuck *me*. How long have I been gone?" Greg asked himself in disbelief. "Okay, well, let's go and do this search. Anything else can wait. You cool with that?"

Rhett nodded. "Yeah."

"Do you want to take one car, or a car each?" asked Greg, still uncertain about where Rhett's comfort level was.

"Let's just take mine," Rhett replied. "I can drop you back here when we're done if you think you still want to be here instead of the city."

Greg took a moment to consider that. Did he want to be back in the city? He'd go and search towns and cities for his cousin's son, but what would he do after that?

"Okay, that sounds good," he said. "Give me five. I'll just throw some clothes together."

Left alone on the veranda, Rhett turned and looked out over the lake below. It was a remote location, but he could see why Greg liked being there. There was peace in solitude with only the sound of birds, a running creek, and rustling trees around. He'd always been a city kid, but standing there, at that moment, he wondered if getting away from it all wouldn't be good for his soul after all.

"All set," he heard Greg say as he walked out again. "Do you want anything from here? I can bring some packet or canned food…"

"Beer," Rhett said. When he saw Greg grin at his reply, he felt drawn to kiss him again. He fought that urge. They had to get on the road and start focusing on something other than themselves.

"Beer coming up," Greg said, chuckling as he went inside to grab some cans from the kitchen. "Shall we go?" he asked on his return.

Seeing Rhett nod and start to walk toward the car, Greg took his time checking and locking the cabin. It was risky, leaving his car there and the cabin stocked, but he'd take the risk. He hadn't seen another person in the area since he'd arrived. He was confident nobody would be around while he was gone.

As he climbed into Rhett's car, he pushed their kisses from his mind again. He suspected he and Rhett were in two different areas of thought regarding that. He'd never been attracted to men, but he'd definitely been affected when Rhett had kissed him. He was open to exploring that further, even if the thought of any kind of sex with a man wasn't an arousing thought. He was open to them experimenting, but he would let Rhett decide if that was anything he'd ever want to do. They were friends. That overruled anything else.

CHAPTER 13

The first place they stopped, Greg and Rhett didn't expect to find out anything about David. It was impossible to know where he could be. For all anyone knew, he could have been lying in an unmarked grave somewhere, or not even that.

"Holy fuck, can it be?" the two men heard a deep voice call out to them. "Rhett fucking Beaumont! I can't believe it."

On hearing the voice, Rhett grinned. It belonged to the exact person he'd hoped to find. When he turned around, he was pulled into the arms of Nick Guthrie, an acquaintance from shadier times of his life.

"How the fuck are ya?" Nick asked as he pulled away. "It's been what? Five years? What's taken you so long to get here?"

"You know how it is. Life gets in the way of fun sometimes," Rhett replied. "Hey, Nick, this is my mate, Greg," he said before facing Greg. "Nick and I shared a cell for my six-month stint…"

"A *fucking* long time ago," Nick said, chuckling. "Good times, my friend. Good times," he continued as he turned toward his house. "Come inside and meet the love of my life."

"You're still married then," Rhett teased. "She didn't kick your sorry ass to the curb after prison?"

Nick laughed. "Nah, she's used to my antics. I think I told you we've known each other since high school. There's nothing about me that she don't know," he said as they entered the home. "Tasha, this is Rhett."

"Pleased to meet you, Tasha," Rhett said, addressing the woman who'd joined them.

"Rhett Beaumont," Tasha said, grinning at him.

"Oh, I've heard quite a bit about *you*, let me assure you."

"Only the good stuff is true," Rhett replied, chuckling. "Anything bad he said was probably actually about him."

Tasha laughed and nodded. "Yeah, you could be right in that. This man of mine is nothing but trouble," she said, moving closer to Nick and ruffling his hair in affection. "Hi, I'm Tasha," she said as she held out her hand to Greg.

"Oh, this is Greg," Rhett said.

"I'm pleased to meet both of you," said Tasha. "Your timing is perfect. We've got a roast cooking, if you wanna join us. There's more than enough."

Rhett looked to Nick for guidance. He was pleased when Nick nodded and agreed they should stay. The smell of the roast was unlike anything Rhett had eaten in months.

"Is there anything you want help with, Darlin'?" Nick asked.

"Nope," Tasha replied. "You grab some beers for these lads, and I'll shout out when the grub's ready."

Nick ushered the two men out the back door to sit at a large picnic table in the yard. When they were all settled with an open beer in hand, he turned to them.

"I'm glad you're here, Rhett, but I'm sensing there's a reason," he said. "What do you need help with? I should say that, for that gorgeous woman in there, I'm clean. I don't want to get into anything illeg…"

"No, nothing like that, Nick," Rhett said. "To be honest, we're looking for someone. Another mate's son has gone missing. We think he's on the run, but I said I'd try and find him."

"And you think he passed through here?" asked Nick.

"I have absolutely no idea where he went, so I'm going to just look around as far as I can," replied Rhett. "It's possible we won't find anything, but I figure there's no harm in trying."

"True, true," said Nick. "He's on the run from the cops?"

"We think he *thinks* he needs to be, but he doesn't," Rhett said, pulling out two photos. "This is a photo of him in front of his car, and this is a close up of him. It was taken about a year ago, but he hasn't changed that much since then."

Nick took the photos and studied them before shaking his head.

"I don't remember seeing the face, but more importantly, I *know* I'd remember seeing that car," he said. "That a Valiant?"

"Yeah," replied Rhett.

"No, I haven't seen any sign of the car or the person you're looking for, but I don't venture out so much anymore," said Nick. "There is a pub in town. You might have more luck there. Is he a drinker?"

"Not that I know of," Rhett said, instantly looking at Greg.

"No, I haven't seen David drink - not seriously anyway," Greg added. "Then again, whatever he's doing, I'm guessing he isn't living his normal life at the moment."

"Yeah, being on the run makes people assess things and make changes sometimes," Nick said. "I did it for over a year in my late twenties. There was an initial thrill of being able to go where I wanted, when I wanted, and be *who* I wanted. It gets lonely, though." He paused to look at the photos one more time before passing them back to Rhett. "Sorry I can't help you with that. What's your plan for finding him? You really got no idea where he might have gone?"

"None," said Rhett. "His older brother said he looked around a bit, in places where they'd spent time together when they were younger, but he doesn't know where he'd go."

"He's not shacked up with a missus?" asked Nick.

"He could be," Rhett replied. "There was a rumor that he was seeing someone, but nobody's ever seen her or met her, so we don't know if that's true or not."

Nick scoffed as he chuckled. "You're looking for a needle in a haystack," he said. "He could be just shacked up with some pussy, with the car in her garage."

"He could, but if she was someone he cared about, I think David would be a bit more savvy than to risk leading law enforcement to her," Rhett said, nodding. "It could definitely be a possibility, though. Having nothing to go on, I figure we have nothing to lose by asking around the people we know anyway."

"Fair enough," Nick said as Tasha appeared from the house.

"You boys wanna come and grab some food?" she called out. "Grab a plate, and then we can all sit out here to eat."

Greg needed no further encouragement. At the cabin, he'd done some hunting but generally had been living from canned and packet foods. He hadn't missed meat, but the smell and thought of it was incredible.

Sitting down together with plates in front of the four of them, they moved off the topic of David. Wherever he was, he likely wasn't in the small town that Nick lived in. Rhett and Greg had made a mental note to visit the pub before they moved to the next town. Before that, they would relax and enjoy the simple bliss of good food, good beer, good company, and good laughs.

~~~~~

"Where are you headed now?" Nick asked when they'd eaten, talked, and laughed for hours, and were making their way back to the car.

"We'll head up north a bit and see if anyone's seen him or his car up there," said Rhett.

"You okay to drive, man?" asked Nick. "If not, go to the pub and ask there. They do cheap-as rooms. Don't
~~~~~

go having no fucking accident."

Rhett smiled. "I'm cool," he said. "Thanks for everything. You haven't changed a bit!"

"Yeah, well, make sure you bring your butt up here again, Beaumont!" Nick called out before Rhett started the engine.

"Will do!" Rhett yelled back before they exchanged a wave, and the car eased away. "Pub, here we come," he said, turning to Greg once they were on the road.

"Let's ask about a room for the night," Greg said. "Sitting in the sun, drinking beer, has definitely affected me, and you look like it's got to you, too."

"No, I'm fine to drive," Rhett answered even though he could feel the effects of the alcohol. "The pub's just up here."

After parking the car and getting out, Greg saw Rhett stumble. It wasn't a lot, but it was enough for him to be sure he wasn't the only one in the initial stages of intoxication.

"If they have rooms here, we're staying the night," he said. "If they don't, we're crashing in the car."

"No, I'm..." Rhett started to argue. Greg cut his words short.

"No fucking arguing!" he said and saw Rhett give a mock salute and grin in reply.

Inside the pub, they approached the bartender and showed the photos of David and his car. In response, the bartender shook his head. Seeing only three patrons in the bar, Greg and Rhett approached each of them. None of them had seen anything.

"Let's give it up for tonight," Greg said, walking toward the bartender again. "Do you guys have rooms to stay the night in?"

"We do, and you're in luck," the bartender said as he looked at a diary on the counter. "We've got one left. Want it? Thirty bucks and it's yours."

Greg didn't hesitate. He was used to drinking, but the combination of good beer and the heat of the sun always seemed to accelerate things, even with a big meal. He happily paid the cash and took the key.

"Checkout is at ten," the bartender said before dismissing them.

Walking into the room, neither expected much. They'd stayed in pubs before. Some had been nice. Some, not so much. They didn't care. A bed was a bed.

On opening the door, both were relieved that the room had twin beds. They'd slept in the same bed enough times for it to not mean anything normally. Recent happenings had left both wary and not particularly wanting to be that close until they sorted out what was going on and how to deal with it.

"I'm gonna crash," Rhett said before lying down on one of the beds, not even bothering to take off his boots. "We didn't get any closer to finding David, but it was still a great afternoon."

As Greg sat on his bed, he watched Rhett go quiet and then drop off to sleep. He grinned. He'd seen his friend fall asleep that easily so many times over their decades of knowing one another. He'd never taken time to look at Rhett when he was asleep, but Greg found himself doing just that. He remained still, perched on the edge of the bed, looking and listening. As he did so, he tried to analyze his feelings. They needed untangling, but it all just felt like one big mix-up of emotion. He felt content and discontent at the same time. He equally felt happy and unhappy, positive and negative, and lonely although not alone. In truth, he just felt confused. He'd known Rhett almost his entire life. They'd always been close friends. They'd had years of knowing one another before they'd kissed. Why had the need for it happened when it had? That was the question he found played on his mind most of all - when and why had things changed?

CHAPTER 14

At the Stonewarden home, excitement was in the air. The youngest brother, Fitz, had sourced intel on another job. It wasn't always Fitz who found possible jobs, but with his high degree of technological know-how, he was the one who usually heard about things first.

As he sat in the living room with his father and four brothers, he pushed down the dislike he felt for them all. They were his family, but he never felt a part of them. It had always been the same for him. He didn't know why. When he'd been younger, he'd had no choice but to be among everyone. Since he'd grown into his adult years, he spent no time with any family except when they were planning and carrying out a job.

"Which part of town is it in?" his third oldest brother, Regan, asked. The two of them could have been close since they both lived at home. Fitz didn't care. He was able to make his own choices, and he chose to hardly ever be at home. There were always other places to stay. If it wasn't for the jobs, he'd gladly walk away from his entire family altogether.

"East side," Fitz replied. "It's a new boutique jewelry store that's on the top level of a two-story building."

"What's underneath it?" his father, Mitchell, asked.

"Indian restaurant," Fitz said.

"That makes things harder," said the oldest brother, Vic. "The restaurant could be open till real late, and the kitchen open with staff doing prep till early hours of the following morning."

Fitz shook his head. "No, I've been monitoring the security cameras of the restaurant and the jewelry store, and the street cameras in the immediate area. I've been watching all of this for seven weeks. I'll keep monitoring it, but I'm pretty sure all of the building tenants have established their routines."

"You said the store is new, though," said Mitchell. "Has it been open the whole time you've been watching the cameras?"

"Yeah, it got my attention when it opened a couple of months ago," Fitz said. "On that day, I started digging into the security and sussing it out. I'm sure it's a go," he added in full confidence. "This is what I think…"

As Fitz went into his usual form of spiel, talking about how to get into the building and what he thought would be the ideal role for each of them, Max's mind began to wander.

The longer that he knew Christy - the girl he'd met at the cop station months earlier - the more frequently that he found himself thinking about her. Two days had passed since he'd last seen her. He was itching to see her again. He still didn't know why he felt such a strong pull toward her. She had a pretty face, but not the shape he'd ever gone for. Sometimes when he looked at her, he almost called her his 'little apple'. Fortunately, he'd never stumbled on that and actually blurted it out. He wished her shape wasn't something that he even thought about. It was irrelevant in his desire to see her again and again. Why did it keep presenting itself as something for him to think about?

He was going to be seeing her that night after the planning session. That was the other part of his conflict where Christy was concerned. She didn't know who he really was, as far as the Stonewarden 'business' went. It was something Max suspected he'd never tell her about. She was good and had almost a pureness about her. He didn't think it likely she'd accept he was a jewel thief. He could be proven wrong. Ash had accepted the Stonewarden family ways when he'd married Charlie.

The situation wasn't quite the same since Charlie had fitted into the family business in another way, managing the large ranch that was a disguise for a getaway place for any Stonewarden needing to hide. Regardless, Ash had still married Charlie, even knowing she was a part of a family of thieves. Maybe it wouldn't be such a bad thing to share with Christy…

"Max!" he heard his father say with his usual strict and firm tone. "Focus!"

Max instantly shifted his thoughts to what Fitz was talking about. He didn't usually get distracted during their planning times. He put it down to being in the odd position he was in, being the one who wanted to do the chasing instead of being the one who was being chased. He suspected James was in a similar position. He, too, had seemed distracted in recent times whenever they had crossed paths. There was a rumor that a girl was behind that too, although James only ever gave Max a hard time about his love life and never mentioned his own.

He put his dilemma down to the shooting and having been in the coma. That had changed some things inside of him, including making him question how he truly wanted to live his life. It was the only life he'd get - getting shot had reminded him of that. He wanted it to be the very best life it could be.

Once again, he had to force himself to refocus. He'd see Christy later that night. There was no reason for her to be on his mind during something so important as their planning session. During those times, everyone had to focus. To not do so could result in something going wrong and someone getting hurt. Since the gala event, when they'd all walked away when gunshots had begun, they'd done a few jobs, mostly at residential homes. There hadn't been any hiccups at all with the whole team getting out and the gems successfully going through whatever they went through after his dad took them.

He fought to do it, but he managed to shift his

attention. He heard Fitz answer questions from Regan, James, Vic, and their dad. The job was three weeks away. There would be plenty of planning sessions before that night. That was what made the Stonewardens so successful. They studied and they planned, figuring out every worst-case scenario before they did anything. If something didn't look 100% doable, they walked away and didn't look back. It was no bother doing that. There was always another job that could be done.

"Okay," Mitchell said, standing. "That's enough for tonight. Who's working when in their regular jobs? James? Vic?"

"I'm on Wednesday to Friday nights only at the moment," James replied.

"I'm still working weekdays, eight to five," said Vic.

"Back here tomorrow night then," Mitchell said to them all.

As soon as he said that, Fitz was gone. He had nothing to say to his father or brothers, except for anything to do with the jobs. When those discussions were over with, so was the attention he gave to anyone in this family.

"Vic," Mitchell called out to his oldest son before he could leave. "I know I haven't given you any training yet."

"That's okay," Vic said as he shrugged his shoulders. "You've been busy being a granddaddy," he added cheekily.

"She is adorable, your little niece," Mitchell replied, grinning. "But it's time. I want you to come with me after this job, to see what happens with the gems after we get them. The job is on a Monday night since that seems to be the quietest night for the restaurant. Will you be able to come with me straight after that?"

"Yep," Vic replied.

"It can take a while…"

"Yeah, no problem. Tuesdays are usually quiet at work. Even if I'm out late, I'll be fine for work on Tuesday morning," Vic said. "I'm ready, Dad."

"I know you are," agreed Mitchell as he placed a hand on his son's shoulder. "You're ready to take it over, and I'm ready to hand it over *to* you. After this job, you can see what happens that night, and then I'll start showing you the admin side of things so you can begin managing all the accounts as well."

"Okay," Vic replied. "I gotta go. See you tomorrow night."

Mitchell looked at the remaining sons in the room. "You guys alright?" he asked Max and James, only noticing then that Regan had slipped away as silently as Fitz had.

"Yep. I'm heading out," Max said, making his way toward the front door.

"Got a date again, Max?" James asked, still intrigued by his younger brother's love life.

"Leave him alone," Mitchell said, chuckling. "*Both* of you have met someone who's changed your love-all-women ways, it seems!"

"Yeah?" Max asked, grinning. "*You* got some gossip to share, big brother?"

"Shut up," James said, making Max and Mitchell laugh out loud.

Max continued to smile as he walked out of his family home. He was going to see Christy. Why that made him so happy, he had no idea. All he knew for sure was that something about her delighted him. It wasn't a word he generally used, but it perfectly described the way she affected him.

Climbing into his Mustang and starting the engine, his mind returned to the job that he was going to be doing with his brothers and father. He'd been in the business for several years. Over that time, he'd done all the jobs just as he'd been instructed to do. It hadn't played on his conscience before the shooting. Since he'd been shot, he'd had a change of heart about the Stonewarden ways. He knew there was some kind of honor to be appreciated from taking from the too-rich and sharing that wealth among the poor. It was a good intention, but the method didn't sit well with him.

Before, when he'd just seen girls for a short amount of time, and mostly for physical enjoyment, what he did for work hadn't been an issue. In those situations, he'd never invested any substantial amount of time in getting to know those women. With Christy, it was different. He'd been spending time with her for quite a while. They didn't have sex, but she was the only woman he felt like spending time with.

The more time Max invested in her, the more he grew wary that at some point, he was going to have to do some explaining. He didn't know how or when that needed to happen. They weren't serious, so the time hadn't arrived yet, but he was drawn to her. Usually, he enjoyed jumping right in and getting as much pleasure out of someone as he could. With her, he felt protective. He didn't want to hurt her, so he held back in many ways. It wasn't usual for him to not want to rush to the good stuff, but he respected Christy. He suspected from their kissing sessions that she wouldn't mind moving things forward physically. Regardless, he felt like she deserved better. She deserved to be treated like a queen.

As he drove to her home, he resolved that all he could do in the present moment was enjoy the time he had with her. Having been shot had made him realize there might not be a tomorrow, so it wasn't worth worrying about too much. Prepare for it, but don't be obsessed with it. He'd heard a lot of things going on when he'd been in that hospital bed, unable to move or speak. It had all left him resolved to live the best life he could and be the best person he could be. His family's ways conflicted with that, but he would keep doing what he had to do.

When he arrived at her apartment block, he sat in his car for a long while. He was eager to see her. He was equally eager to not hurt her. There was a fine line between enjoying her company, but not encouraging her to enjoy his to a degree that she'd be hurt if something happened to him. His logic told him to not dwell on such things - there was no point in doing so - but sometimes, it took conscious effort to prepare himself for seeing her.

By the time he'd arrived at her apartment door, he was back to his usual carefree self. When she opened the door, he didn't have to pretend to smile. Always, when he saw her, his face did it naturally.

"Hey, Max," Christy said when she saw him in her doorway. Although she'd spent quite a bit of time with him in preceding months, she still didn't know why he kept spending time with her. It didn't seem to make sense.

Her mind had a lifetime of experience in telling her that she was too fat and ugly for anyone to want to know her. Since meeting him, she'd proactively fought her mind's verbal abuse inside her head. If Max Stonewarden wanted to use her for anything, he was sure taking his time getting to the point of whatever that was. He had only treated her as a friend. He hadn't asked her for anything. He even tried to have sex with her. It made no sense to her, but she continued to seize every moment with him, expecting one day soon he would disappear. When he did, she'd have some happy memories to cherish from their time together.

"Hey, you," Max said as he took a step inside and kissed her gently on her cheek. He watched as she closed the door. Sometimes it was hard not to seize her in his arms and show her how passionate he felt in her presence - and he *definitely* felt passion for her. That had begun the moment he'd seen her long eyelashes and perfectly kissable mouth. She never did anything to intentionally turn him on, but she certainly did affect him that way. Max had more than once wondered if the way his body reacted to her was what the whole 'animal magnetism' thing he'd read about felt like.

"How was your family get-together?" Christy asked as she sat on her sofa and watched him settle down beside her.

"Same as always," Max replied, appreciating that she never asked for specific details about *why* his family were having get-togethers so regularly. "Nothing to share there. How has your day been?"

It had taken time for Christy to begin to open up and talk about herself. As she sat and relayed what she could about her day - which wasn't too much since she worked in the local cop shop and couldn't talk about specific instances - Max relaxed into listening to her talk. Since she'd started appearing relaxed in talking about herself, he'd realized how much he enjoyed just watching her face when she spoke. She'd been timid when he'd met her. She still was to a degree, but she was also highly animated when she explained things. Her facial expressions were easy to watch, just as her words were easy to listen to. The hardest thing was that the longer he looked at her lips moving, the stronger the feeling was that he wanted to kiss her. There was a strange blend of frustration with bliss in those moments.

"Do you want something to drink or eat?" Christy asked when she noticed his trance-like attention. It had been odd at first, making her wonder why he was pretending to be interested. Over time, she'd accepted that he did listen to her when she spoke.

"No," Max replied. "I ate at home, but thanks."

"Do you want to kiss me?" Christy asked, knowing her face would grow deep red as she did, but not caring about that.

Max chuckled. Her stark honesty and straightforwardness were one thing that made her so likable.

"Yes!" he said. There was no denying that truth. "Yes, I always want to kiss you."

Christy moved forward and placed her lips on his. He was the first guy she'd kissed who she didn't think was playing some kind of cruel prank on her. She liked the feeling of her lips against his. They'd kissed a lot already, but every kiss felt like her first all over again.

Max indulged in the immediate feeling of intense arousal he felt as they kissed. It was incredible, but it was also the very reason he tried to keep their time together centered around activities rather than making out. He loved who she was as a person. He wanted that to continue to be their focus, rather than the physical stuff leading the way.

When he knew he was in that same place that he always got to with her - that place of feeling too much of a powerful need to move things forward and well past kissing - he pulled back. He watched as she slowly opened her eyes and looked directly into his.

"I like that," she said quietly, making him grin.

"Me, too," Max replied before giving her one small kiss again. "I like *you*."

Christy smiled and blushed. "And *I* like *you*."

Max pulled away and sat back, unconsciously shaking his head to eliminate thoughts he'd had moments earlier. His body wanted to continue being physical with her. His heart and his head wouldn't let it - not yet.

"What was that scary movie you said you had and wanted to watch but not alone?" he asked.

"Yeah!" Christy exclaimed, remembering. "I put it on to watch it last night. Five minutes into it, I was too scared to continue watching it. Will you watch it with me?"

"Hell, yes! I love horror," he said. "Put it on, and then let me hold you so you're not scared."

Christy smiled at him. There was nothing she'd

rather do.

For the duration, Max enjoyed the movie well enough. What he enjoyed more was the way Christy cuddled into him, encouraging him to keep his arms wrapped around her. She wasn't some chick who pretended to act timid just so he'd do that. She wasn't a chick at the other end of that spectrum who would act tough, always pretending to be stronger than they were. Christy was good and honest. She was who she was. It had been obvious when he'd met her that she didn't like things about herself - her physical self, specifically. Over time, she seemed to have relaxed about that. She was strong and timid all at the same time, and he loved it.

When the credits started rolling, Christy pulled out of his arms and turned to look at him.

"That was okay," she said. "Thanks for watching it with me."

"I liked it," Max said, chuckling. "Those chainsaw scenes were awesome."

Christy burst out laughing as she nodded. "Yeah, I'm glad you were here for those."

Feeling the lateness of the evening, she stretched. When she looked at Max again, she wasn't sure what she was seeing on his face. What she *was* sure about was her desire to kiss him again. She hesitated only a moment before leaning and placing her lips on his once more.

Max wanted to fight all urges flowing through him. That was getting increasingly harder to do. Instead of continuing to think about it, he let his thoughts go. It was kissing. It was something to be enjoyed, not something to stress about.

As he let go of the wall he'd kept up the entire time he'd known her, his arousal grew to a whole new level. He didn't stop himself from kissing her as passionately as he'd wanted to since the moment he'd met her, until he felt like he was at breaking point.

Harshly, he broke away and stood up.

Christy remained dazed for a moment before she realized what had happened. In her mind, the time had finally come. Since the moment she'd met him, she'd been asking herself why he wanted to spend time with her. She'd told herself it must be some sick joke or prank for someone so good looking and popular to want anything from her.

Since they'd been hanging out, she'd kept remembering her days in high school, when kids would set her up, making her think some popular boy or other liked her, so that they could then humiliate her in front of everyone. There was no audience anymore, but as she sat on the sofa and thought about the degree to which Max had just pulled away, she waited for the punchline. It had all been a joke. *She* was a joke. She fought to hold back the tears that felt like they were bursting to get through. All she could do was wait for whatever was to happen next. Wait, experience it, and then move on with life as if Max Stonewarden had never entered it.

Max looked at her as he cleared his head of all sexual thoughts. It was painful, how much he wanted her but also didn't want to do anything to hurt her. He'd never experienced anything like that.

When he focused on her face, he could see he had somehow upset her. She was working hard to not let those tears through, but she wasn't succeeding. Max felt his heart break for her. From hints she'd given him about how she felt about herself, he suspected her mind had instantly gone to a bad place.

He sat back down, took one of her hands in his, and raised the other to her chin. Forcing her to look up and right at him, he leaned forward and kissed her gently.

"Sometimes when we're kissing, I feel ... *more* with you than I've ever felt with anyone else," he said. "It's ... *incredible* ... but it's also real scary for me."

Christy watched him as he spoke. Her mind was

already in her self-loathing place. It took time for her to push that aside and hear what he was saying. Even when she processed his words, she didn't comprehend what he was actually trying to tell her.

"I don't understand," she said, unable to stop one tear that finally escaped. "I pushed myself on you when you don't like me…"

Max smiled at her.

"You're telling yourself that, but you've got it backward, Christy," he said, caressing her cheek. "I like you a *lot*." He paused as he studied her attempting to understand. "I like you beyond *any* level of liking someone before, and when we're kissing like that, you definitely aren't doing anything wrong!"

Christy sat quietly, continuing to listen but not hear his meaning.

"Christy, I love our kissing a bit too much," Max continued. "I know you don't see yourself as attractive, but believe me, I am *incredibly* attracted to you. My body *screams* at me that it wants to have you when we're together."

"But you pull away…" Christy responded. "I repulse you…"

"No! Oh, Christy, can you really not see? I pull away because I feel too much. I want you," said Max. "I want you, but I don't *want* to want you - not because I'm not attracted to you, but because I don't want to go there with you and then end up hurting you." He watched as her look of self-disappointment changed into confusion. "I told you I've been with lots of girls," he said and saw her nod. "I've used a lot of girls for sex. I don't want us to get physical in case I'm doing it for that same reason. Having sex with them and then not having anything more to do with them wasn't right, but it was what it was. The thought of having sex with you and then not continuing to spend time with you … it's … it's just not something I want to risk."

Christy finally began to hear what he was saying. As she listened, her self-loathing thoughts slipped away. They were replaced with an inner strength that had been growing slowly inside of her.

"You say that as if only you get to decide," she said out of the boldness she felt at that moment.

"What?"

"You're saying that we can't have sex because you don't want to risk us not spending time together afterward," she said and saw him nod. "Why do you get to decide that on your own? Why don't I get a say in that decision?"

Max looked at her in surprise - and an even greater level of respect than he'd had for her before that moment.

"You want us to openly talk about us having sex or not having sex?" he asked, curious.

"Yes!" said Christy. "If what you said is true - that you pull away from me because you don't want to hurt me - shouldn't we just talk about it so that I can tell you what *I* want?"

"Yes," said Max. He'd never had such a discussion in his life - not with even one woman previously. It was weird, but it was highly invigorating. "Tell me you want."

"What I want from you? And me? Together?"

Max grinned and nodded, feeling oddly excited by the conversation they were embarking upon.

"Yes! Tell me exactly how you see you and me, and what you want," he replied.

"I want…" Christy began as she studied his eyes. "I … I like you, Max. I love spending time with you, and I love kissing you. When you kiss me, I feel … things in my body that I've never experienced. I know that these feelings might be just a natural bodily thing and nothing to do with my heart, but I don't think they are. I love spending time with you, no matter where we are or what we're doing."

"I feel the same way," Max said. "When I'm with you and we're kissing, I know I want more physically, but, Christy, I think about you all the time. I like when we get out and do things - go for drives or meals or walks. During those times, I know that I'm enjoying you for just being you, and not because of any kind of lust thing." He watched her face. It was always a pleasure to see it relax. "I am very in lust with you. I can't deny that, but please believe me when I say that if I'm pulling away to stop that progress, it's because of how *much* I like you, not because of how little."

"Okay," Christy said, nodding. She paused and took a moment to consider what she wanted him to know. "I'm a virgin."

"Then you have something special to look forward to," Max said in almost a whisper.

"Max, I'm ready," Christy said. "Whenever you kiss me, I know I'm ready, and I want it with you."

The thought of having sex with a virgin didn't bother Max. He'd done that plenty of times during his senior high school years. It equally didn't appeal as something he *particularly* wanted to do, like he remembered some of his mates wanting to do as if it made them some kind of champion. His only consideration was hurting Christy.

"Are you sure?" he asked and saw her nod. "You don't want to wait for … I dunno … marriage or something?"

"I want to have sex when I feel like the time is right, and when I'm with someone who I feel is right," Christy said. "I don't have any beliefs about no sex before marriage or anything like that."

"Do you want to plan … a time…?" Max asked.

Christy chuckled and felt herself blush. That she was talking to a gorgeous man about the two of them having sex was an entirely new experience for her in so many ways.

"No," she said. "I want … I want it to happen naturally, but I *do* want it to happen, Max. Please - no more stopping because you worry about hurting me. If it feels right and we're both enjoying this, why should we stop? We're not teenagers. I might be a virgin, but I still know how I truly feel."

"Okay," Max replied. At that moment, he realized that he wasn't in any way aroused, but his emotion was high. Every word that came out of her mouth pushed up his respect and admiration for her. "You are so incredible."

Christy smiled sadly at him. "No, I'm not, but thank…"

"Stop that," Max said, cutting her words short. "Stop arguing with me. When I tell you that I think you're incredible and sexy and amazing to spend time with … just believe me. I'm not going to lie to you about that. Stop arguing with me, and *start* arguing with that brain of yours," he continued as he gently touched the top of her head. "What it tells you - all those negative things - they're just not true."

On hearing his speech, Christy felt tears threaten. She didn't try and hold them back. She knew her brain was her toughest critic of all. It was abusive toward her. It always had been. She knew as well as he did that she had to keep fighting to keep her negative thoughts repressed.

She nodded, unable to respond with words.

"It's late," Max said, regretful of the fact but also respectful about her having to work the next day. "I know you have to get up early."

Christy held back the thought that wanted to break through - that Max was making an excuse to be away from her. She nodded, smiled, and kissed him.

"I do," she said as she stood. When he stood up, she was glad to be pulled into his arms. She knew it was an ongoing struggle for her to accept good things in her life and nice things being said to her. It was also a fight she was determined to win.

Max hugged her and then followed her to the door. There, he pulled her close again and kissed her. It wasn't a kiss of passion, and it wasn't a kiss of sympathy. When he kissed her, it was purely from his heart, knowing that, outside of his mother and his sister, she might be the most amazing woman he'd ever met.

Breaking away, he smiled at her and then kissed her cheek.

"I'd like to sweep you away on Saturday," he said. "Do you have plans that day?"

"No," Christy replied, smiling. "What will you sweep me away *to*?"

"That'll be my little secret," Max teased while grinning. "Sleep well."

The kiss he gave her was welcome to Christy. Doubts plagued her, but all she could do was continue to counterattack them.

When the door had closed, she turned off everything in the living area and went into her bedroom. There, she stood and looked in the full-length mirror. It was a difficult thing to do. She did it each morning before work, only as a check that everything was in its place and she was tidy. Taking time to really look at herself was hard. It was another thing she was determined to force herself to do. She was who she was. Max had helped her to see that whoever that was, she deserved to stand tall, be proud, and own it.

She set the timer on her phone. It would have seemed a silly idea to anyone else, but forcing herself to stand and look at herself from head to toe for five minutes was something she wanted to do every night. The short, round girl in the mirror was her - and she was okay.

CHAPTER 15

When Greg woke the following morning in the pub bed, he was surprised to see Rhett awake and looking at him.

"Hey," he said as he began to sit up. Then the day before hit him in the form of an extreme headache. "Oh, *fuck!* Did we only drink beer yesterday? Shit, that stuff hit me hard. I feel like I drank a couple of bottles of bourbon last night."

Rhett chuckled. "Yeah, I'm suffering too. Either Nick put something in those beers, or we could just need some of that weird stuff called water."

"I've grown to like water, thank you very much," said Greg as he sat up fully. "From the spring near the cabin, it's good."

"I'll have to take your word for that," said Rhett.

"Where do you wanna go today?" Greg asked. "Are we working in a planned direction? Unless he's been out in public - and I don't see that being likely - I don't know how we're going to find him."

"I know," replied Rhett. "But I told Mark I'd give it a go, so I will. Even if we just drive around for a week or two."

"Yeah, alright," Greg said. "I need a decent breakfast before we go anywhere."

"And a bucket of coffee," Rhett added. He was glad things appeared normal between them. Anything could have been suggested with them sleeping in the same room together. Nothing had been. He was relieved about that. He wasn't anywhere near having processed how he felt about his best friend. Until that happened, he wanted it to be left as something not to be talked about.

"Let's go see what the breakfast options are."

CHAPTER 16

Inside a boatshed on the edge of a lake up the coast from where Rhett and Greg were, David Leadbetter woke with the same feeling he'd had almost every day for the previous four years. Sometimes he wondered if it had always been inside of him, slowly festering until it had finally broken through the surface of his conscious thought.

He wanted to kill. He didn't know why. He just did. So far, he'd only given into that desire one time. Fortunately, he hadn't been successful. He felt the primal need to kill, but he equally felt the humane desire to restrain himself. It was like something he needed but didn't want. Some people felt an intense level of arousal that made them need to orgasm. David Leadbetter felt an intense level of having to kill someone.

After the supermarket shooting, he'd had no trouble covering his movements that day. The cops had questioned him, just as they'd questioned everyone in their household. There had been nothing for the cops to find, or that they could prove. He'd needed to kill that day, and in the moment, he had wanted to. He'd been glad to hear that the only person who'd been hit by one of his bullets had survived. He knew it was a weird contrast inside of him. He wanted to kill, but he didn't want anyone to die because of him. He didn't understand it, but he'd fought for a long time to control it.

He'd thought life had moved on and was peaceful again. Then that night of the gala had happened. If only he hadn't hidden the gun in the house. If he'd gotten rid of it, or at least hidden it elsewhere, Rex wouldn't have found it. If Rex hadn't found it, he wouldn't have pulled a gun at the event, and things would have been different.

There was no point in dwelling on that. It had happened, and there was no changing it. The cops would have the gun, and their ballistics testing would have shown that it was the same gun that had been used in the supermarket shooting. They'd be searching for him everywhere.

He regarded himself lucky to have been able to get away when he had. It had been annoying seeing Sasha at the house that day, but perhaps that was for the best. At least their parents would know he was alive, assuming she'd relayed to them that she'd seen him. He regretted having had to run away from his family. He wasn't that close to any of them, but he'd never had any problems with them either. He'd always done what his father had directed him to, as was the Leadbetter way.

His father had been the leader of the Leadbetter gang for as long as he could remember, until that moment when he'd decided to stand down. He'd stood down, and Pete had taken control. That was what had created the unfortunate series of events on the night of the gala. Fucking Pete Leadbetter. When David had first left town, he'd caught a glimpse of news on a gas station television. He'd seen that Pete had been killed. He wasn't sad about that. He wondered who would have since stepped up to keep the entire Leadbetter clan in line. Had his father resumed that role, or had someone else? Not that it mattered. David was on the run. For the foreseeable future, he wasn't a Leadbetter any more than he was a Smith, a Jones, or anything else. He was a nobody.

He thought about the life he'd left behind. The hardest thing had been walking away from Kasey. He hadn't even said goodbye to her. It was a horrible thing for him to have done, especially since they'd been together for almost five years. He hated himself for the hurt he would have caused her, but the only alternative would have been to tell her what he'd done and where he was going. He hadn't wanted her to know anything. If she knew nothing, she couldn't be charged for withholding information if the cops went to her, asking about him.

Since he'd left, he'd continuously felt lonely. He hadn't thought he would. In his family home, there had been hundreds of times when he'd wished he could be on his own. Being alone hadn't proven as enjoyable as he'd always expected it would. He didn't have Kasey. He couldn't drive his car. He didn't even have any of the family members who he'd found annoying.

All of his life, he'd held down urges inside of him that constantly fought to break free. He knew he'd always been considered polite and quiet, especially compared to others like his sister, Sasha. Compared to her, with her constant exhibitions of anger, people thought he was a saint. If only they knew the depths of destruction he imagined inside of his mind all the time.

The darkness was always trying to consume him. He wanted to feel the satisfaction of killing. He wanted to feel blood on his hands and hear a last breath. That he felt that way horrified him. He didn't want to be that person, but he *was* that person.

Turning over, he switched his view to the small amount of sky and sunshine he could see through a meager window. He wasn't comfortable in body - sleeping in a sleeping bag on the hard wooden floor of the boatshed was anything but nice - but at least he was out of sight. In the time that he'd been hiding out there, he'd seen nobody come near the boatshed, let alone inside. If whoever owned it appeared, he wasn't sure what he'd do. Pretend to be just a homeless squatter who was harmless, he guessed. That was what he thought in his positive times. In the moments when his darkness successfully pushed through, he wondered if anyone walking through that door might end up suffering whatever fate his mind turned to at that moment.

CHAPTER 17

Mark Leadbetter stood at the kitchen window, looking out into the large yard. He told himself that he was assessing the woodpile to check if he should get more firewood to chop and stack before winter. His mind fought against such an unexciting thought. Intermingled with the concerns about heating the house in winter were further thoughts about his sons. It was never a cheerful thing to think about, but when the emotions hit him, he chose to let them happen. Once they were set free, he found he could then get on with getting through another day.

Feeling the loving arms of his wife, Stacey, wrap around him from behind, he smiled. That was one area of his life that never changed. They had their ups and downs, as all couples did, but they'd stuck together and loved one another for three decades. He knew he was lucky to have the love of such a wonderful woman.

"What are you thinking about, my gorgeous husband?" Stacey asked him before she kissed the part of his neck that she knew affected him.

Feeling her lips on his skin made Mark's smile grow wider. He'd never thought that two people could keep desiring each other for their entire lives. It continued to surprise him just how much lovemaking they both still enjoyed.

"You know I can't think much at all when you do that to me," he said, ensuring she heard his suggestiveness through his voice. Feeling her repeat the action made him moan.

"Where are the girls?" Stacey asked as she smiled, pulled away, and moved to stand beside him.

"Sasha's gone to spend the morning and have

lunch with Nicky," Mark replied as he moved his hand down onto his wife's butt.

"And Anya?" Stacey asked. She only had one thing on her mind, and the thought was intensifying by the minute.

"Out with her 'BFFs'," Mark replied as he turned to face her. "Said she'd be back for dinner."

That was all the confirmation Stacey needed. They were alone, and she felt like she was on heat. It was one of many things she loved about being a middle-aged woman. Her body always felt like it was on fire. She knew she was fortunate to have a husband who did not mind that at all.

"Need a hand with something, huh?" Mark asked, grinning when he saw the look on her face. He knew her face and her body well. When she wanted sex, there was no missing it or misreading it. That particular desire always emanated from her like a huge neon sign.

He wasn't surprised when she didn't reply with words but instead pushed him up against the wall. Feeling her body press hard against him and her mouth forcefully take his own, he was sure he must be living in heaven. Growing up, he'd always thought people would have stopped having sex by the time they turned fifty. Oh, how wrong he'd been in that.

It took only seconds for him to be hard. That was always the way, no matter how his body aged and changed. After he felt her hand reach down and unzip his jeans, he lifted the hem of the sundress she had on. He had the intention of slipping his hand into her panties. On firm instruction from her, he instead slipped them down to the ground. While he did enjoy foreplay, and they did indulge in that most times they had sex, when she gave her next instruction, he had no desire to deny her.

He watched as she moved to the kitchen bench, turned around, and bent over, holding her dress hem up.

"Fuck me," Mark heard her say. He didn't need her to say anything more. Easily and swiftly, he moved up behind her and edged inside. Jeans down to his knees, he felt like they were back in their late teenage years, trying to fit in a quickie before they got caught behind the bike shed at school.

"Fuck, yes," he heard her say. It wasn't nice, soft sex she needed then. He knew her sexual moods. He gladly increased his tempo and the force with which he started slamming into her. With every increase in both, he heard her moan louder. Before he could climax, he reached around and touched her clit. It was only seconds before he heard and felt her reach her orgasm. He let go straight afterward, the power of such an intense and quick joining leaving him slightly light-headed.

"Holy *fuck*, woman," he said, making her giggle.

They stood together, still joined, for a few minutes while Mark lovingly caressed one of her hips with one hand and one of her still-covered breasts with the other. Kissing her neck and breathing in her scent was a simple pleasure he loved.

After a long while, he pulled out of her and resurrected his clothing as she turned around. Pulling her into his arms, he was in no hurry as he kissed her.

"Thanks," Stacey said, grinning. "I needed that."

Mark laughed. "Any time, my beautiful wife," he said before kneeling. "You're missing something, though. How about I help you back into these."

Prompting her to step into her panties, he took his time lifting them into place. As each hand moved a side of them higher, his lips and tongue found and caressed the skin of her shins, knees, and thighs. Higher he moved until he stopped the movement of her clothing. Instead of moving her panties into their final spot, he used his hands to spread her folds before moving his head forward and lapping at her.

Stacey rested a hand on his head as she enjoyed

the sensations. She never tired of having sex with her husband. Anything and everything they did, she was turned on by. She'd just had an orgasm. Regardless, she wasn't surprised when his tongue prompted her to move her to climax a second time.

As he felt and heard her body shudder, Mark smiled to himself and finally moved her panties up. Taking his time to lower her dress hem and ensure it looked tidy, he stood. The post-orgasm look on her face always made her look even more beautiful.

Stacey wrapped her arms around him and kissed him. It was easy to do. She loved him. He was everything to her. If anything ever happened to him, she couldn't imagine she would ever recover.

They stood together for a long time, holding each other and lightly kissing until they heard a knock at the door.

"Expecting someone?" Mark asked her.

"No, not at all," Stacey replied, equally curious.

Opening the front door, both saw a young woman standing before them.

"Can we help you?" Stacey asked, seeing the serious look of almost distress on the young woman's face.

"Is ... does David live here?" the young woman asked. "Do I have the right house?"

Mark and Stacey looked at one another. They were part of a family of lifelong criminals. They knew that not everything was always as it seemed. The woman was someone neither had ever seen. Was she an acquaintance of David's - or might she be a cop, disguised in the hope of finding out where he was so they could arrest him?

"Who are you?" Stacey asked.

"Is ... this is the Leadbetter house?" the woman asked. "I'm trying to find my boyfriend, David. I haven't seen him for ages, and he isn't answering my calls."

Although he knew there was a chance she was in law enforcement, doing some undercover act, Mark prompted her to enter the house. If she *wasn't* a cop, she might hold clues as to where David had gone.

"Sit down," Stacey said. "I'm making some coffee. Would you like some?"

"Yeah ... yes, please," the woman said. "I'm Kasey. Are you ... his mother and father?" she asked.

Mark studied the young woman's face. To him, she looked almost panicked, and definitely out of her comfort zone. He nodded.

"We are," he said. "I'm Mark, and this is Stacey. When did you last see David?"

"It feels like too long," Kasey said as she felt tears begin. "I thought we were good. Everything seemed fine, but then he left my place one night, and I haven't seen him since. It took me ages to remember which part of town he lived in, and I had to ask around to find out where Leadbetters lived..."

"Well, now you have found us," Stacey said in a tone that she hoped would calm the young woman.

"Does ... does he *live* here?" Kasey asked. "He stayed at my place a lot. I'm not even sure if I'm remembering right that he said he lived at home still."

Stacey smiled. "He does," she said, holding back tears that threatened for her as well. "We ... we haven't seen him in a while."

"We actually thought he might have been with you," Mark said.

"I wish he was," said Kasey. "I wish I knew where he went ... and why. Did he say anything to you about why he stopped talking to me? I don't know what I did, and now I have something I need to tell him..."

Mark and Stacey both wondered what it was. When the young woman didn't offer any explanation to them, Stacey used her bold-is-best approach to ask straight out.

"What do you need to tell him, if you don't mind me asking?" she asked.

Kasey felt panicked. It had only been since David had disappeared that she'd realized she was pregnant. It hadn't been intended, but it had happened. She'd thought she knew David. If that were true, she would have anticipated his leaving, or at least expected him to talk to her about it if he was unhappy.

"Is he okay?" she asked. "You said you haven't seen him for a while. Should we be worried? Do we need to call the cops and report him missing?"

"No!" Stacey said automatically at the same time that Mark also reacted to Kasey's question.

"No cops have been to your place?" Mark asked tentatively. He couldn't ask the question without asking it directly. He didn't know what the young woman might or might not know about their family.

Kasey shook her head. "No," she answered. "Why would they?" After a moment, she looked from Mark to Stacey and back again. "Is he in some kind of trouble?"

"Can you tell us what happened the last time you saw him, Kasey?" Stacey asked without answering the question just presented. "Did something happen between you?"

"No, not that *I* know of anyway," Kasey replied. "He went out one night for something to do with someone in his family - not you guys, I don't think. He didn't say parents or mother or father, so I think he meant someone else. He went out that night, he came back, and then the next day, he left. He didn't say he was never going to come back or talk to me again."

"How was he before he left that day?" Mark asked.

Kasey looked at each of them again. Inside her gut, she felt a deep feeling of dread. Something had happened, and the father of her unborn child was missing. She closed her eyes and rested her head on her hands. They'd seemed so happy. Where had things gone so wrong that he'd leave her like that?

"He was ... he was a bit different, I guess," she answered when she roused herself out of her thoughts. "David's usually pretty easy going and happy. He has his moments when I see him looking serious - like *real* serious - but then he seems to snap out of it, and he's his usual carefree, loving self."

"But that day?" Stacey asked.

"He was quieter than normal, but like I say, he has moments of seriousness, where he looks like he's thinking about something not good," Kasey said. "But I thought he was happy with *us*. He didn't say anything before he walked away..." She hoped either of David's parents would offer some kind of explanation, but they didn't. "Look, if he just isn't wanting to speak to me, can you please tell me so that I know to get on with my life? If it's something else - if something's happened to him - I'd like to know that too. He's going to be a fa..."

Although she'd stopped speaking, Stacey and Mark could both imagine what she'd been about to say. They looked at each other before Mark lowered his head. On top of everything else that had happened...

"You're pregnant?" Stacey asked for clarification. When she saw the young woman nod, she needed more clarification still. "You're pregnant with David's baby? Our grandchild?"

"Yes," Kasey answered. "And if he doesn't want to be a part of our lives, that's fine. It doesn't make me happy, but I'll respect that. I just want to know he's okay."

"We don't know, Kasey," said Mark. "We haven't seen him either. Wherever he is, he hasn't contacted us to share that with us either."

Stacey reached out with her hand and grabbed Kasey's.

"Him not being in touch with you isn't something

you need to take personally," she said. "He's disappeared from all of us."

"Well, then, we need to report him miss…"

"Kasey, we can't do that," Mark said. "I don't know what David has told you about our family, and I'm not going to get into that now, but the cops are familiar with us."

"Not David…" Kasey said, hoping she was guessing correctly. When neither parent replied, she felt her heart begin to pound. "No, David has his moods, but he's *good*. He wouldn't be in trouble with the law."

Stacey's mind was cast back to when she'd realized what the name Leadbetter meant. It had taken her time to accept that was who Mark was. He'd told her before they'd married and before any children had been born so that she had time to really assess if she wanted him in her life. When she thought about their thirty years of marriage, she had no regrets, but she could remember just how difficult it had been to decide to stay with Mark when she'd learned that news.

"Kasey, don't think about that for now," Stacey said. "You need to concentrate on you and your baby. How far along are you?"

"Long enough for me to know that I'm keeping it," Kasey replied, unconsciously placing both of her hands on her belly. "I won't get rid of it."

Stacey was alarmed at the realization that the young woman might have thought that was why she'd asked.

"Of course, you won't," she said. "Being a mother is the greatest thing in the world."

Kasey looked from one parent to the other and then stood.

"I was hoping to find David here," she said. "I'm worried about him, but I … I'll go now. If you hear from him, will you please ask him to contact me? Even just one text message to say he's okay. If he wants nothing more, that's fine. I just … I just want to know what to tell our baby about its father when it's born."

"Does David *know* about the baby?" Mark asked.

"No," said Kasey. "I just found out a couple of days ago. I've been hoping he'd contact me or turn up at my place so I could tell him."

Stacey stood and tentatively approached the young woman. When she perceived that the woman was comfortable about being hugged, Stacey indulged.

"I don't think his not making contact has anything to do with you and your relationship, Kasey, but if we hear from him, I'll make sure to tell him to call you and tell you what's going on," she said.

"Thank you," Kasey said as she walked to the front door. She hadn't found out anything to tell her where the man she'd fallen in love with had gone. She didn't even know if his parents were telling her the truth when they said they didn't know where he was. Either way, she had no choice but to go home and start preparing to be a solo mother.

"Kasey," Stacey called out as the young woman walked down the porch steps. "Don't be a stranger. If you need support with the baby, or just someone to talk to, you're welcome here."

Kasey smiled before turning and walking away. She didn't know if she'd bother seeing David's parents again, but it was nice to know that she could if she needed to.

"Another mixed blessing?" Mark asked Stacey when they were alone again.

"Yeah? How so?" she asked.

"I guess we know that David's not with her," Mark said.

"But we still don't know where he *is*."

"True, but the more possibilities we can eliminate, the closer we'll be to finding out what's happened," Mark replied.

Stacey placed her head on his shoulder, needing to feel the strength of his muscular body.

"What's the other side of that then?" she asked. "You said *mixed* blessing."

"We've got a first grandchild on the way," Mark whispered.

Stacey pulled away from him and looked into his eyes.

"If she's far enough along to know she's pregnant, her baby will be born before any that Phillip and Daisy could have," she said.

"True," Mark agreed, nodding. "The order doesn't matter, though. Any children that our children have will all be loved and welcome in our lives, Stace."

"I know," Stacey said. "It's just … I wonder if we will *have* that child in our lives." She rested her head on Mark again. "Oh, David, where are you?"

Mark wrapped his arms around her and held her tightly. Everything was messy, but he chose to maintain hope that David was still alive. If he was just hiding, that was fine, as long as he was alive and he was safe. They just had to maintain hope. He hadn't shared with Stacey that Rhett was looking for David. He knew the odds of that bringing any joy were slim. There was no need to create false hope in her. He didn't often keep things from her, but that tidbit of information, he would.

"I love you so much, Mark," he heard her say against his shoulder, her voice and the movement of her body betraying her beginning to weep.

"I love you too, Stace," he said as he kissed the top of her head. "So much."

They stayed like that for a long time, feeding strength to and from each other. Regardless of how long they'd been married, they each continued to know and appreciate just how lucky they were to have one another.

CHAPTER 18

Over three days and nights, Rhett and Greg drove from place to place, asking if anyone had seen the black Valiant. It seemed a pointless exercise, but Rhett didn't want to stop until he'd given it at least a decent effort. If someone didn't want to be found, he knew it was pretty easy to hide away. Regardless, he was determined. If he couldn't tell Mark when he returned that he'd found David, he'd at least be able to say that he'd searched far and wide.

On the fourth day, they stopped at a gas station and went through the same routine of showing the photos. The response they got was finally different from those that they'd received previously.

"Oh, I remember *that* car," the young guy behind the counter said. "My dad used to show me photos of his old Valiant. I'd never seen one in real life till that one drove in here. It was a beauty, too. The guy who owns it obviously loves it."

"When was this?" Greg asked.

"Umm, probably two weeks ago … maybe?" the young guy suggested.

"Did the driver talk to you?" asked Rhett.

"Yeah," replied the attendant. "He was a bit jumpy, like he was on edge about something. Kept looking around him. I didn't ask any questions."

"Did you notice which way he was driving?" asked Greg. "Which direction?"

"North," the attendant replied. "Up toward the lake, I think."

Greg and Rhett looked at each other. It still might turn out to be nothing, but it was enough to give them a little hope. After thanking the attendant, they jumped back in the car. Before they pulled away, Rhett's phone rang.

"It's Mark," he said, looking at Greg. "Hey," he continued, answering the call. "Haven't found anything yet. I'm just on the road right now. I'll call you back later," he said before hanging up.

"That was brief," Greg teased him. "Does he know I'm with you?"

"Nope," answered Rhett as he eased the car out onto the road. "I know you want to be away from everyone, so I'm not going to share that information. If you want him to know, you can tell him."

Greg appreciated and believed his friend's word. Things weren't 100% normal between them, but that didn't affect how much he trusted Rhett. It didn't feel good not being honest with Mark, but there was hope that they might be getting closer to David. Whether they found him or not, Greg knew he'd have to decide what he wanted to do as far as hiding from the world went. If they found David, he'd know. As Greg looked out the window of the car, he wondered once more what exactly he was even hiding from.

"There's a lake," Rhett said, breaking Greg out of his thoughts. "I wonder if that's the one that guy meant."

Easing the car into a parking area right on the waterfront, they glanced around. There was a scattering of small touristy shops, a café that had signs indicating it might also be a grocery stop, and a kayak rental place.

"Well, I can't imagine David renting a kayak or going shopping for cheap souvenirs, but *that* place might be handy to ask in," said Greg, pointing at the café. "If he's been around, he might have gone in there for food."

Rhett nodded and climbed out of the car. As they walked into the café, a couple of people glanced at them before resuming their meal.

"Can I help you?" a voice called from the counter.

"Yeah, umm, actually, we're looking for

someone," Rhett said as he pulled out the photos.

"You two cops?" the attendant asked, wary.

"No," Rhett replied, chuckling. "We're looking for a friend's son who's gone missing. Have you seen him or this car?"

As Greg studied the attendant's face, he could see nervousness. That was a good sign. It meant that the person knew something and had possibly seen David but didn't know whether to say anything.

"If you'd rather not say, that's okay," he said, attempting to put the attendant at ease. "We'll wander around. Who knows - maybe we'll find him."

Rhett looked at him as if he was crazy. A question had been asked but not yet answered. He didn't understand, but he followed Greg's lead when he walked out of the café.

"That woman obviously knew something," he said when they were outside. "Why did you suggest we leave before she told us anything?"

"Rhett, she wasn't going to say anything," said Greg. "Didn't you see how nervous she was? It's okay. Her body language said enough. He's here somewhere. Let's stop here and hang around for a bit."

"Looks like there's a camping area over the other side of the lake," Rhett said as he started the car. "Let's go around there. Weather looks okay. What do you think? Sleep under the stars?"

Greg grinned. It seemed like a lifetime since he'd done that.

"Sounds good," he said.

As they drove slowly around the lake edge, they kept their eyes open, looking in all directions. It seemed unlikely that David would still be driving around in his car. Maybe he'd been driving it through the previous town, but wherever he stopped, surely he'd either ditch it or hide it. If he truly thought the cops were after him, the latter seemed the obvious choice. Then again, it had become evident in recent times that David might not think the same way as other people did. In truth, he could be doing anything anywhere, and it could be something that nobody else would think to do.

On reaching the far side of the lake, both men climbed out of the car and moved to sit on the bonnet. From where they were, they were able to look directly at the small scattering of buildings they'd just left behind, just across the water. If David or anyone else pulled in there, they'd be able to see.

"I feel like *we're* cops, trying to find a criminal," Rhett said, breaking the silence. "I don't even know why David's running."

"He possibly hasn't seen the news since he left," said Greg. "That's the only thing that would make sense. He thinks the cops are after him. He hasn't heard that Rex was killed *and* is now the suspect of the supermarket shooting."

"Yeah, maybe," said Rhett as he lit up a cigarette. "Want one?"

"Nah, I'm clean of that shit," Greg replied.

"Since *when*?" Rhett asked, chuckling.

"Since I've been in the cabin," Greg said. "Ran out and didn't feel like seeing anyone, so decided to not buy another pack."

"Just like that?"

Greg burst out laughing. "Not just like that! It was torment for about three days. Since then, though, it's been easier. I don't think about it now."

"But here I am, having one in front of you again," said Rhett.

"Yeah, but oddly enough, even seeing you have one, and smelling the smoke, it isn't making me feel like one," Greg said. "I think I'm clean of it. I may as well stay quit of it now. I don't have much money, but what I have, I don't want to waste."

"Fair enough," Rhett said, nodding.

They sat on the car bonnet for a long while, monitoring the comings and goings of the café. As the day began to turn cold, they finally moved.

"Let's find some firewood," Greg said, climbing down. "May as well set ourselves up for the night."

An hour later, they sat on a waterproof blanket on the ground, staring at the flames.

"You know, if we find David, he's going to see you, and he'll likely tell Mark that you're here with me," Rhett said as he gazed up at the darkening sky.

"I know," Greg replied. "I know it's time I made contact with Mark. He didn't do anything to deserve me disappearing."

"I did the same," Rhett said, turning onto his side and looking at Greg. "I went back, but I wasn't there for them when they lost Rex either."

"Well, we can make up for it after we've done this," Greg said. "First, we have to find David. He might have just passed through here and not be here at all."

"There aren't many places to hide here," Rhett said, glancing around. "There's hardly any homes, and if he's gone bush, there's a lot of that. We'd never be able to find him out there," he continued, pointing around the hills.

"True," said Greg. "I just hope he either goes home because we find him, or he goes home because of his own decision."

"And soon, cos I'm fucking hungry," Rhett said, making Greg laugh. "Why didn't we get anything at that café shop while we were over there?"

"I've got some food in my bag," said Greg as he jumped up. "Hang on."

Coming back with two cans, he pulled out his pocket knife to cut the top off each, then sat them on the edge of the fire.

"Canned pork and beans?" Rhett asked, laughing. "You're a fucking *legend*, Greg Leadbetter!"

CHAPTER 19

David Leadbetter woke in the middle of the night after having a nightmare. He wasn't surprised by it. The same nightmare had been entering his mind during the nighttime hours for years. Although it was recurring, the only person he'd ever talked to about it was Kasey. Sleeping next to her, he'd woken her so many times that there hadn't been any reason to hide it from her.

When he'd explained to her that in the dream, he was killing masses of people, he'd worried that it would scare her. The images he saw in his head weren't like what he imagined when he had a strong urge to kill, but they still resulted in people dying. It was yet another angle of the feelings he sometimes experienced that confused him. That need to kill, combined with no desire to prevent someone from living, was a weird contrast. He couldn't imagine that people who went on to be killers ever felt bad for having taken someone's life.

Although the nightmare was something he'd visited in his sleep so many times, he didn't take it as any kind of premonition or plan. In some ways, it reminded him that killing people would be the most horrendous thing. That was the reason he accepted the nightmare when it visited.

Kasey knew about the frequency and content of the nightmare, but David had never shared with her his occasional desire to kill. For a while, he'd worried that if he felt like that at the wrong time when he was with her, she might suffer from that. He hadn't held that concern for a long while. He loved her, but he'd left her. When things had gotten tough, with expectation of the cops being on his tail, he'd packed a bag and left, and not even left her a note to say why. In his heart, he felt bad about that. He also deeply missed her. She was one of the few people in his life that he truly trusted and believed was willing to see the real person that he was. He'd never felt that with his family. They seemed to regard him as some kind of angel. If only they knew what his mind was really like.

Glancing at the window, he could see the beginning of dawn. It was that moment in time that happened by miracle every day, when the dark began to just melt away. Shuffling over inside of his sleeping bag, he felt a familiar loneliness. He couldn't go on like he was. It was okay as a temporary measure, but did he seriously want to keep hiding for the rest of his life? What kind of life was that going to be?

He knew his mother and father would have been worried about him. His brothers and sisters probably didn't miss him so much, but he conceded they would have wondered if he was okay too. They weren't a close family, but they'd always looked after one another. If one of them was in trouble, someone would step up and provide assistance.

He wondered what his mother and father would think about him having been the supermarket shooter. He hadn't killed anyone that day, but he'd felt like doing so. It was only a fluke that he hadn't. Would he have rejoiced if he had? He didn't think so. He'd regretted having done it but felt fortunate to have gotten away with it. How long would that be for?

For a moment, he considered leaving the boatshed, jumping in his car, and driving to a police station. He dismissed that idea. He accepted he would be picked up at some time. He wasn't going to hasten the process of being arrested for attempted murder or illegal possession of a firearm.

When his stomach growled, he decided it was time to move. The café opened early to cater for long haul truck drivers passing through after their night of driving. The earliness of it suited David. The few times he'd gone to pick up a few groceries to see him through for a while, he'd been able to go in and leave again before any tourists arrived or the café got too busy.

He knew he had about twenty bucks in his wallet. That was the last of the money he'd been able to grab before he'd left town. It wasn't much, but he wasn't a fussy eater. It would get him a few cans of veges or fruit, at least. He'd been surviving on one can of food a day. It wouldn't have sustained him before he'd left town. His belly seemed to have adapted to it since.

Climbing out and readying himself, he quietly stepped outside. Instantly, he could smell the scent of the lake water. It was a pleasure of each day. He knew he'd lucked out, finding the tiny township and the abandoned boatshed. It was home to him and his car, but he'd leave the car safe within the boatshed's walls. It wasn't too far to walk to the café, and refreshing first thing in the morning.

Walking in, the young woman behind the counter gave him a smile, just as she had on each occasion he'd been in there.

"Morning!" she called out to him as she watched him move around the aisles.

David didn't want to talk to anyone, but he politely returned the greeting as he grabbed a few items into his hands. When he walked to the counter to purchase them, the young woman leaned close to him.

"Some people were looking for you yesterday," she said quietly, even though she appeared to be the only other person around.

"Who?" David asked, not wanting to converse but not able to stop his curiosity.

"Two men," the young woman said. "They had a photo of you and a photo of a black car."

"Cops?" David had to ask. It might not have been wise, but he had to know.

"No," the young woman said, chuckling. "They were two older guys, and pretty rough. Looked more like they'd fit into a gang rather than law enforcement."

"Do they know I'm near here?" David queried. "What did you tell them?"

"Nothing," she replied. "Whatever that's about, it's not my business. I said I hadn't seen you or the car."

"Thanks," said David. "I'll just take this lot," he continued, pointing at the groceries.

The young woman proceeded to process the purchase, not looking at him again until he'd paid.

"Be safe," she said to him before he walked out. All he could do was give her a sad smile and then leave. If someone was watching out for him, they'd probably seen him walking to go into the café. There was no undoing that.

He walked to the lakeside to take in the view. If he was going to be picked up and put away for a long time, he needed to appreciate all of the beauty that was currently available to him. As he looked around the lake edge, a vehicle caught his eye. It probably wouldn't have if he'd seen it from the distance he was at, and he'd not just been told that two older guys had asked about him. The combination of both made him wonder…

The sun was only beginning to creep up in the sky. He resolved to walk back to the boatshed and drop off his purchases before skirting around behind the vehicle and seeing if his suspicion might be true.

Walking into the boatshed, he placed the paper bag down and then stood still, weighing up his options. The people looking for him could have been law enforcement. Seeing a car that looked like Rhett's gave David hope. Rhett and Greg? They'd fit the description the young woman had given. It was also very possible that they were looking for him on behalf of his father.

He halted only a moment before walking out again.

CHAPTER 20

Greg woke to the annoying feeling of a bug crawling over his cheek. He swatted it away, only to find it then on the other side of his face. Swatting at it a second time, he was greeted by the sound of a chuckle. For a moment, he fought to wake up as he tried to remember where he'd heard that particular sound before.

On opening his eyes and peering upwards, he saw the face that he and Rhett had been searching for. He wasted no time before jumping to his feet and throwing his arms around David. He couldn't remember ever having hugged Mark's second son before. He didn't care.

"Thank fuck!" he exclaimed as he saw Rhett rouse himself and slowly realize who was in front of them. "David, what have you been doing? Your ma and dad are so worried about you."

David hung his head. That had been one of his concerns since the day he'd left.

"I know," he said. "That night … fuck, that night … I just … I know the cops must be after me."

Greg smiled sadly at him. The news he had to deliver would be so bittersweet with the extremes of joyfulness and incredible sadness.

"No, they're not," he said. "David, they think Rex was the supermarket shooter."

"What?" David asked. "I don't…"

"Was it you?" Rhett asked as he approached. Seeing David's reluctance, he nudged him. "David, was it you who fired into the supermarket that day?"

David nodded as he felt tears well up in his eyes. He hadn't told one person it had been him that day. It felt both scary and empowering to say the words.

"It was," he said. "That was me." He paused and

thought about what Greg had just told him. "If they think Rex did it and he's going to get in trouble for it, I need to..." he started to say before Greg cut his words short, placing one hand on David's shoulder.

"David," Greg said, feeling a tear threaten as he prepared to deliver the news. "Rex won't be getting in trouble for it. That night ... the night of the gala ... Rex was shot. He didn't survive."

As David heard the words, he refused to believe them. Rex was his kid brother. He was a pain in the butt almost all of the time, but he was his brother, and he was only a kid.

"No," David said. "I saw him there when I left. He was *fine*."

Greg watched David's disbelief. He understood it. He'd found it equally difficult to believe when Rhett had told him.

"He had ... my gun?" David asked both of the men standing before him. Seeing them nod, he felt a new emotion flow over him - guilt. "The cops shot him?" he asked and saw the nods again. "Because ... he used ... my gun?"

It was heartbreaking for Rhett and Greg to watch as David dealt with that realization.

"It's all my fault," David started to say. "I had that fucking gun in the house, and he took it..."

"David, this isn't your fault," Rhett said. "That whole night was fucked up. You know it, and I know it. Pete had no plan but to use a gun and try and get someone to hand him the diamonds. I'd always thought he wasn't sane, and that night proved that. Unfortunately, Rex got caught up in that."

"Even if it was your gun that he used, David," said Greg. "None of this would have happened if it wasn't for Pete. That's who this is all on, not you."

"If Rex hadn't found that gun in my room..."

"He would have done something equally stupid to

prove himself to Pete," Rhett said. "As soon as the cops took Pete down, Rex would have done something that still could have had the same end result."

"Everyone must hate me…"

"No!" said Rhett. "Your father and mother know it was a bad job all round. If Rex hadn't had your gun, he could have easily gotten another one. Pete was armed and ready to fire at anyone who got in his way. It's possible he had more guns with him, ready to distribute for the others to use."

"David, they just want you home," Greg said. "Nobody holds you in any way responsible for what happened to Rex, and the cops think it was him who used that same gun in the supermarket shooting. They aren't looking for you. You can go home."

David understood what was being said to him, but he was wary. Just because it didn't seem like the cops were looking for him didn't mean that they weren't.

"I don't know," he began to say. "How do you know for sure?" he asked Greg.

"I only know what Rhett's told me," Greg said. "I left town straight after the gala, too. I only heard about things a few days ago, and I haven't seen your dad."

"Your dad sounded pretty sure, David," Rhett added. "The cops have publicly announced that Rex had used the same gun in the supermarket shooting and the gala event. They haven't been looking for you. There's no reason for them to. On the security footage, you didn't look like you did anything wrong, your dad said."

"No, I didn't," David agreed. "I only got as far as walking around and looking before everything got crazy. I just got the hell out of there as fast as I could. I didn't touch anything or anyone."

"You still got your phone and your car?" asked Greg.

"Not my phone," said David. "I ditched that before I left town. My car is hidden where I've been sleeping. I haven't been driving around in it, just in case."

Greg nodded. "Good."

"You wanna call your dad?" Rhett asked, holding his phone out.

"I can't," David replied. He didn't want to face talking to anyone at home. He also didn't want them to keep worrying about him. "I don't mind *you* letting him know I'm okay, though."

Rhett smiled, nodded, then took a few steps away to call Mark.

"News?" Mark asked as soon as he answered the call. He knew it was unlikely, but he had to maintain hope that his second son was alright.

"We're with him," Rhett said. "He's here, and he's fine."

Mark breathed out a long sigh.

"Thank God," he said. "Can you put him on?"

"He doesn't want to talk right now, Mark, but he does want you to know he's alright," Rhett replied.

Mark felt desperate to talk to David and know for sure that he was alive and well. He paused a long while, reassuring himself that Rhett wouldn't lie.

"Okay, but give him a message?" Mark asked. "Tell him Kasey came here, and she needs to see him. She has some news for him."

"I'll tell him," Rhett said. He was just about to hang up the call when he heard Mark make one more request.

"And please … please tell him that we love him and we want him home with us."

"Will do," said Rhett. "I'll contact you again soon."

"What did he say?" David asked when Rhett walked back over to them.

"He said … that … he loves you and wants you home," Rhett said. "Also seems that a young lass by the name of Kasey has been trying to get in contact with you. Apparently has some news that she wants to tell you."

David's mind cast to Kasey. What news could she have that he would want to hear? That she'd accepted he was gone and wasn't returning? That she'd already met someone new and was moving on with her life? He missed her like crazy, but was she safe with him? Was *anyone*?

Greg watched David's face. He couldn't miss that the young man wasn't as happy about the news he'd learned as Greg had thought he might be. There was sadness in having lost a brother, but Greg didn't think that was what was driving the morose mood he was observing.

"What's up?" he asked, keeping his voice soft and encouraging.

"I can't go home," David said, looking directly at him. "There's something wrong with me."

When he didn't elaborate, Greg pushed him to continue.

"What do you mean?"

"I ... I have these thoughts and dreams about killing people," David replied.

"Yeah, so what? They're just dreams," Rhett said.

"No, well, maybe, but it's not just that," said David. "I ... that day that I went to the supermarket with my gun, I went with the idea that I wanted to kill someone. I *wanted* it!"

"You didn't kill anyone..." Greg said.

"But I wanted to!"

"Sure, but tell me this," Greg continued. "Since that day, have you been glad that you hurt nobody, or angry that you didn't hurt anyone?"

"Glad!" David exclaimed. "I can't explain it. I wanted to kill someone, but I didn't want anyone to die."

"Well, I'm no shrink, but that sounds to me like

you're someone who has a heart, after all," said Greg. "Truly bad people don't feel emotion like that, as far as I know. Maybe - and, like I say, I'm no shrink, so could be talking complete crap - but maybe, that's something you could just get help with handling, David."

"Maybe," David muttered, not sure what to do.

"You know, your sister used to be one angry young woman," Rhett said. "She's changed - a lot! If she can go from being that angry to actually looking happy now, I don't think you should give up hope about yourself. Go home, David. Tell your dad about your thoughts and your fears. Let them help you if you need some help. If you stay running, you're not even giving that healing process a chance."

David listened to all that the two men said to him. Although he appreciated all that they had to say, he was a grown man. He'd need to make his own decisions and not be swayed by what anybody else suggested he did.

"I shot at people," he said, his emotion getting away on him again as he began to weep.

"Mate, we've all done things that weren't good," said Rhett. "Welcome to the wonderful world of Leadbetter. The person you ended up shooting is now recovered. It could have been much worse. At least you don't have a murder on your conscience. Trust me, you're lucky in that."

David wanted to ask if Rhett had killed someone. He held back. He didn't want to know. That their family was so entrenched in any type of crime was a source of frustration for him. Admittedly, they didn't generally hurt anyone. When his father had been in charge of the entire Leadbetter clan, he'd made sure everyone knew that violence was not okay. Then again, Mark Leadbetter was different from other Leadbetters, especially the ones who were like Pete. David had bad thoughts, but, in general, he *knew* they were bad.

He nodded. He needed his family. He'd go home.

CHAPTER 21

Reversing the Valiant out of the abandoned boatshed, David felt the same level of anxious pounding in his heart as he'd felt when he'd left home. He had no reason to not trust what Rhett and Greg had told him about the cops not even looking for him, but was their intel right about that? Just because it didn't look like the cops weren't after him didn't mean they weren't.

No matter what lay ahead, he knew it was time to go home again. The things in his head had always plagued him enough throughout his life, but most of the time, he'd been able to distract himself from his thoughts. The time he'd just had in solitude had meant no distraction. The heaviness of his natural desires had been weighing on him day in, day out. All of it had to be dealt with. If that meant him being arrested and put in prison, he'd deal with it. At least in there, everyone around him would be safe.

Greg and Rhett had said they'd accompany him home, driving in Rhett's car but staying close to him. David appreciated that. If the cops pulled him over on his way home, he had witnesses who could report the incident to his parents so they'd know what had happened. He also realized that if he panicked, changed his mind, or wanted to run and hide, it was going to be much harder with this father's closest friends at his side.

It was a long trip home. He had a lot of time to think about what he'd done, who he was, and who he wanted to be. He had to find a way to change things inside of him. He knew he needed help with that. There were many things in life that he believed people could work out themselves. The images in his head, he didn't believe were one of them.

CHAPTER 22

"You think we're doing the right thing, encouraging him to go home like this?" Greg asked Rhett as they drove along behind David's car. When Rhett glanced at him with a surprised look on his face, Greg continued. "It's easy for us or Mark to tell him that everything's okay, but what if it's not? What if the cops *have* been waiting for him to return to town?"

"I think - from what David's said - that he's thought about being arrested," said Rhett. "He seems to have prepared himself for that possibility."

"Yeah, but should we be helping him along in that?" Greg asked. "I know Mark and Stacey want their son back, but…"

Rhett thought about all that David had told them he'd done and felt. The aspect of David having shot into a supermarket in broad daylight to kill people wasn't the thing that concerned Rhett. They were Leadbetters. They'd all done criminal things, to some degree, although some much more than others. Doing the crime and doing the time wasn't all that surprising among anyone they knew.

What had caught Rhett's attention more was the degree to which David had talked about his self-described need to kill. That was something of an entirely different magnitude.

"He sounds like he needs help," Rhett said. "Not with the law, but with his head."

"He has a few bad thoughts," said Greg. "Who doesn't now and then?"

"If he thought they were nothing, he wouldn't have talked about it so much," said Rhett. "He needs help, Greg. I just hope Mark actually hears that, if David tries to explain it to him."

"Yeah," Greg said, his mind moving on to the possibility of seeing Mark and Stacey again. He knew he didn't have to. He could ask Rhett to stop the car at any spot and let him out, but what was he afraid of? He'd needed time out, and he'd taken it. He still needed more of it. The idea of being an active member of the Leadbetter gang, doing whatever the current leader said he should, didn't appeal. That novelty had worn off a long time earlier.

He continued to consider his options until they entered their home town. As if reading his thoughts, he heard Rhett ask the exact question he'd been asking himself.

"You want me to drop you off somewhere, or do you want to come back to Mark's?"

"I do want to get back to the cabin, but yeah, I'll go in with you," Greg finally said.

"Okay, I can give you a ride back to your wilderness later," said Rhett as he glanced at Greg and saw the seriousness on his face. "Hey, don't worry about this. I was away for ages too, remember. Mark was only happy to see me. He didn't ask about where I'd been or what I'd been doing. He'll only be glad to see you too."

"Yeah, I know," said Greg. "I just … I feel like I abandoned them when they probably needed me…"

"We didn't know anything had happened to Rex," Rhett reminded him. "And besides, you know Mark better than that. He wanted to get away from the family himself. That was why he stepped down."

Greg knew Rhett was speaking truthfully. There was no reason either of them had ever needed to leave, and there was no reason why Greg wouldn't be welcomed back, just as Rhett had been. Regardless, the closer they got to the street where the Leadbetter home was, the more anxious Greg felt.

~~~~~
~~~~~

When they approached the home, they saw Mark and Stacey both appear outside the front door. Rhett and Greg watched as David hesitated before getting out of his car and instantly being enclosed in the hold of both of his parents. For a moment, Stacey and Mark didn't appear to be aware of Rhett's car right behind David's.

When Mark turned and saw Rhett's vehicle, he grinned at Rhett. Then he noticed the person sitting next to Rhett. He felt torn for a moment, needing to see and hear about the journey of his cousin as much as his son's. As he watched, he saw both of his closest friends climb out of the car and walk toward him. He was glad enough to see Rhett. Seeing Greg was enough to push him to rush forward and pull him close.

"Where the fuck have you been?" he asked, feeling like his emotions had been pushed to the limit within what seemed like only seconds. "It's good to see you. It's good to know you're *alive*."

Greg grinned as he pulled away.

"You thought I was dead?" he teased, appreciating the ease and happiness he felt to be in his cousin's presence again. "If I was dead, I'd have haunted the crap out of you, believe me!"

Mark turned to move toward the house. When he realized his two friends weren't moving, he stopped and faced them again.

"You guys coming in?" he asked and saw Rhett shake his head.

"This one…" he started to say.

"This one needs a little bit more time away from things," Greg finished. "I'm okay, Mark, but I want time away right now. I need it for me."

Mark nodded. He understood the need to escape.

"I'm glad you're okay," he said before hugging Greg again and then turning to Rhett. "Thank you for bringing my boy home."

"I'll see you again soon," Rhett replied.

CHAPTER 23

On entering his family home, David felt panicked. It was good seeing his mother and father again, but he felt vulnerable. It was a feeling he didn't like. It was hard to let go of his fears about the cops arresting him. Being in the house also reminded him of the last time he'd been there. He'd seen his sister, Sasha, that day. The very moment that he'd seen her, he'd been feeling like hurting someone - anyone. He'd told her to leave, and she had. Nothing had flowed on from his thoughts, but he could still remember how he'd felt at that moment.

At the end of the hallway, moving out from the kitchen, he saw his youngest sister, Anya. Usually cheerful, he was thankful that she held back. He knew how chirpy she could be. He couldn't feign joy at that moment. He gave her a sad smile and appreciated the quietness of her mirroring that and not saying or doing anything more.

There were no other family members to see. He was glad.

"I'll fix you something to eat..." Stacey started to say, fully aware of the uncertainty about what David would want. She'd known plenty of people who'd returned from being on the run. Some needed to talk. Some needed silence. Although he was one of her babies, she held back from smothering him the way she naturally wanted to.

"No ... thank you," David said quietly. "I just want to ... can I..."

The front door opening again behind them caused all three to turn around.

"Is that David's car?" Sasha called out as she passed through the doorway before she saw him. When she did, she walked up to him, looked at him for a brief moment before she wrapped her arms around him. She didn't say anything to him.

David found the interaction odd but strangely welcome. The action was abnormal for her, but Rhett had told him that Sasha had changed and left behind her angry moods. She'd been constantly angry, but she'd changed. Perhaps she would be one person who could at least begin to understand how he felt.

Mark glanced at Stacey. Seeing their kids hugging each other was a new thing in their household. Seeing David hug Sasha seemed particularly unexpected. Despite the strangeness of it, they walked through to the kitchen, leaving the two young people in the hallway.

"He's changed," Stacey whispered to him when they passed through the kitchen and out into the sun-bathed yard. "He even looks different."

Mark pulled her close and nodded.

"But he's home," he said. "He's alive, and he's home. Let's give him space. When he's ready, he'll talk."

"We have to tell him about Kasey," Stacey said, pulling away and looking him in the eyes. "He needs to know…"

"And he will," said Mark. "Just give him a minute to breathe," he teased her. He was able to portray feeling easy-going on the outside. It was far from what he felt on the inside.

~~~~~

In the hallway, Sasha pulled back from her brother. She didn't know what had inspired her to wrap her arms around him. They'd hardly ever interacted in any way at all, he was so quiet and withdrawn all the time. Something about the way he'd looked had made her think he needed it - not just a hug in general, but a hug from *her*. As she looked at his face when she pulled away, she didn't see any discomfort at all.

"Will you tell Ma and Dad that I just want to be
~~~~~

alone?" David asked her in almost a whisper. He suspected his mother, especially, would want to coddle him. He appreciated the sentiment but didn't want that.

"Yeah," Sasha said. "If you want to talk…"

"Thanks," David replied before he turned, made his way to his room, and closed the door.

Inside, he walked to his bed and lay down, appreciating the simple pleasure it produced in him. He'd been sleeping on a hard floor for ages. Before the gala night, he'd hardly slept at home, spending most nights at Kasey's. It had been easy to forget just how comfortable his childhood bed was.

Kasey. That was the next thing he had to think about. He owed her an explanation. According to Rhett's message from his father, Kasey wanted to tell him something. Was it that she'd moved on? If she had, could he handle that? Of course, he would. He'd decided to leave without talking to her. She deserved more happiness than he could provide if he did that.

Turning over, he knew he needed sleep. Everything seemed just that little bit better when he was fully rested and not stressed or overtired. The stress, he couldn't control so much. The rest and sleep, he could.

~~~~~

As Sasha walked out into the backyard, she could see the worried looks on the faces of not only her mother and father but also her younger sister. It wasn't good. When Anya wasn't happy, there had to be something seriously wrong.

"Where is he?" Stacey asked her daughter.

"He's in his room," Sasha replied. "He's asked to be left alone."

"How are things with you?" Mark asked Sasha. Although they lived in the same house, their paths crossed surprisingly little.

"All's good with me," Sasha said. "Nothing new to tell in my world."
~~~~~

"And *James?*" Anya asked, emphasizing his name in a posh tone and grinning as her usual chirpy self pushed through the somber mood of the previous few minutes.

Sasha smiled at her younger sister. The two of them even talking was relatively new. The far-too-happy outlook of her sister still annoyed her on occasion, but nowhere near as often as previously.

"I think it must be about time *you* started talking about boys," she teased. "You got someone you want to share some news about, Anya?"

Anya giggled at her sister's effort to change the subject but didn't pull Sasha up on it.

"I like everyone," she said in full honesty. "Boys … girls … I don't care. If someone's friendly to me, I'm friendly to them."

"That's question avoidance if ever I heard it," Sasha said, grinning. "But I'll let you away with it."

Mark and Stacey watched the interaction. Everything about Sasha's changes was something to see. Watching her grow and flourish since meeting James and little Nicky had been one thing. Her change in how she interacted with her youngest sibling was a surprise of a different degree. As sisters, they always should have been close. They never had been. It was possible they never would be, but seeing them smiling and speaking to one another was a good start.

"He let you hug him," Stacey said, remembering.

Sasha was confused for a moment until she realized what her mother was talking about.

"It felt … right," she replied. "I told him I'm here if he wants to talk to me."

Stacey felt tears begin to well. She wanted to be the one that her second son would talk to, but she knew she probably wouldn't be. David was a grown man. She didn't doubt that he loved her as his mother, but it had been a very long time since he'd needed anything from her. When he was ready to talk, he might talk to Sasha, or he might talk to Mark. If he didn't need or want to talk to his mother, it saddened her, but she accepted it. She'd raised her kids in accordance with the Leadbetter ways. Part of that had been telling them to harden up when things seemed tough. It meant an entire childhood of no hugging or saying they loved each other.

She knew there was no point in dwelling on the past. She'd raised her kids that way, and they'd grown up as they had as a result of it. A time had finally arrived when all of them had started to warm up more to each other, and treat each other better. If David felt comfortable hugging and talking to his sister, Stacey knew she had to be happy about that. He was her son, and he was alive. That had to be enough. That *was* enough.

"Anya, aren't you meant to be going to meet up with your friends?" she asked her youngest daughter.

"Yeah, but do you want me to stay?" Anya asked.

"No," replied Stacey. "Go, and enjoy your day, little one."

"Okay," Anya said as she stood and moved to her mother for a hug. She was old enough to not need them, but she still liked them. She also appreciated how much her mother seemed to need them. "Bye," she added before walking out.

"What are you going to do today, Sasha?" Stacey asked.

"I just got home!" Sasha said, a sliver of her previously-always-annoyed tone slipping through. Seeing her mother and father both smile at it, she chuckled before standing. "Nah, I'm gonna go and watch some movies in the lounge. I'll be around here for the rest of the day if you need a hand with anything."

"No *James*?" Mark cheekily asked, copying the posh voice Anya had used to say his name.

Sasha rolled her eyes at her father.

"Haha, very funny," she said before grinning. "Think I'll watch a *slasher* movie or three."

Mark chuckled. It was a weird dynamic, having lost a son, not knowing how to help another, while also seeing his always-angry daughter looking happy and easy-going.

When he and Stacey were left in the sunshine alone, his mind was active.

"What are you thinking?" Stacey asked, him seeing the contemplative look on his face.

"It doesn't seem that long ago that the biggest thing I was thinking about was finding jobs to provide us with cash to survive," Mark said. "So much has changed, and over such a short amount of time."

Stacey nodded. She couldn't argue with what he'd said. They'd lived a life that entailed stealing and interacting with a huge circle of people who were doing the same. That hadn't been an ideal lifestyle, or one that other people would want, but it had been their norm.

"One thing hasn't changed at all," she said, taking his hand in hers and raising it to her lips. When he looked at her, she elaborated. "My love for you."

Mark leaned forward and kissed her softly.

"Or mine for you," he said before raising his hand, pulling her closer, and kissing her with the deepest passion that he felt for her as the woman he'd always loved, and always would.

Everything had changed and would continue to change, but he never stopped appreciating that he was married to one of the most incredible women in the world.

"We should let Phillip know," Stacey said when they pulled away.

"I'll text him," said Mark, picking up his phone. "I'll let him know David's asked to be left alone, at least for the moment. I don't want him rushing over here."

Stacey watched as her husband typed the message

and then set his phone back on the table.

"No, especially with them being newlyweds," she said as the memory of her own post-wedding days flowed over her. She and Mark hadn't had a honeymoon, but they hadn't needed one. They'd had a home to set up. Just being in it together without anyone else around had provided more than enough enjoyment for them.

Glancing at the house that had been her home for all of the years since her wedding, she felt happy. Things weren't ideal in all areas of their world, but she was lucky. Other women wouldn't have wanted the existence she'd experienced over her adulthood, but many other women also wouldn't have had such a great love as she'd had with one man who had an incredible heart.

"You getting all soppy at the thought of them being newlywed?" Mark asked, grinning as he watched her expressions.

Stacey chuckled, then leaned in to kiss him just as passionately as he'd just kissed her.

"Yeah, and the knowledge that I've been blessed in my marriage," she said. "I hope all of our kids experience that."

A shadow passed over each of their faces as they considered that one child would never experience that. It was a fleeting moment. There was a future that they needed to focus on.

"We need to decide how we're going to handle the knowledge we got from Kasey," Mark said.

"Let's just give him a couple of days to settle in and relax," said Stacey. "You told Rhett to tell him she'd been here, right?" she asked and saw him nod. "Hopefully, he'll contact her, or he'll ask us what was said. We can take it from there. It should be her that tells him. Hopefully, he'll give her a chance to."

No more was said as they sat and basked in the warmth of the sun, silently telling themselves they were happy, and they just needed to sit tight and be patient.

CHAPTER 24

Sitting in Rhett's car on the way to his cabin, Greg was thoughtful. He'd just seen his cousin. Despite how nice that had been, he knew he needed more time in the bush, away from family stresses. He was glad to have been a part of finding Mark's son and encouraging him to go home to his parents. Seeing the reunion had been enough to make Greg ponder the life he'd lived. He'd had plenty of opportunities to settle down and start a family. When he'd been younger, it hadn't been something he'd wanted. Seeing Mark and Stacey together, it was easy to regret his earlier decision to go through life as a single man.

"You're quiet," he heard Rhett say beside him. "What's up?"

"Just thinking about Mark and Stace," Greg replied. "I used to use our lifestyle as a reason to never get attached to anyone, but when I look at them…" he began to say. His words drifted off. He wasn't sure why he was so contemplative.

"They do have something unique," Rhett agreed. "Their relationship, I think anyone would be envious of - criminal or not."

"Do you regret not having started a family?" Greg asked.

Rhett was surprised by the question. There had been plenty of times when they'd sat down together and had some form of heart-to-heart or other. That particular question had never been voiced.

"Regret? No. I don't tend to regret things. Life's too short," said Rhett. "Do I sometimes wonder if I could have been happy if I'd chosen one of my past girlfriends and actually tried to make it work for the long haul? Yeah, of course. I think anyone who gets to our age, who hasn't settled down with someone, asks that question. When we're younger, we stupidly think we'll have the same life of fun forever. It's not till we're older that we wake up and see that there might be decades ahead of us yet, and we're possibly going to be alone for them."

"You had a few long-term girlfriends who were definitely willing to tie the knot with you, if I recall," Greg said, remembering their years.

Rhett laughed. "Yeah. I liked all of the women I've been involved with, but fuck, when they used to drop that marriage bomb, that was my moment to get the hell out of there."

"None that you now think you could have been happy with?" asked Greg.

"Yeah, of course," said Rhett, casting his mind back over the long list of women he'd had some form of involvement with or other. "They probably all were wife material, and I could have been real happy with, settling down and having some kids. But I didn't want that then, and it's in the past now."

"You're not too old," Greg said.

Rhett turned and looked at him, surprised by the comment. "I wouldn't want kids now!" he said. "No way. Not for me. Is that what you're thinking about? You want to go out and find a woman to settle down with?"

Greg thought about the possibility. It had been a long time since he'd even had the energy to have sex. The thought of having a lover wasn't appealing, let alone investing time into a full-on relationship.

"No, I think I'm past that," he said.

"You sound like you're doing some mid-life crisis analysis or something," said Rhett. "Is this to do with … us?" he asked, gulping while broaching the subject face-on.

"I dunno," Greg said. "Maybe."

Both remained quiet for the rest of the journey to the cabin. Rhett had raised the subject. Greg didn't know if he was going to continue it, or if he even wanted to. In the car hadn't been an ideal place to talk about it. As they pulled up beside the cabin, he prepared himself for anything to happen or be said.

"You staying a while?" he asked, deliberately not suggesting a timeframe. If Rhett wanted to stay for a few nights, that would be cool. If he wanted to stay for a few minutes, that would be okay too.

"Yeah," said Rhett as he climbed out of the car. "I'll hang around for a bit. It is peaceful here."

Greg unlocked the cabin and went inside. He'd only been gone for a few days, but he was glad that everything looked secure and just as he'd left it.

"I'm just gonna get some firewood in and get the fire ready to light before it starts to get dark," Greg said.

"I'll give you a hand," said Rhett, following him outside. "Tell me what to do."

Greg smiled to himself. Rhett sounded relaxed. That was a relief. He'd run away once when things had been uncomfortable. Greg didn't want him to do it again. Their friendship was far too precious.

"Okay, you wanna fill that basket with a couple of loads of wood and stack it inside? That'll be enough for the night," Greg said. "I'll go and fill some water bottles."

Rhett watched his friend walk into the house and then away again through the bush with an armful of large bottles. Once left alone with the firewood, Rhett stood still for a moment and just listened. All he could hear were some birds chirping and the trees rustling in the slight breeze. He'd spent time in nature in his earlier years, even going completely bush at one stage. Standing as he was, he remembered how soothing nature was.

Refocusing, he began his chore of carrying the firewood inside. It was getting late in the afternoon. As he performed the actions, he was aware that he might have to choose whether to stay or go. The choice might not be something to worry about in the end. Greg might not invite him to. If that was the case, all good. If an invitation *was* extended, though, he needed to think about what he wanted to do.

Stacking the last of the wood in a neat pile near the fire, he was undecided. What did he want? He knew he didn't need to stress about Greg pressuring him for anything. They'd just spent almost an entire week together, sleeping close to one another. Nothing had happened between them. It wasn't an issue. They were friends. That wouldn't change, no matter what did or didn't happen.

"You dazed after all that effort?" he heard Greg's voice tease him from behind. "Hard work wear you out?"

"Fuck off," Rhett threw back, making them both chuckle.

"Beer?" Greg asked, handing out a can. "This one's not cold, but the next ones will be."

Rhett took the can. Before he opened it, he looked at Greg. He knew Greg was against driving after drinking. It was easy to imagine that the beer was given to him as a way to make him stay.

"I can make you a coffee if you'd rather have one of those," Greg said. "I just need to light the fire and get the water on to boil…"

"Beer's good," Rhett said.

"Come outside and watch the sun go down," said Greg. "It's something to see."

The two of them going onto the veranda and sitting in the two chairs that resided there felt normal. They'd sat there for a short time after the gala event. It had felt okay then until Rhett had left, obviously stressed and worried about things.

"I do see why you like being here," Rhett said after a long period of silence. Relaxing right back into the seat and closing his eyes, it was almost magical listening to the sounds of nature while breathing in the fresh air.

"Yeah, it's good for the soul, that's for sure," said Greg.

"You think you'll go back to your house in the city? You seem pretty settled here."

"I think … fuck, I don't know," Greg admitted. "I like it here. It feels more right being here than being there, at least for the moment." He took a long swig of his beer before turning to face Rhett. "You know you're welcome to stay and hang out here if you want."

Rhett heard the suggestion. It was an attractive offer. He didn't know why it worried him. When they'd been searching for David, neither of them had mentioned their previous kisses or done anything physical. He knew there was no pressure on him to do anything. Greg had been his friend for almost all of their lives. He'd never tried to make Rhett do anything.

"Yeah," Rhett said, not elaborating what he was referring to.

"I'll light the fire soon and get the cabin warm," said Greg to veer the conversation away again. He didn't want to risk freaking Rhett out. The offer had been made. No more needed to be said about that. "It can get cold here real quick once that big yellow thing in the sky completely disappears."

He sat a moment longer, sculling back the last of his beer before standing and moving inside. He left the door open. That was his message to Rhett that he didn't mind if he stayed or he went. Whatever Rhett decided, it was very okay with Greg.

Rhett stayed where he was, not at all minding the momentary solitude as the sun began its descent. He was still in conflict. He could stay, or he could go. If he stayed, it would be as Greg's friend, no matter if they kissed again or they both put that behind them for good.

Once more, he considered how his life could have

been different if he'd made different choices. If he'd married any of the many women who had crossed his path, would he still be married now? Would he have still been drawn to kiss Greg? It was a useless thing to think about. The past couldn't be changed, and in reality, would he want it to be? He liked his life. He had his times of loneliness, but who didn't? It was a normal part of being human.

He focused to turn off his thoughts as the sun lowered further in the sky. He was in a place where he could be at peace. That rarely happened in the city with so many different Leadbetter families around, all expecting different assistance at different times. He knew he needed to appreciate it while he could.

Inside, Greg took time setting up and lighting the fire. Designed for heating the cabin and cooking food, he loved the simplicity of the daily ritual that he'd established since going to the cabin on the night of the gala event. It was soothing, getting things right so that the fire would go well when he lit it. After that, it was hypnotic, watching the flames take hold. He didn't have a fireplace in his city home. He'd never missed having one before. He suspected he would when he returned.

When? Or if? He didn't have any set plans. Since Phillip was newly married, Greg suspected his home was empty at least most of the time. That was something to think about. No property was good left unattended, especially when Leadbetters knew about it. Family homes should have been off-limits. He knew from experience that they weren't for some members of the extended family. A home with things in it was a home with things in it for the taking. It was a sad truth.

As he knelt, staring at the flames, he heard Rhett enter.

"I'll hang out here for the night if you're cool with that," Rhett said.

"Yeah," replied Greg, casting a glance at his

friend. "Bring in anything you need to from your car, and let's get that door closed. It won't take long for this to make the place toasty."

Rhett nodded and walked to his car. On opening the door to get out his bag, he contemplated one more time if he was doing the right thing, staying. He shook his head and scoffed at himself. He hadn't been consciously thinking about the kisses he'd shared with Greg. His doubts about whether to go or stay indicated that the subject was still present in his subconscious.

"It's getting dark real quick," he said when he walked into the cabin again and closed the door.

"Yeah, there's little sunshine here because of the trees, but I like the seclusion," Greg said. "I'm sure lots of people would chop down the trees and open it up. I can't say that I have any desire to do that."

"Fair enough," Rhett replied. "What can I do?"

Greg chuckled. "Do? Grab a seat and enjoy the warmth from this, first off. I'll make us some food soon."

They sat in silence for a long while, staring at the flames while enjoying the heat that emanated toward them. As Rhett sat on a small chair to the left of the fire, he naturally moved his eyes from the flames to where Greg knelt in front of it. His lifelong friend. Had things changed from him being that? Rhett guessed not. They weren't in a 'relationship' or anything. They'd just kissed a couple of times. Granted, they had been amazing kisses, and they'd aroused him. When they'd stood together, he'd also felt how aroused Greg had been. It had been a shock at the time. As he considered that moment, he was surprised to find himself slightly heated at the thought. It was confusing. He didn't know if it would ever *stop* being confusing. The unknown for him was whether it would be better to keep ignoring what had happened and vow to never do it again, or face the feelings straight-on and see what happened.

On sensing Rhett watching him, Greg turned and

smiled.

"You in a trance?" he asked, wanting to break whatever serious thoughts his friend was indulging in.

"Just thinking," Rhett replied, shifting his sight back to the flames again.

"You did good, going out and finding David," Greg said as he placed another piece of wood on the fire.

"We both went…"

"Yeah, but it was you who wanted and decided to," said Greg. "If you hadn't, he'd still be on the run."

"I wonder how he's going to move forward with what he told us," Rhett said. "It definitely sounded serious."

"And he shot at people that day in the supermarket," said Greg. "That takes his dark thoughts to a whole other level."

"Well, fortunately, he didn't kill anyone," Rhett said. "I guess even if he had, the cops would have still put it down to Rex having done it since he had the gun that was used."

Greg nodded. "It was fortunate that David had cleaned it of all his prints. If he hadn't, the cops might have taken a bit more notice. Really, it's pure luck on his part that they didn't pursue him anyway."

"Well, they never could prove it was his car or him driving," said Rhett. "But I agree. Luck was on his side for him to get away with that."

"I'm not so sure he feels lucky, the way he was talking," Greg said. "I think it might weigh on him, what he did."

"Not a typical Leadbetter," Rhett half-joked.

"Not at all," Greg replied as he smiled.

"I thought Mark and Stacey seemed pretty happy, considering all they've been through," said Rhett. "I guess they'll never forget, but they seem okay."

"Yeah?" asked Greg. "That's good. Seeing one of their kids get married must make them happy, especially

Stace. She'll be itching for grandkids."

Rhett laughed. "Yeah, Mark'll love being called Granddad - Pops," he said.

Greg laughed as he stood and moved toward the well-stocked floor to ceiling pantry.

"Right, what are you in the mood for?" he asked.

"What are the options?" asked Rhett as he stood and walked to where Greg stood. As soon as he positioned himself behind Greg so that he could also peer into the space, he grew aware of their closeness. It was crazy how it could turn on so quickly, but the desire to be closer was there.

"Umm," Greg said, unaware of the inner turmoil that had just begun again in his friend behind him. "I've got cans of stew, which I can cook up with some rice, or I can cook up one of these ultra-delicious packets of instant macaroni cheese."

When he didn't get an instant response, he turned around. The look on Rhett's face was undeniable. Regardless, Greg ignored it, holding up the two meal options in his hands.

"Stew? Or mac'n'cheese?" he asked, gulping. He hadn't been thinking about anything to do with bodily pleasure. The look on Rhett's face was enough to fuel him, even though he only wanted to hide his arousal away.

Rhett forced himself to look at each food item. His body was trying to get his mind to act in a way that he didn't want to. Focusing on the food, he smiled.

"Hmm, mac'n'cheese from a packet," he said. "That's just an entire meal I can't possibly resist."

Greg grinned and nodded. The moment had been broken, and he was glad. If Rhett had been sure about whatever he was feeling, he would have acted. He hadn't. That told Greg that it wasn't the right time for anything to happen.

"Done!" he said as he put the can of stew back in

the large cupboard and closed the door. "This culinary feast will take only a few minutes."

He was happy to have the diversion of preparing the pot and placing it over the fire to cook.

Rhett sat back down and watched the flames. His earlier inner question about whether it would be best to pretend there was nothing between them or face it straight-on, he had an answer to. Ignoring it wasn't making it go away. He needed to confront it.

It had been a long time since he'd thought before acting when it came to anything physical with someone. Usually, it grew from a natural flow of events. Thinking in advance about kissing Greg after they ate their meal was something he found invigorating. Instead of thinking about how much the idea of two men being sexual together turned him cold, he focused only on kissing Greg's lips again. That was enough. That was all they needed to do to gain a better understanding of how they both felt.

He was surprised by how easily he grew semi-hard while contemplating the idea. Generally, he never thought about that stuff ahead of a situation happening. When it happened, it was good. Any other time, it just wasn't something he thought about. He'd always been fairly active sexually. There had never been too long when he or Greg hadn't had one woman or another throwing themselves at them.

There had been several times throughout the years when they'd had sex with a woman each in the same bedroom but different beds. They'd also had occasions when a woman had asked for both of them to join her, and they'd obliged. They'd never touched each other at all during those times. In the threesomes they'd been in together, it had always been about pleasuring the woman. That was something they both enjoyed. On those nights, they'd just happened to do it together.

Rhett pushed his thoughts aside as a way to

control the arousal that was intensifying the longer he thought about sexual pleasure.

He watched as Greg stirred the pot of instant meal. It was a further distraction and a welcome one.

"Hungry?" Greg asked as he removed the pot and began filling two bowls. When he handed one to Rhett, he deliberately didn't meet his eyes. Something was going on in Rhett's mind. Greg chose to ignore recognizing it.

"Thanks," said Rhett as he received his bowl. "Yum," he added, making Greg chuckle.

"Food is food, right?" Greg said.

"Yeah, I'm not sure this stuff is actually classed as real food, but it does taste good."

After putting on a pot to boil some water in, they sat in silence, peering at the flames while not sharing their thoughts. Food finished, Greg jumped up with the hot water.

"I'll do wash duty," said Rhett, eager to do anything other than sit still with his mind going to the places he'd rather it didn't.

"I just wash in this and then throw the water out in the morning," Greg said, handing over a dish scrubber to Rhett. "Not as glamorous as a dishwasher."

Rhett smiled and got on with the job.

"You know I don't care about glamour," he said.

As Greg sat up on the other seat by the fire, he thought about Mark and Stacey. They'd had a great love for three decades. In that time, they'd experienced many highs, and then the lowest low they possibly could when Rex had died. No matter what they went through - good or bad - they continued to have each other's back. They weren't always happy - Greg had seen them have some epic shouting matches over the years - but they always worked through things and continued to love one another. He was happy for them, and incredibly envious.

"All done," he heard Rhett say. "Where do you

want this water put?"

Greg grabbed the hot water and moved it to its designated nightly storage place. When he stood up and turned around, he was surprised by how close Rhett was standing. He wasn't moving, but his facial expression once again held that indication that something was on his mind, and it was causing confusion in him.

Greg took a step closer and raised his face so that they were almost nose to nose.

"Wanna make out?" he asked in a light-hearted way to ease the tension.

Rhett couldn't help but laugh softly. He'd been feeling intense. Greg's joking manner relaxed him. He knew Greg's ways of defusing situations when it was needed. He had the skill of inserting humor whenever it might ease things between people.

Greg was pleased to see his friend relax. He led Rhett back to the fireplace. He was about to sit down again when he heard Rhett speak from behind him.

"Greg," Rhett said, knowing something had to be confronted.

When he saw Greg turn around, he leaned forward and kissed him. It was a tentative move at first. When the lips under his responded, he didn't hold back.

Greg didn't have any conscious thought from that moment. As soon as Rhett's lips were on his, he once again tuned out to everything else. It was a great passion that flowed between them. It was natural, it was powerful, and it was beautiful.

For a long time, they stayed where they stood, kissing deeply but not moving away from the spot. Greg's mind wasn't active. Rhett's mind was.

Knowing how he'd reacted to feeling Greg's erection against his the previous time they'd kissed, Rhett moved forward. He eased into closing the gap between their bodies as he wrapped his arms around Greg. Once again, through their two pairs of jeans, he could feel the very defined shape and hardness. As he continued to kiss Greg's lips, Rhett pressed forward, forcing himself to ascertain whether the two of them having erections was something to be scared of. He moved a little, subtle in experiencing the feeling of his hardness moving against his friend's. He was pleased that he did. It was different from holding and pressing against a woman, but it wasn't intimidating or scary at all.

He heard Greg moan as he enclosed Rhett in his arms. Rhett didn't want to fight the feelings. He'd always loved the feeling of being turned on. It was a feeling he'd never found hard to find, no matter what woman he'd been with. He'd made it to fifty with all working parts intact. His body had always worked just as it should, when it should.

It wasn't very long since he'd last been with a woman. Regardless, kissing Greg, Rhett felt like it had been forever since he'd been sexual with anyone - or at least since he'd last climaxed. With a fairly easy-going string of women in his life over the decades, he'd never been one to need or want to self-pleasure. His libido could lie low for ages until it reacted to another body. He couldn't deny that his libido was fully alert when it came to kissing his closest friend.

He didn't know what he wanted or where they could go with their undeniable passion. Determined to at least give it a go, Rhett moved his hands down to Greg's butt and rested them there before he summoned the courage to move one hand around to the front of Greg's jeans.

Hearing Greg moan further at his touch, Rhett moved his palm over the bulge. It was new but surprisingly exciting, like being on a new journey of exploration. Moving his hand around, he could feel the shape of Greg inside his jeans. He was then surprised by the mutual pleasure of feeling Greg's hand begin doing the same to him. Rhett wanted his head to stop thinking, but he kept finding himself analyzing everything. It was odd but exhilarating, feeling up another guy. It was no different being felt up himself. He guessed a hand was a hand, no matter which gender it belonged to. The quick analysis pushed him forward in kissing with more passion, finally accepting that he was kissing his best friend, and he was loving it. Despite the prejudice that had been instilled into him as he'd grown and lived with the Leadbetter gang, he didn't feel like what he was doing was wrong. It all felt very, very right.

Greg rejoiced. He'd never thought about being intimate with a man. With it being the third time they'd kissed, he only wanted to keep exploring. He was so turned on that he thought he might burst. Not only did he like the way he felt with Rhett's hand rubbing him the way it was, but he was also enjoying the feeling of Rhett's erection through his jeans. He'd never thought about how it must have felt for any of the women he'd been with, to hold him in their hands. Feeling the sign that someone was obviously turned on was enthralling. He liked touching the shape of Rhett through the denim. He wasn't against the idea of touching him without the denim in the way. They'd been naked together many times over the years. There was nothing to hide or be embarrassed about between them.

For a fleeting moment, he thought about unzipping Rhett's jeans. He immediately decided against that. Rhett had turned away twice. Greg didn't want to do anything to make him turn away a third time.

"I need to loosen up," Rhett said, pulling away from Greg's lips and making him laugh as he adjusted his jeans.

"Me, too," Greg said quietly. He studied Rhett's face to try and identify any panic or regret. He saw neither. "Pull it out," he boldly suggested. At first, Rhett looked surprised. The look quickly disappeared as Greg watched Rhett then undo his jeans and set himself free. Greg didn't hesitate to reach out and touch him. They'd see each other's bodies plenty of times. There was no surprise in what he saw. What it felt like in his hand was new - and he liked it.

As he continued to stroke Rhett, he felt his own jeans being undone and pushed down just enough for Rhett to have access. Feeling Rhett's hand stroking him, Greg felt like an itch he'd had for a while was finally being scratched. The stroking was simple but effective. It was a short time before Greg felt himself head toward the glorious edge of pleasure.

"Fuck, I'm gonna cum any minute," he said before kissing Rhett again. Once their lips began playing together again, that was all it took. Greg moaned in exquisite release.

Rhett removed his hand and focused on his arousal. It wasn't in any way as horrible as he'd always thought being touched by a man would be. There was nothing uncomfortable. It took only another couple of minutes before the movement of Greg's hand was successful.

"Fuck!" he said as the powerful release that had been building was finally set free.

Both men stood where they were, not sure what to say or do. When they looked into each other's eyes, they smiled in quiet disbelief but also relief.

As Rhett tucked himself in, he felt sheepish and shy. When he and Greg had both resurrected their clothing, he pushed himself to take a step forward and kiss Greg's lips again.

"You really turn me on," he said quietly as he grinned. "Fuck, I needed that."

Greg returned the kiss. "You turn me on too."

"I don't know what to do now," said Rhett.

"It's getting late," said Greg. "Let's crash."

CHAPTER 25

For his first night back at his family home, David focused on sleeping. It was intermittent, but it was needed. Every time his body woke up and tried to persuade him it was time to get up and do something, he turned over and forced himself to relax so he could sleep some more. The thoughts were worst when he was tired. He was prepared to sleep for a week if it meant he'd be back to a happier and healthier self.

The next day, he finally left the confines of his bedroom, lured by the aroma of his mother's amazing roast pork. He knew the smell well. She'd never been an affectionate mother when he'd been growing up, but she'd always made sure her kids were well fed.

As he walked to the bathroom, he heard Sasha call out down the hallway.

"You okay?" she asked.

David turned toward her, nodded, then resumed walking to the bathroom.

"Was that David?" their mother, Stacey, asked as Sasha entered the kitchen.

"Yeah, he's going to the bathroom," Sasha replied. "Looks like he's been sleeping for months."

"Or *not* sleeping," said Mark. He was worried about his son but equally glad that David had returned.

The black Valiant was parked on the street out front. If the cops had been searching for David, they had a clear indicator that he'd returned home. Mark waited for a knock on the door. He didn't think it would come. He truly believed that they'd closed the supermarket shooting case with Rex as the shooter. Regardless, he thought it better to be prepared for the possibility than not.

Mark was pulled from his thoughts by a phone notification. After glancing at the screen, he looked at Stacey and smiled.

"Phillip and Daisy are wanting to come over," he said.

"Well, why is he messaging instead of just turning up?" asked Stacey.

"So, I'll tell him yes?" Mark teased her, loving seeing her smile.

"Tell him to be here in thirty minutes so they can join us for this," Stacey said, grinning. "It'll be good to have everyone here."

As always, when she said the word 'everyone', her heart felt like it threatened to drop out of her chest. In her household, the word 'everyone' now referred to 'all but one'.

Mark saw the change in her joy. He quickly sent his reply and then stood to take her in his arms. There had been many years when they'd hidden their intimacy from their kids. As Sasha and Anya both sat at the table, Mark didn't hold back from giving their mother the support and love that she needed at that moment.

Stacey hugged him back and then pulled away. The sadness about Rex would never go away, but she would keep living each day while she could.

"What can we do to help, Ma?" Sasha asked after viewing the tender moment between her parents.

"The meat and roast vegetables will be done in half an hour," Stacey replied, refocusing. "Sasha, can you open up that can of apple sauce and put it into that jug? And, Anya, you can set the table ... for seven? Unless James is coming too..."

"No," said Sasha. "I've told him I want to be home at the moment, just in case David wants to talk to me."

It wasn't a lie. It just wasn't the whole truth. Sasha was aware that David was the brother who had fired into the supermarket that day and put James's younger brother in a coma. She didn't particularly want them to ever be in the same room together. It wasn't probable that she'd be able to prevent that from happening if James stayed in her life, but for the moment, she could.

Stacey hugged her oldest daughter.

"I'm so proud of you, Sasha," she said before turning to Mark. "Sit outside for a while?"

"Yep," Mark replied, swiftly taking her hand in his and leading her to the front porch. Once settled onto the sofa swing they'd spent hours upon hours on during their long marriage, he pulled her close. "Are you okay?"

"Yeah," Stacey said as she faced him and leaned her head close to his. "You know what I'm thinking about when I have my moments."

Mark nodded. "I do. I think about him too."

"At least we got one back," said Stacey. "That's something to be grateful for."

Mark silently agreed as he kissed the top of her head. Glancing out toward the street, he focused on David's car. How his son had gotten away with the shooting when the cops had known that it was that exact type of car that had been involved was difficult to fathom. It was just one of the many criminal things that a Leadbetter had gotten away with.

The Leadbetters. They were his family, and he'd always lived by their guidance and rules. When he'd been in charge, he'd tried to stomp out any violence, whether it be from members to others, or from members toward their own. For a large part, he'd thought he'd succeeded in changing the ways of the extended family. Pete's typical criminal stupidity and use of a gun made Mark think that he probably hadn't changed things at all.

So far, nobody new had been selected to lead the family. It wasn't a role he wanted again, but if whoever was suggested was a criminal of the same caliber as Pete, he was resolved he'd try and fight for that place again. He still felt guilt on occasion about having stepped down. If he hadn't done that, so much that had happened since never would have.

"You're tense," Stacey said as she pulled away and looked into his eyes. She was surprised to see his eyes looking like they were welling up. "What's up?"

Mark studied her face for a long time, reaching up and gently running one finger along her jaw to rest on her cheek.

"I shouldn't have stepped down," he said in almost a whisper.

"Oh, Mark, if you take full responsibility for Rex's death, I have to as well," Stacey said. "I was the one who wanted you to step down. You couldn't foresee what was going to happen any more than I could. Please don't keep going back to that place in your head. We're here, and the rest of our children are here. That's … that's what we have to focus on - the future, not the past."

Mark slipped his hand into her hair and pulled her close, seizing her mouth with his.

"Once David seems more his usual self, let's slip away for an afternoon," he said to her, his voice low.

"Slip away … where?" asked Stacey.

"Somewhere peaceful," Mark replied before kissing her. "Away from people." Another kiss. "Away from everything." Yet another. "Just you and me in nature, alone."

Stacey grinned. "Do you have naughty thoughts?" she asked in a whisper near his ear.

Mark burst out laughing. "Maybe I do."

"I like that thought very much," Stacey said. "But let's wait and see if and how David might need us."

"Okay," Mark said, nodding. "Here's Phillip now," he continued, seeing Daisy's car entering the street.

The two of them watched the newlyweds get out of the car and walk up the path.

"You look so comfortable," Daisy said, grinning.

"Yeah, he takes a bit of getting used to, but I think I'll keep him," Stacey said, joking about her husband.

Daisy laughed. "I got one of those too."

"Oy!" Phillip said sternly but with a big grin. "Yum, I can smell that pork from here," he said to his mother. "We brought dessert," he went on to say as he held out a boxed cheesecake.

"My favorite?" Stacey asked and saw her oldest son nod. "Oh, thank you! Come inside. It's almost time to eat."

When Stacey and Daisy entered, Mark purposely held back and turned to Phillip.

"How's he doing?" Phillip asked with his voice low.

"I don't know," said Mark. "He hasn't spoken to any of us. Came home, went into his room, and has been there ever since. I'm hoping he'll join us, but no guarantees."

"I'll try and get him talking," Phillip said. He was the closest to David in age, but they'd never had much interaction. Regardless, he was his brother. He'd do whatever he could to help David settle back into normal life.

Mark nodded and led his oldest son inside. He hoped that Phillip might be able to get David to ask for help or support. He was hopeful that all he'd needed was a good catch up on sleep. He wondered if it could be that easy to get back the son who'd always seemed more at peace than any of his other kids.

CHAPTER 26

While in the shower, David took his time to appreciate the simple joy of being able to get clean. It was something he'd not done while on the run. Enjoying the hot water flowing over him, and the smell of shampoo and soap, he felt more normal than he had done in a long time. The thoughts were still there, but he felt stronger. He needed to get help, and he would. First, he'd take some time to be with his family.

He'd woken to the smell of his mother's cooking. As he thought about that, he began salivating. After finishing in the bathroom, he quickly moved to his bedroom to get dressed and then made his way to the kitchen. He was surprised by the two extra people who were there.

"Hey," Phillip said as he approached David. "Let's chat after lunch."

David was surprised. They never 'chatted'. Despite his surprise, he nodded.

"Oh, David," Phillip continued. "This is Daisy - my wife."

"You … you're … what the *fuck?*" David asked, making everyone laugh before he remembered his manners. "Sorry," he said to Daisy. "I'm pleased to meet you … sister-in-law?"

Daisy grinned and nodded. "I am pleased to meet you, too, brother-in-law," she said.

She knew he was the one truly suspected by his family of having shot at the supermarket. The action went against everything Daisy had thought she believed in when she'd studied to be a lawyer. It was another level of change that had been made in her thinking since she'd met Phillip. The whole family were criminals, but she loved him, so she accepted them.

"Come and sit down," Stacey said, rounding everyone up.

As David sat among the people he'd grown up with, he felt an ease flow over him. It was noticeable to him that someone was missing from the table. It played on his mind, serving as a reminder that he'd had a gun and that person had not only used it but also been killed in the process. He fought back the anger and shame that he felt when he considered that. There was nothing that could be done to change the outcome. All he could do was focus and try to do better for the future.

"I'd like to say how good it is to have you back again, David," Mark said. "It's … it's good."

Stacey smiled at him. He'd stood up, intending to make a confident speech. It was always nice to see his emotions surface and counterattack the confidence. She knew she was more fortunate than many women with that kind of man for a husband.

"Hear, hear!" Anya said out loud while banging her hand on the table, making everyone smile.

Once everyone began eating, Stacey looked around the table. It was almost complete. One was missing, but she was hopeful it wouldn't be long before a new little one would be around to fill that place.

As she thought about the possibility of Daisy and Phillip having a baby, she remembered that David might not yet know that he was going to be a father too. She knew he'd been told that Kasey had left a message for him to contact her. Had he?

"Crackling, Ma?" she heard Anya ask, shifting her thoughts to the present moment.

"Yes, little one," she said, smiling at her youngest. "Thank you."

When she looked at Mark, she saw him grin at her. It was the type of family mealtime that they always should have enjoyed - happy and at peace.

~~~~~

When the meal was over with, David retreated to his bedroom. He guessed it should have been nice being around so many people again. Instead, it just felt overwhelming. The overt displays of happiness intermingled with an underlying degree of sadness made for a dynamic that left him uncomfortable. He could see that his parents were trying to move on from Rex's death. He could equally see that they still thought about his baby brother and how much they missed him.

That was what kept playing on David's mind most of all - in an indirect way, he'd contributed to Rex's death. That consideration made him want to roll over on his bed, go to sleep, and never wake up.

A knock on his door made him sigh. He didn't feel like talking to anyone. Nobody would be able to understand anything that was going on in his head.

"Yeah?" he called out.

Phillip opened the door and showed his head.

"Just me," he said. "Can I come in?"

"Yeah," David replied as he sat up on his bed. "What's up?"

Phillip took his time closing the door and going to sit on the bed. He hadn't gotten any useful information from anyone about David's situation. Nobody knew where he'd been, what he'd done, or what he'd been thinking.

"I wanted to ask you the same thing," he said. "Where have you been, David? And why did you run?"

David shrugged his shoulders. "I thought the cops would be after me."

"Was it you? The supermarket shooter?" Phillip dared to ask. He'd heard the theory. It was difficult to believe.

"It was," David admitted as he looked his older brother directly in the eye. "If you're gonna ask why, please don't. The reason ... it's not something you'd
~~~~~

understand, and even if the cops aren't charging me, believe me, I'm living in hell with the knowledge that Rex was shot because of me…"

"What?" Phillip asked, unable to see any logic in what he knew. "Why would you think that?"

"Phillip, he pulled out *my* gun," said David.

"So? If he hadn't had yours, he would have got one from someone else," said Phillip. "Pete was armed with several weapons. He was a total psycho. He would've handed Rex a gun if he'd known Rex was trigger-happy. And even if he hadn't, Rex obviously wanted to use a gun. He would've probably taken one of Pete's if he didn't have one on him already."

Phillip watched the countenance of his brother. It was easy to see the level of guilt that David carried.

"This wasn't your fault, David," he said. "Nobody thinks that it was."

"Yeah?" asked David. "You sure about that?"

"Yes!" replied Phillip. "Who would blame you for anything to do with that night? It was screwed up. It was a bad job, and even worse was the management of it. Pete wasn't someone who should have ever been in charge of anything. He was a murderer." He took some time to see if anything he said produced any effect on David. He felt dismayed that it didn't seem to. "This is *not* your fault. You know what Rex was like. He *wanted* trouble. He sought it out. If this hadn't happened that night, it still would have happened some other time. I know … I know he was our brother, but you've got to get past this. You're a good per…"

"No, I'm not!" David said as he jumped up and walked to the window. When he turned around, he could see that Phillip was trying to understand. "You don't *know*, Phillip. You don't know what goes on up here every single day," he continued, pointing to his head.

"Tell me," said Phillip as he watched David turn toward the window again.

"Every day, my head is full of these thoughts ... these images of horror that I know I've caused," David said. "I haven't done them, but they're not just nightmares. When I'm awake, and they appear, they're *ideas*." He turned and faced his brother again. "I feel like killing people - not all the time, but enough for me to know that something's not right with my head. It can't be right to see these images all the time. It *can't* be."

Phillip processed what he was being told. It was a surprise. David had always seemed peaceful and quiet. There had never been any hint of darker things going on in his mind. Other than Anya, he was the only one of the family who'd never been in trouble with the law.

"You're serious," he said quietly.

"Of course, I'm serious," David replied as he moved to sit on the bed again. "I think I need help."

"Then get it," said Phillip.

"You're not going to tell me to harden up?" David asked. It was the usual advice anyone gave anyone in the Leadbetter family. That was the very base of the Leadbetter way.

"Fuck, no!" Phillip replied. "I know we've been told that all of our lives, but no. You know your mind better than anyone. If this really is something that plagues you…"

"It does."

"Then get it sorted. Find a shrink and go and see them," Phillip continued. "It might be nothing, or it might be something that's fixable. Whatever it might turn out to be, wouldn't it be better to know?"

David nodded. "Yeah, *I* think so. It's not how we do things, though, is it."

"Who cares? We're supposed to all love and be proud of this fucking Leadbetter name," said Phillip. "It's the very reason I took Daisy's name when we married, instead of her taking mine."

"What?" asked David, slightly amused. "You used

your girlfriend to get rid of your name?"

"Yep, I am officially no longer a Leadbetter," Phillip said as he smiled in relief to see his brother relax.

"What's your name then?"

"I am..." Phillip said, standing and bowing. "Phillip Leefton."

David laughed, and it felt good. He'd never been particularly close to his older brother, but it felt good to be interacting with him. It felt even better knowing that Phillip had proven he was beyond some of the Leadbetter ways as well.

"Fuck," said David. "How did Dad take that news? He must have been downright *pissed* about that."

"No, actually, he was really good," Phillip said. "He and Ma have seemed happy with me taking Daisy's name. I think he's wanted to be out of the family for a while himself. That's why he stepped down."

The brothers looked at each other in silence for a while. It wasn't a naturally friendly relationship that they had, but it equally wasn't one that had ever been tense.

"Is there anything I can do to help you?" Phillip finally asked. "Whatever I can do - or Daisy. She's been a lawyer. She probably has contacts."

"Thanks, but I'd rather keep this quiet, at least for now," said David. "I will talk to someone, but in my own time. Don't worry. The thoughts that I have, I don't like. I'm not having them and thinking that I want to go and do those things."

"But the supermarket..."

"Yeah, that wasn't my finest hour," David responded. "I ... I can hardly remember what I was thinking that day. It's like my mind wanted me to do it, but then it wanted to try and make me forget that I had."

"Sounds scary," said Phillip.

"You think that deep inside me, I might be a murderer, like Pete?" David asked. "Maybe it's something that runs in our family."

"I'm no expert about this stuff, so I don't know, but my non-professional opinion is that you aren't anything like Pete," Phillip said. "He was someone who enjoyed hurting and killing people. From what you've said, you have the thoughts, but you don't want to follow through and make them reality. So, no, I don't think you're the same as Pete, but I guess a professional would be able to provide you with the right kind of consultation to assess something like that."

He saw David nod but not reply.

"Weren't you seeing someone before you went away?" Phillip asked.

"Yeah," said David, nodding. "Kasey."

"Is everything okay there? What did she think about you skipping town?"

"I haven't talked to her," David replied. "I need to. Apparently, she came here looking for me."

"Oh, she didn't know you'd left town?"

David shook his head. "No, I didn't want to risk going to her or calling her in case the cops were on my tail. I didn't want her mixed up in anything, so I haven't made any contact with her since I left."

"Would you want to go back there?" asked Phillip.

David looked at his older brother for a long time as he pondered the question.

"She was ... we were really good together," he replied. "She knew about the nightmares I have that are real violent. She was understanding about them, but I never told her that those same kinds of things are in my head all the time, not just as nightmares. She thinks I just have bad dreams. How can I tell her the extent of this stuff?"

"I guess it depends on whether you think she's worth putting yourself out there for," said Phillip. "It's not the same thing, but I had to tell Daisy - a lawyer who puts people like us away - that I was a part of a criminal family. It wasn't easy, and I did expect her to walk away."

"But she didn't," said David.

"No, she didn't," Phillip said. "I think it's been harder on her than she's let on, but she wants to be a mother, so she's made the choice to leave the legal profession and focus on that."

"You're gonna be a dad?"

Phillip grinned. "Hopefully," he said.

"The fun's in the trying, right?" David said, grinning and making Phillip chuckle.

"Oh, yeah!"

"I'm gonna be okay," said David. "You don't need to worry about me."

"Maybe not, but I do," Phillip said. "You're my brother - now, my only brother. We all need to look out for each other. Everything's changing."

"Yeah, especially with you getting married," said David. "Shit, I didn't even see that one coming."

"Me neither," joked Phillip. "I don't think me meeting and marrying Daisy is as weird as Sasha and her boyfriend, though. That has been the most unexpected thing for me."

"Sasha's got ... a boyfriend?" asked David. "Seriously?"

"Yeah," Phillip replied. "But, David, there's something about him that you probably should know," he said and took a moment to formulate his words. If David was in such a bad headspace, Phillip didn't want to upset him any further, but he did want to prepare him. "He's the brother of the guy who was shot in the supermarket that day."

David had to play the sentence over in his mind several times before he fully understood what Phillip had just told him.

"Sasha's seeing the brother of the guy I shot?" he asked for clarification that he'd heard correctly.

"Yeah," replied Phillip. "I don't think he holds any animosity toward our family for it. He was here for my wedding and seemed pretty relaxed, and he's been real good for Sasha, but, yeah, just know that he does know it might have been you that delivered that shot."

David put his head in his hands in disbelief.

"Fuck, could the universe get any more fucked up?" he mumbled. "How am I supposed to deal with that if I see him?"

"I dunno," replied Phillip. "You might want to talk to Sasha. She knows more about James and what he knows than I do."

"Okay," David said, nodding. "I need to figure out what I'm doing - with Kasey, with this *boyfriend* of Sasha's, and with my life."

"I'm here for you, however you need me," said Phillip. "I'm working regular hours now, but my boss is easy going. He wouldn't hesitate to let me get away if you need my support with anything."

"Thanks," replied David. "I do appreciate it."

"Okay, I'm gonna leave you and go find my wife," he said, making David chuckle.

"Wife," David said. "I still can't believe you're an old married man now."

"Quit with the old," Phillip said as he stood up to leave. "I mean it about reaching out to me if you need help of any kind, David."

"I know. Thanks."

When the door had closed, and David was alone again, he thought about the conversation. It had been good talking to his older brother. Phillip hadn't freaked out when he'd heard about David's thoughts. He'd said to get help. He'd also said that he'd be there if David wanted *his* help. That was new, but it was good.

Lying back on his bed and staring at the ceiling, he considered the choices he had to make. Contacting Kasey was the biggest conflict. If she'd moved on and was happy, he didn't want to interrupt that. He also didn't want to freak her out if he had some head work he needed to get sorted.

The other thing that had settled into his mind was Sasha's boyfriend being who he was. The potential for things to get ugly there seemed huge. He wasn't close to Sasha, but he didn't want to make things uncomfortable for her. Thinking about that, he stood and made his way out of his bedroom to seek her out.

When he entered the kitchen again, he saw only his mother and father.

"Is Sasha still here?" he asked.

"She's sitting out in the sun," Stacey replied, still feeling shy around her second son.

After she and Mark watched David walk outside and close the back door behind him, she turned to her husband.

"I hope that's a good thing," she said quietly.

"Yeah, that's not going to be an easy situation, I don't think," said Mark. "Assuming he knows who James is."

~~~~~

When David walked outside, he saw Sasha sitting alone at their outdoor table. He was glad.

"Hey," he said. "I ... think I need to talk to you."

Sasha wasn't used to talking to him, but she'd prepared herself to be there for him.

"What's up?" she asked, keeping her tone casual.

"I ... umm ... Phillip said ... told me ... who your ... boyfriend is," David said, forcing the words out. "I mean, with him being..."

"It was his brother who was shot, yes," Sasha said. "His brother's fully recovered now. You ... you shot him, but you didn't kill him."

"Yeah," David said, feeling tears begin to flow. "I'm so sorry about that. I don't know what I can do to make things right..." he tried to say before the tears
~~~~~

made it too difficult.

"David, are you okay?" Sasha asked, surprised by his weeping. "What's going on with you?"

David wiped his eyes, partly to stop the tears from flowing down his face, but also to bide time while he wondered what he could talk about with his sister.

"People keep telling me that you've changed," he said. "I … I've only ever seen you angry. How did you change?"

"I don't know," Sasha said in almost a whisper. "I think that all of the years when I was real angry, I lived in my own head too much, if that makes sense?" she said and saw David nod. "When I met little Nicky, I found it really sad that someone so young had no confidence. She made me want to be a better person and want to change. It didn't feel right that someone so awesome couldn't understand how amazing they were. I think … I think that looking at her from my point of view made me look at me as well, as if from someone else's point of view. I dunno. I just wanted to be different."

"And you've done it," said David.

"I have changed, but I still have moments when my brain takes me back to that feeling of being angry and hating the world," Sasha said as she pondered her own changes. "It's still there, but I'm not … I'm not letting it show itself so much, I think."

"When I went to the supermarket that day, I wanted to hurt people … I wanted to *kill* people," David admitted to her. "I keep having these dark thoughts. I don't want to have them anymore."

Sasha was surprised by what he said, but on some level, she understood what he meant.

"You feel it, but you don't want to feel it," she said.

"Yes!" David exclaimed.

"I get that," said Sasha. "I get it completely."

"I don't know what to do about it," David said. "I

don't know if it's something I need to do something about or not."

"You shot at people," Sasha said. "I mean, I've knifed a few people in the past when I've been real angry, and they've pissed me off. I guess it's not much different. We've both caused people bodily harm."

"I wish I hadn't," said David. "Since then, I've still had the same thoughts about killing someone, but I've been able to not actually do anything. I don't know why that particular day I went ahead and did what I did."

"Maybe we're just wired differently," Sasha suggested as she shrugged. "That doesn't excuse what we've done, but it's inside of us. It's part of who we are."

"I don't want it to be part of who I am."

"Then do something to change."

David studied her. Even her body language and facial expressions had softened since he'd previously seen her. He'd thought people must have been exaggerating when they'd said she'd changed. He could see that they hadn't been. As she was, sitting and facing him, it was difficult to imagine her as an angry person at all.

"Yeah," he said, thinking. "How did your boyfriend accept who you were? He knows it was me?"

"He knows it *might* have been you," Sasha replied. "He didn't know who I was when we met. It was a slow thing, just bumping into each other at different places. It was the night of the gala that we met up and started to really get to know each other, but it was after Pete was on the news that James clicked," she said. "When that happened, he told me it was his brother who'd been shot that day. It made things messy for a bit. I didn't expect to see him again after that."

"But?"

"But he heard about Rex dying, and he sought me out to make sure I was okay," Sasha said. "I don't know how he'd react to seeing you, David. He's been here a few times. He's met Ma and Dad, and Phillip and Daisy. I don't know what he's thinking inside when he's around any of us, but he appears to be okay with who we are. Whether he'll accept you or not, I don't know."

"Does he know I'm here?" David asked and saw her shake her head.

"I haven't told him," Sasha said. "No matter what, you're my brother. I will put you first, ahead of him, if he can't accept you're here."

David heard the passion in her voice. He hoped she wouldn't have to make any such choice about who to have in her life. It was easy to see that if her boyfriend was visiting their family home now and then, it might be best if David withdrew from the house altogether. He was old enough to never live at home, and for the most part, he'd stayed with Kasey most of the time before he'd left town.

"Thank you, but that's not right," David said quietly. "You shouldn't have to…"

"I know, and it might not come to that," said Sasha. "But just know that I'm here for you. I know what it's like to have demons that keep trying to push through my consciousness, making me be someone I don't want to be. I'm happy to listen to you whenever you need to talk - especially if you feel like you might actually do something."

David nodded. "It would be good to have someone I can talk about my feelings to as they're happening."

"What about your chick? What's her name? None of us even know…"

"Kasey," David replied. "I haven't spoken to her since I ran. I don't want to hinder her happiness."

"Then I suggest you call her because from what I hear, she's been pining for you for a long time."

CHAPTER 27

"Kasey," David said when he heard her answer her phone. "It's me … David."

"David! Oh, is it really you? Oh, baby, I've been trying to find you!" he heard her almost yell down the line. Hearing her voice was enough to make him smile, even as tears flowed down his face.

"I know," he said. "I'm so sorry."

"Are you okay? Where are you?" Kasey asked.

"I'm at home," said David.

"Did they tell you?"

"What?" asked David.

"Oh … will you come over? We need to talk."

"Okay," David replied. "Now?"

"Yes! Please!" Kasey said. "Please, I need to see you."

"On my way," said David.

For a moment, he said on his bed, unmoving. He was going to see Kasey at last. While a part of him didn't want to hear what she had to say to him, he knew he had to face up to that fear. She was entitled to move on with her life. He was the one who'd left. If she'd found someone new, as much as it would hurt, he'd wish her happiness and good luck for the future.

He roused himself to prepare for whatever was going to happen. When he started the engine of his car, he felt a familiar panic. It was the car that had been used in the shooting. The cops must have known that for sure, even though they'd dismissed it as a possibility when the shooting had happened.

Regardless of the risk he felt as he sat in the car with the engine idling, he prompted himself to pull out and begin the journey. If he was going to be arrested, he was going to be arrested. It was all in fate's hands.

As he pulled up to the tall block of tiny apartments, he took a deep breath. High up on the third level, he could see Kasey standing on her small balcony. He returned the wave she gave to him, and pasted on a smile that he hoped would hide the intense anxiety he felt.

Before he reached her door, he saw it open, and Kasey run to him. He happily welcomed her into his arms but kept his guard up. If he was about to be hurt, he wanted the hurt to be as minimal as possible. For that, a wall had to be built around his heart, at least for the moments to follow.

Kasey said nothing as she held him and then took his hand to lead him into her apartment. Once the door was closed behind them, she couldn't help but kiss him with all the passion that she'd always had for him. He'd run away and left her, but she had to know if it was because he didn't have any feelings for her.

David tried to keep his wall up, ready for whatever heartbreak was about to hit him. The way that she kissed him, he knew the wall couldn't stay up. He also had to let himself believe that if she was kissing him like she was, she couldn't have met someone new.

He broke away, needing answers from her, and needing to provide some explanations of his own.

"Kasey," he said, studying her face and gently touching her cheek. "I need my head straight. Can we sit down?"

Kasey led him to the small sofa. When they were seated, she took his hands in hers.

"Where did you go? Why did you leave? Were you unhappy?"

"No ... Kasey, of course, I wasn't unhappy," he reassured her. "I had ... other things going on. I had to leave town, and I didn't want you involved."

"Your parents said ... you ... your family ... are

known to the cops," Kasey said and saw him nod. "Is that why you ran? Did you do something?"

"It's a really long story," David said. "There's a side to me, Kasey, that I've tried to keep hidden from you."

"Why would you do that?" she asked. "Don't you trust me?"

"Yeah, of course I do!"

"Then why hide things?"

"Because … because they're things that I don't … I have feelings sometimes that I don't want but are there, inside of me," David tried to explain. "They're not good. I don't want to hurt you."

Kasey lowered her head and sat silently before raising her head again and looking into his eyes.

"You hurt me when you disappeared without telling me why," she said. "I assumed you'd left me because you didn't care…"

"I'm so sorry," David said. "Please understand that I didn't leave *you*. I left *town*, and I didn't want to involve you. I couldn't do that to you."

"But David, I need you," said Kasey. "I *love* you. I've loved you for ages, and I can't just stop loving you because you decided you needed to go somewhere without me."

"I know," said David. "I screwed up. I wasn't thinking straight." He studied her face. The expression on it was one of disappointment. That saddened him deeply. "You asked if my parents had told me something. What were they supposed to?"

"I'm … we're … pregnant," Kasey said, studying his face as she said it so she could gauge his reaction. As usual, his face was calm and revealed little. "I'm having a baby, David. *Your* baby," she added to make sure he understood.

It took some time for the news to sink in. As David realized what she was saying, he grinned.

"You're going to be a mother?" he asked and saw her nod. "I'm going to be a dad?" He saw her nod again as she grinned at him.

"Are you happy?" Kasey asked.

"Yes!" said David. "But … is this what you want? Are *you* happy?"

"I am," Kasey said. "I love you, and I'm ready to be a mother. If it's too much for you, I can do this on my own…"

"No, you won't," David said. "No way. But, Kasey, there's something I want to share with you. I wasn't sure I'd share it, but I guess your news makes it pretty important that I do. You need to know this before we decide anything about … us. Either way, I'll be here as a dad, but please listen and think about what I'm going to tell you."

Kasey felt panicked by his words but nodded.

"My mother and father told you that we're - well, there's no sugar-coating it - we're criminals," he began. "It's the way that my father was raised, so the way that me and my brothers and sisters have been raised, too. Generally, I haven't done things unless under strict instruction from my father or another senior Leadbetter, but sometimes I do think … things … that aren't pleasant. I sometimes feel like I want to hurt someone … badly…"

"Me?" Kasey asked but saw him shake his head.

"No, never you," said David. "It's never a thought to hurt a particular person, or for any particular reason. It's more of a … I dunno … I guess a *pull* to hurt someone."

"And have you?" Kasey asked. In response, she saw his head drop low.

"Do you remember when the big supermarket in town got shot up?" he asked. When he saw her nod, he waited for the moment she understood what he was about to say.

"You?" Kasey asked. "You did that?"

"Yes," David admitted.

"But why? Why would you do that?"

"I don't know," said David. "I told you that I have nightmares, but I have these thoughts during the daytimes too."

"You want to hurt people? That's what that day was about?"

"Yeah, I know it's probably hard to understand because it's hard for *me* to understand, but that day, I wanted to hurt someone, and I gave into that feeling," David replied. "I don't know what it is or where it comes from, and it's not something I want. That's the only time that I went with the feeling, and I wish I hadn't, but I did. I can't undo that."

"No, you can't," Kasey said, not hiding the sadness she felt at what she'd heard. "But, David, we're going to have a baby. What do you want us to do? You say you love me. Do you want to be with me still?"

"Yes!" David replied. "I mean it when I say I love you. You're the best thing that's ever happened to me. Please believe that I only left to *protect* you, not because I didn't want to be with you. I want to be with you, and I want to be a father to our baby. My biggest fear is that you can't accept who I am - who I *really* am - and I understand if you can't."

Kasey raised a hand and cupped his jaw as she looked into his eyes. They'd been together for a long time. In that time, he'd had his moments of looking like he was in serious thought about something. He'd had moments when he looked like he was down. One thing he'd never done was hurt her or make her feel like he wanted to hurt her.

"I don't know what should be done about your thoughts - if anything," she said. "What I do know is that I love you. I've loved our time together, and I don't think you'll hurt me. I like that you've told me about your thoughts and how they scare you. I hope that when they happen, you know you can trust me enough to tell me that it's happening. If you can do that, I can assess if I need to worry about you - or me - or our baby. You've never given me any reason to fear you."

"And I don't want to," David said.

"I believe that," said Kasey. "I don't know if you need help or not. The person best to talk to about that could be your mother. She must know you better than anyone..."

"No, she doesn't," said David. "She doesn't know this side of me."

"Maybe, but ... I dunno ... maybe she's worth talking to anyway," Kasey said. "Regardless, if you're asking me if I will accept you as you are, with all that you've told me, then yes, I do. You've had these feelings and thoughts for a long time? Right through our time together?" she asked and saw him nod. "Then I don't feel any differently. I accept what you say about your family's ways, and I accept you. Do you accept me? Do you accept our baby?"

"Yes."

"This isn't a situation I want you to say yes to just because you think you should," Kasey continued. "I'm happy to raise our baby alone, and you still be a part of its life if you want. I'd rather that than be in a situation where you resent being there because you wish you weren't."

"No, Kasey, you are everything to me," said David. "I'd do anything to keep you and our baby safe."

"Are you sure?" Kasey asked.

"One hundred percent," David said, grinning. "I want to make this work and I'll get whatever help I need to, if it looks like I do."

David watched Kasey relax and smile. He had to maintain hope that although his thoughts seemed big inside his head, he'd lived with them for a long time but only gave in to the feelings once. Once was one time too many for it to be acceptable, but he held onto hope that someone would be able to help him eliminate the demons in his head.

"Take me to bed," he heard Kasey say in almost a whisper. "It's been so long."

David grinned more. That was the easiest request she could have made, that he could very easily fulfill without worrying about anything else.

~~~~~

Lying together on Kasey's bed after an intense but long session of mutually pent-up passion, neither spoke for a long time.

"I need to sort my life out so that I can provide for you," David said, his mind shifting back into gear. "I've done shelf stacking before. I can do that again. It's not much, but it's something. I've been drifting for far too long."

Kasey lifted her head and looked at him.

"Our baby won't need much except for us," she said before kissing him softly. "I'd rather give them our time than things. We can get by just as we have been."

"Kasey, for ages, I've been staying here without contributing to your bills," David said. "I'm sorry. I just didn't even think…"

"If I had ever wanted you to, rest assured - I'd have let you know," Kasey said. "Get work if you want to contribute. Who knows - maybe it'll be good for you to have something to keep your mind occupied too."

"How do you accept me so easily?" David asked.

Kasey smiled. "Because I love you, and I do believe that you love me. I wasn't sure when you were away. I choose to believe everything you've told me."

"I wouldn't lie to you," said David. "I've kept things from you, but I've never lied."

"We'll be okay, David," Kasey said. "If we both truly want this, we'll be okay. We don't need anything."
~~~~~

CHAPTER 28

With each morning that Rhett woke early in Greg's cabin, he felt the same conflict in his head. They'd spent time together and gone past the simplicity of just sharing a kiss. More than once, they'd gone that one step further and touched each other, using their hands to give and receive pleasure. In the moment, it continued to be exhilarating. During the hours around those moments, it was too easy for familiar thoughts from years of brainwashing to resurface. He didn't like prejudice, but it had been drummed into him hard as he'd grown and matured amongst the Leadbetters. He wished it had never affected him, but it obviously had.

He remained still in the small bed he'd been sleeping in. The thought of him and Greg sleeping in the same bed hadn't inspired either to do it. They'd shared beds in the past. Back then, there had never been any thought that there might be something to them doing it. With them having crossed the line from platonic friends to friends who were attracted to one another, everything had changed. What he wasn't entirely certain about was whether it had changed for the better.

During the daylight hours, they'd been doing all the cabin chores of wood chopping, water gathering, and resetting the fireplace for each night's lighting. They'd done some hill walks through the bush around the cabin, and they'd trekked down to the lakeside a couple of times to sit and listen to the water softly lapping at the pebbly edge of the land. Nothing bad had happened between them. Rhett knew there was no reason for his panic button to feel like it had been pressed. Regardless, with each subsequent morning that he woke, he was aware that he expected to be more relaxed about everything - and was anything but.

When his bladder demanded that he move, he quietly did so, taking care not to wake Greg. As he walked past his friend's bed, Rhett glanced down at the face he knew so well. Even just glancing at Greg for that moment, Rhett felt the now-familiar pull to kiss him. It continued to confuse him, not knowing where it came from. Physical attraction was usually something that he'd felt within the first few minutes of being in someone's company. He'd never heard of it developing and showing itself after more than thirty years of friendship with someone. It was weird all round. No doubt about it.

After dealing with his morning need, he quietly worked to bring the fire back to life while intermittently preparing cups and water for the much-needed making of coffee. Hearing Greg's deep but steady snoring made Rhett smile. It was an annoyance sometimes, but there was also a comfort that came from it.

Coffee made and no sign of life from his friend, Rhett sat outside on the verandah. The sun was only just beginning to rise, but the birds of the bush and trees around them were well awake. It was something he'd grown to enjoy over the short time he'd been at the cabin. There were no sounds of vehicles or people. All he could ever hear in that spot were birds and the rustle of trees swaying in the wind. He could see why Greg liked it. The experience produced the feeling of being in a different universe with no stress, no violence, no crime, and only peace.

Although there was no reason not to stay at the cabin, Rhett knew he was getting itchy feet. He liked being there, but his feelings and confusion about Greg continued to play havoc with his mind. He needed a breather. Maybe they could continue on that journey in the future, but he needed to take some time to distract himself again and get back to normal life. It wasn't an easy decision, but he knew it was the right one.

When he heard Greg get up, Rhett remained where he was. The view was good. The air was fresh. The coffee was just as he liked it. There was no reason to move.

"Hey," Greg said as he walked out. "You're up early."

"You say that every morning," replied Rhett, smiling. "You're just a lazy bum."

Greg grinned but nodded. "No point in denying that," he said as he sat down, coffee in hand. "Thanks for making this."

Rhett chuckled. Greg knew Rhett had made the pot of coffee for his own use. Rhett couldn't help but be amused by his friend's cheekiness in implying Rhett had made it for him instead.

"You've got that look," Greg said, seeing Rhett's face.

"What look?"

"That look of being ready to go and do something," replied Greg. "You gonna head off?"

"Yeah, I have been thinking about that," Rhett said. "I like it here, but I do feel like I need some space."

"Sometimes, it's just what we all need," Greg said. He'd enjoyed the time alone with Rhett, but he knew his friend well. As close as they'd always been, they'd both had plenty of times when they'd needed space from one another. "When will you go?"

"Soon," said Rhett. "I'll pack up my gear shortly and then head off. I want to go and see Mark today to see how he's doing and how David's going."

Greg didn't reply. He knew he'd soon be heading back to his house in the city as well. He didn't mention that to Rhett. He wanted there to be no expectation about that.

After a long while, with the two of them sitting in silence, Rhett stood.

"Another?" he asked, pointing to Greg's coffee

cup.

"Yeah, thanks," replied Greg as he looked up at Rhett's face. For a sliver of time, it seemed to him that Rhett was about to say something. The moment passed.

Left alone on the veranda for several minutes, Greg considered that he was going to be alone in the cabin again. It had been good having some company. It had been good having his best friend there. It had also been good that they'd confronted the odd natural desire that had shown itself to be mutual. It had proven strange to touch another man but also highly exciting.

The more that Greg thought about how the two of them had expanded the boundaries of their friendship, the more he realized his arousal was growing. He didn't want to act on that in any way. Rhett had said he was leaving. Greg wouldn't try and convince him to stay. Their lifetime as friends had proven that no matter how long they were apart, whenever they were next in each other's presence, they easily adjusted to being best friends again. It was a reassurance that all was fine.

His thoughts were disrupted by Rhett handing Greg's coffee cup back, then sitting beside Greg once again.

"I'm not leaving because of … us," said Rhett.

"Okay," replied Greg, nodding.

"I … I am still confused, but I … I have really enjoyed this time," Rhett continued. "I don't know what to do with it, or about it, but I definitely need some time to process it."

"I know," said Greg. "No matter what, you're my mate."

Rhett smiled and nodded while resuming his stare out toward the lake. What he'd said, he'd meant. It had been a good time, hanging out with his friend. When he thought about their intimacy, he felt a pang of regret at his decision to leave. He didn't want to feel that way. It wasn't forever, and they'd still be friends.

After downing his coffee and seeing Greg do the same, he stood, moved to face Greg, and held out his hand.

Greg stood and welcomed Rhett moving forward to pull him close and indulge in a deep and passionate kiss. They hadn't moved toward being completely naked before, but he didn't shy away when Rhett guided the two of them indoors and began removing all of Greg's clothing before removing his own. Seeing Rhett's full nakedness was nothing to Greg. Knowing he was going to possibly be able to touch Rhett's body all over was an arousing thought. Previously, their hands had been constrained to only the specific parts of their bodies needing attention to release. As Rhett continued to kiss him, Greg reveled in being led to his bed, and the two of them lying down side by side.

Rhett didn't know why he felt the need, but he certainly did feel it. He was still not liking the idea of full-on man to man sex, but he wanted it to be more than what they'd been doing. He took his time, running his hands and lips all over Greg's body, just as he had with every woman he'd ever been with. It was a time of exploration, noting the changes in Greg's breathing and body movement with everything that Rhett did.

As he moved down Greg's body, he was confronted. He'd never taken a man in his mouth before. Running his hand over Greg's erection, he was curious. It didn't seem as horrible as he'd expected he might find it as he moved his tongue and lips down over Greg. Hearing a very loud, 'Fuck, yes,' made Rhett smile before he let go and indulged in giving pleasure in a whole new way.

Greg was surprised, but conscious thought left him after his brief consideration that it felt good, and it didn't feel any different than how it had when any of his women lovers had treated him in the same manner. Rhett's tongue licking the length of him, around the warm lips enclosing him, resulted in Greg feeling his orgasm creep up quickly.

"I'm gonna cum," he said, giving fair warning.

Rhett stayed where he was. Women had done it to him hundreds of times over his lifetime. He was determined to at least see what it was like. As Greg ejaculated, it was a surprise being on the receiving end, but what surprised him more was the level his own arousal increased by.

"Fuck," he heard Greg say. "Mate."

Rhett grinned as he pulled away and moved up to eye level again. He'd tasted his friend, and it hadn't been that bad. He could still taste him as Greg pulled him close, kissed him, and then pushed him onto his back.

"Don't think you're the only one who gets to explore like that," Greg said as he began kissing down Rhett's body and wasting no time in taking him in his mouth.

He'd thought about that moment for a long time. Over his many years as an actively sexual adult, he'd wondered how it was for women to have him in their mouths. The wonder was over with as he indulged in the feeling of Rhett's hardness there for the taking. He took his time, experimenting with different ways to move and touch.

"Like that," he heard Rhett say eventually. That was the go-ahead that Greg wanted, to know that he was doing something that felt great to his friend. He continued it until he also got to experience having someone climax in his mouth for the first time.

Rhett felt his body tense in orgasm. He'd had quite a few of those while he'd been in the cabin, but it was always different when produced by a mouth than a hand. When Greg had moved up and settled so they were side by side, Rhett turned onto his side to face him.

"You done that before?" he asked Greg, making him laugh.

"No! You?" asked Greg.

"No, but fuck, that felt good," Rhett said before kissing Greg again.

As they kissed, they realized the passion hadn't quite been extinguished. It wasn't long before both reached down and stroked each other while continuing to kiss, bringing each other to climax again.

When they lay together post-climax again, Rhett shared his thoughts.

"How do we deal with this if we're around everyone?" he asked.

"Nothing needs to change if we don't want it to," said Greg. "We're still the same people. We're still mates."

"You don't think they'll see?" asked Rhett.

"I don't know," Greg replied. "I'm going to stay here for another week and then head home. Mark and the others won't see us together till after then." He studied Rhett's face. It wasn't hard to see the concern on it. "Are you worried about what anyone would think?"

Rhett was surprised by the question. "By this?" he asked and saw Greg nod. "Yeah, of course. I'm … it's not that it's you. It's…"

"That we're two guys," Greg finished.

"Yeah," said Rhett. "I know there's nothing wrong with it, but I know how strongly the family have always felt about it."

"I know, but the only Leadbetters that matter are Mark and Stace," said Greg. "I'm not saying that I'd want to stand up and make any declaration or anything, but I think those two would be more accepting than anyone else in the family."

Rhett nodded and kissed Greg again.

"However things go in time to come, know that I do have really strong feelings for you, and not just as a mate," he said.

"I know," Greg replied. "Don't stress about this.

When you're back in the city, all Mark will want to know is that you've been okay. You know he's not one to ask personal questions."

"Yeah," said Rhett before kissing Greg one more time. "I'm going to get going."

Greg said nothing in reply, only smiling as he watched his best friend climb off the bed and dress. Although their closeness and physical intimacy had increased, the confusion caused by it hadn't lessened. He was glad they were going to have more time apart.

Saying goodbye on the veranda, they held each other tightly.

"See you in a week or so?" Rhett asked as he began walking to his car.

"Yep," replied Greg. It wasn't much of an answer, but it was all that was needed.

He watched as Rhett's car reversed and soon disappeared. For a fleeting moment, he felt incredibly alone and regretful he hadn't left with Rhett. He shrugged the feeling off. At the cabin, there were always chores to be done and things to be prepared. Chopping wood, in particular, was a great source of distraction. It would be a perfect thing to get on with.

As he began to bring the axe down on the first piece of wood, he thought about what Rhett's return to the city might be like. He then thought about what his own return would be like. As much as he loved being at the cabin, he had to concede that it would be good to be back in his city home, at least for a short time. Hot water and easy access to whatever food he wanted, whenever he wanted, was something that definitely appealed.

Yes, it would be good to go home. He was glad that Rhett had gone ahead of time so they could both have time alone to process what had happened, but he equally looked forward to seeing his best mate again.

CHAPTER 29

For David's first week back, Sasha stayed at home at all times except those when she hung out with little Nicky. All other aspects of her life, she was happy to put on hold just in case her brother wanted or needed to talk to her again. She told herself that was the only reason she wanted to be at home so much. In her heart, there was a much more serious reason.

Even though she and James exchanged text messages every day, she hadn't told him that David was home. In truth, she didn't particularly want to. It was something she dreaded him finding out, and she wasn't sure how well she could keep it hidden if she was in his presence. She knew it would be perfectly understandable for James to want to do something about the situation. He might even be driven to go to the police and tell them that he believed it was David who'd shot his brother, and that David was home. It was a risk that Sasha didn't want to take.

Sitting alone in their backyard, she took some time to think about James. There was no official title to whatever it was that they were doing. When they were together, they kissed, and he'd always encouraged her to build on her comfort with touch, but things hadn't gone beyond that. He never pressured her. For that, she was grateful. She was always aware that her level of relaxation about touch had changed, and she'd started to enjoy it far more than she'd ever thought she could. She'd also changed from being absolute in her desire to not ever have sex again, to being open to it.

They'd been getting on well, not spending too much time together, but meeting up at least a few times a week. She didn't know what he thought about her having avoided the last couple of suggested meets, making one excuse or another. It was a difficult place for her to be in. She didn't want to see him, but she so much did.

"You look so serious, Sasha," she heard her mother's voice say. When she turned, she saw her mother approach and sit beside her. "Do you want to talk about something?"

Sasha took a moment to think about that. Talking to anyone in her family was still new for her. She kept trying to open up, but it had been a long process.

"I was thinking about James," she finally said.

"Ahh, and how is he?" Stacey asked. "We haven't seen him for a while."

"No," replied Sasha. "I … I'm not sure what to say to him right now."

"Is this something to do with David?"

"Yeah. I don't want to have to lie to him about what's been happening with us, but I don't want to talk to him about David either," Sasha said. "It feels like the easiest thing to do is to avoid him."

"But you miss him," Stacey guessed.

"A bit," said Sasha. "I want to see him, but what do I say? What do I do to seem normal, so he doesn't ask me anything specific about this?"

"Does he usually ask you questions about us?" Stacey asked, curious.

"No, not at all," Sasha replied. "We both generally avoid talking about family stuff."

"Then maybe it isn't an issue at all," Stacey said. "Sasha, if you want to see James, go and see him. Make the most of what time you can have with him."

As Sasha heard her mother's words, she also heard the same sad tone that indicated her mother's attempt to hold back tears. She was thinking about Rex and how his death was a reminder of how short life could be.

Sasha smiled. "Okay. I'm heading out soon to take

Nicky to see a movie, but I'll message James after that and see if we can hang out."

"Is everything okay between you, other than that?" Stacey asked.

"Everything is … easy, I guess," said Sasha. "I like him."

"And from what I've seen when he's been around, I think he likes you too - a lot," Stacey said, happy when she thought about the looks she'd seen James giving her previously-angry daughter. "I think he's one of the good ones."

"I do, too," Sasha replied, grinning. Sometimes it still surprised her how it had happened, but she couldn't deny that the pretty boy's efforts to get to know her had paid off. He'd melted the coldness around her heart in a way that no other person had ever been able to do. "I need to go," she said, standing up and walking away.

Readying herself to go and meet up with little Nicky, she felt happy. The eleven-year-old had made such an impact on Sasha's life that she was a priority Sasha wouldn't cast aside. As much as it was Nicky's highlight each week to hang out with Sasha, the reverse was also true.

"Hey, hey, Nicky-kid!" she said when she met Nicky and her mother inside the mall. She always laughed with Nicky when they did their unique hand greeting. Hearing the giggle of her small friend was something to always make her even happier herself.

"I'll be back at three to pick her up, if that's okay, Sasha?" Nicky's mother, Susan, asked.

"Yep, that's cool," said Sasha. "That gives us time to see the movie and have a look around the shops too."

"Yay!" Nicky said, jumping up and down. "Will James come too?"

Susan chuckled. "Your *friend* has made quite an impression on Nicky, Sasha," she teased.

Sasha grinned and faced Nicky.

"Nah, it's just you and me today, Nicky-kid," she said. "You cool with that?" she asked and saw Nicky nod enthusiastically. "Alright, then. Shall we go?"

As the two of them walked into the cinema, Sasha felt her phone vibrate in her pocket. Pulling it out, she saw a message had arrived from the very person she'd been trying to avoid.

'Hey you, what are you up to?'

Sasha felt nervous but knew she had to get over that. She couldn't hide forever, and in her heart, she didn't want to.

'Taking Nicky to a movie right now'

It took only seconds before her phone vibrated again.

'I have to go to Dad's tonight, but do you wanna come with me to the beach after your movie?'

'Susan's picking up Nicky at 3'

'Pick you up outside the mall after that?'

'Yep.'

"Is that James?" Nicky asked.

"Sure is," Sasha replied, chuckling. "But let's hurry and get our tickets and seats. What munchies do you want today?"

~~~~~

After lots of giggles during the movie, and some time in the mall food court, Sasha walked Nicky outside.

"I'm going to a birthday party tomorrow," Nicky said as they waited for her mother to pick her up.

"You are?" Sasha asked, grinning. "That's so awesome, Nicky! How are you feeling about it?"

"Okay," Nicky replied. "I'm a bit scared. What if the other kids don't want to talk to me?"

Whenever Sasha heard Nicky say or ask things like that, she felt sad. She crouched so they were face to face.

"If they don't, then that's okay, but I think you might find that if you say hello, they will say hi back,"
~~~~~

she said. "You're doing so well, Nicky. I'm proud of you for taking such a brave step and accepting the invitation."

Instead of Nicky replying, Sasha welcomed her young friend wrapping her arms around her neck.

"Thank you, Sasha," Nicky said. "I'm gonna try and be brave."

"You got this," Sasha said. "You're awesome."

In the distance, they heard Nicky's mother call out to them. When they both turned, they saw Susan approaching.

"You two have fun?" Susan asked.

"Always," said Sasha. "This cool kid was a right Miss Giggles in there."

Nicky giggled again. "*You* were!"

Sasha grinned. Getting to hang out with Nicky always made her feel happy.

"Do you want a ride somewhere, Sasha?" Susan asked.

"No, thanks," Sasha replied.

"She's gonna see James," Nicky said in a mock whisper to her mother.

"Ahh, I see!" said Susan, winking at Sasha. "Okay, little miss, we have to get going, so say goodbye to Sasha," she said to Nicky before looking at Sasha again. "See you next week?"

"Sure thing," Sasha replied, smiling. "And *you* have fun at the party!" she said to Nicky. "Remember - just be you."

As the two walked away, Sasha watched them until they were out of sight. She remembered feeling strongly that she'd never be a mother. When she'd spent time with Nicky, her enthusiasm about that changed a little at a time.

Her pocket buzzing woke her out of her thoughts.

'I'm on the north side of the carpark. Where are you?'

Sasha looked in the direction he'd given and saw his car.

'I see you. I'll be there in a min.'

As she walked across the carpark, she felt anxious. She'd already decided she wouldn't share the news that David was home again. She'd often considered that she knew little about James's family, so there was no real reason for her to share a lot with him about hers. They always had plenty to talk about without delving into family dramas. She was grateful for that.

"Hey," James said when he saw her approaching.

Sasha grinned. Seeing him leaning against the boot of his car made her think he could be a model on a professional photoshoot. She had to push the thought aside. She'd never seen guys' looks as a reason to like them, and it wasn't James's pretty face that had chipped away at her heart. It was so much more than that.

"Hey yourself," she replied as she was engulfed in his arms.

Happily, she wrapped her arms around him. It had taken her a long while to be able to do that. Since that first time, she sometimes felt like she'd never stopped hugging him.

James held her close. She was a tough chick with a hard exterior, but he was glad she'd learned to relax enough to be so close to him. He was in no hurry to move things along physically between them. She was the first woman that he could remember having wanted to know him *without* wanting sex from him. It created a different kind of dynamic, but a good one.

Looking down into her eyes as they pulled apart, he couldn't help but kiss her. He'd been looking forward to that all day, every day, since he'd previously seen her days earlier. He didn't know what had been keeping her so distant, and he wouldn't ask. If anyone knew about things sometimes being not good or wise to talk about, it was him. He'd still not told her anything about the

Stonewarden family business. He wasn't sure he ever would. He guessed it should have made things uncomfortable, keeping something so big from her. It didn't. He had an entire lifetime of keeping things about his family secret from everyone. He knew her family was also in crime. He suspected that meant there would be a lot that he'd never learn about the Leadbetters either, and he was quite alright with that.

"Yum," Sasha said as she pulled away from their kisses. The smile he gave her then was incredible. She'd never before believed in the concept of someone actually feeling something in their heart when they looked at a loved one. Although it had been unexpected, that was exactly how she felt when she was in his company. Her guard wasn't completely down. There were still days when her negativity jumped in and tried to question what he truly wanted from her. She'd started to teach herself to ignore those questions.

"Yum, indeed, Sassy Girl," James said, enjoying the look of happiness on her face. It had taken a long time before he'd seen anything like that. He appreciated how often the smiles now appeared. "Beach?"

"Yep," Sasha said as they climbed into the car.

"How was the movie?" James asked, starting the engine and beginning to ease out of the carpark.

Sasha chuckled. "Really good," she said. "Nicky loved it. She's so cool when she giggles."

"She's a cool kid," said James, smiling at her. "It's cool that you spend so much time with her."

"I always will," said Sasha. "Well, for as long as she wants to, anyway. She's got a long way to go before she's fully sociable, but she's getting there."

James quietly thought to himself that she could have been describing herself rather than Nicky. He kept his thoughts on that to himself. He'd watched Sasha grow and change. It was something to see, but also something to be wary about mentioning to her. She wasn't yet at the stage where she liked compliments. He didn't mind. He still thought she was incredible, even if she didn't want to hear him say that.

"Do you need to get anything from your home?" James asked.

The question was innocent. Regardless, it immediately put Sasha on edge. She didn't want him to know that David was home if she could help it. David's Valiant sitting out front of their home would be a pretty big clue that he was.

"No, I'm good," she said, smiling at him.

"Cool," said James. "I've already grabbed some food, so let's go and watch the sunset."

Sasha laughed softly. "The sun won't be setting for a few hours yet."

"I know," James said, turning and winking at her, making her smile again. "I don't know what these clouds are doing, but I've got some warm gear and a couple of jackets in the back in case it gets cold."

Sasha relaxed back in her seat. The issue of David being home was a non-issue, at least for that moment. She determined not to think about the moment later when James would drop her off at home. That was something she'd have to deal with at that time.

Once they'd settled onto the sand, James laid out food on a blanket.

"This is a feast," Sasha said, teasing him but happy. "Are we expecting guests?"

James laughed. "Better to have too much than too little, right?" he asked and saw her nod. "Summer's on its way out. It's good to make the most of it while we can."

As he lay back, resting on his elbows and peering out toward the ocean, Sasha studied him. Sometimes he mystified her, he was so outwardly confident and poised. He possessed a level of grooming she'd hardly ever seen before. He was such a contrast to her that she often thought people who saw them together must think them a weird couple.

"What's on your mind, Sassy, for you to be looking at me so intensely?" she heard him ask even as he continued to look out toward the horizon. When she didn't answer, she saw him turn and face her. "You okay?"

"Yeah, of course," Sasha replied. "I was just in a daze. Don't get all paranoid and think that I like you or anything," she teased him.

James burst out laughing but nodded at her.

"Okay!" he said before moving his stare away.

Watching the waves lapping at the edge of the sand, he didn't wonder what she was thinking. He liked teasing her about her moments of staring at him, but he didn't analyze it. In many ways, she was like him. She thought a lot, but she didn't necessarily want to talk about her thoughts. On occasion, he'd encouraged her to open up to him if she needed to. Sometimes she had. Sometimes she hadn't. He didn't mind either way, although when she had opened up to him, he'd taken that as an indicator that he'd won at least a little bit of her trust.

"You got chocolate brownies?" Sasha asked when she opened up one of the paper bags laid out on the blanket.

"Yeah, of course," James replied, turning and smiling at her. "They're your favorite."

Sasha felt her heart pound yet again. She fought to hide her feelings at that moment. The pretty boy always made everything so easy and enjoyable for her.

Taking one out of the bag and indulging in a large bite, she then held out the remainder toward James. She wasn't surprised when, instead of taking a bite out of the brownie, he leaned toward her and licked her lips with a big, sloppy tongue, making her giggle.

"Bugger off," Sasha said. "What's in here is mine," she continued, pointing at her mouth.

"What? You had some around your mouth," said James, grinning. "I was just trying to help."

Sasha swallowed her mouthful of brownie and then leaned over and kissed him back. It was intended to be only a brief, light kiss. When her lips met his again, she wanted more. Mindful of the food between them, she carefully moved over and lay on top of him before leaning down and kissing his lips the way she wanted to kiss him.

James eagerly indulged. Since they'd first kissed, and she'd taken time to experiment with how she liked to, she'd definitely begun to excel in it. He didn't hold back from raising his arms around her and pulling her body to him, holding her tightly. They were good kisses, and they were kisses that excited him. With any other woman, he'd have been taking kisses like that as a sign to get right on with the seriously good stuff. With her, he had no such desire. If they ever moved past kissing, it would be her doing. That was what he wanted more than anything - for her to decide when she was ready for sex if that was ever to happen. He knew it might not. For her, he felt sad about that. For him, he didn't mind.

Since she'd started being a part of his life, he'd had no desire to go back to his player days. All of his previous contacts, who'd loved casual sex as much as he had, he'd deleted from his phone. He didn't miss any of them.

Sasha pulled back and looked at him. She was happy that being so close to him no longer scared her. There had been times when she'd laid on him just as she was at that moment, and she'd thought she could feel the obvious sign of arousal in him. It no longer panicked her. She'd always believed that guys only wanted sex from girls. He'd helped her to believe that even if they were turned on by the girl they were with, it didn't mean they were going to hurt her.

"I do like you," she said in almost a whisper.

"Well, that's good, because I do like you too," said James before lifting his head and kissing her gently.

"Back to the brownies, though," Sasha said, chuckling as she pulled off him and moved to her side of the blanket again.

James couldn't help but smile. She was a stark contrast to every woman he'd ever been with. She'd been so angry to start with. Over time, he'd seen her blossom to the point where she could tease him and smile and laugh. In his eyes, everything she did was positive. They could talk together, but they could also be silent together. They could laugh together, but they could just as easily cry together.

"I miss you when we're not hanging out," James said quietly, his mouth speaking from his heart rather than his head.

Sasha looked at him in surprise. Not sure how to respond, she remained quiet. She didn't want her current family dynamic to underlie every interaction she was going to have with him, but she was equally resolved to not share the news about David with him.

"I've got family stuff going on right now," she said. "It's stuff that I won't share with you, but that's why I haven't been around."

"All I care about is whether you're okay and you're safe," said James and saw her nod and smile sadly. "Are you?"

"Yeah, I'm okay, and I'm safe," Sasha replied. "It's nothing that's gonna result in something bad. I just want to be close to home a bit more than usual right now."

"Okay," replied James, not wanting to ask anything more. He had no reason to doubt she was being honest.

"Get eating, pretty boy," Sasha said to change the subject. "Let's clean this lot off real good."

James grinned and sat up to do what she'd asked.

He knew subject-changing attempts, but he didn't mind them at all. She was safe. In his opinion, that was all that mattered.

~~~~~

Food consumed, James ran to the car to get rid of the rubbish and grab a jacket for each of them. He liked the beach. It had always been his place for solitude and peace. He still got that but had to admit that he liked being there with Sasha. The most obvious thing about her was that he could be with her and still feel at peace. There was no requirement for him to keep talking all the time or for any silent moments to be filled by chatter. Despite her initial openly-displayed anger, she calmed him.

"Put this on if you want," he said when he returned and handed a jacket to her.

"Thanks," said Sasha as she accepted it and wrapped herself up in its warmth.

Sitting down again, James moved to encourage her into his arms. It was one of the most amazing ways that he loved being closer to her. Sitting up and peering over her shoulder as she sat between his legs, they fitted together comfortably to both look out at the ocean.

As Sasha relaxed back against his chest, she felt content. Feeling his arms wrapped around her like a security blanket, she liked when he rested his chin on her shoulder, almost cheek to cheek. When they were like that, it seemed impossible for any stress to exist inside of her. Sitting still and watching the sun slowly begin its descent in the sky felt like what she imagined meditation would be like. There was no sound except the small waves in front of them, the occasional seabird passing overhead, and the quiet steadiness of James's breath next to her ear. It was a situation that Sasha imagined the word bliss must explain perfectly.

"Are you warm enough?" James asked. His question was answered by Sasha turning her head far
~~~~~

enough to be able to just reach his lips with her own. James happily obliged the silent request.

"Yep. I'm perfect," Sasha replied as she turned around and settled into her warm and comfortable place.

"Yes, you are," James whispered in her ear. It wasn't a lie. That was exactly how he saw her.

"Kiss my neck," he heard her say. It was always a bold thing when she asked for something physical. Because he knew about the long journey she'd been on to try and grow comfortable with touch, he never took for granted what she asked of him.

Happily, James moved one of his hands to clear aside the jacket collar before he placed his lips on that spot on her neck that they'd both discovered she liked kissed. As she naturally leaned her head sideways, more skin was revealed for his attention. It was such a small thing, but James loved it. It made him sometimes think about all the years he'd been in a hurry to get to sex with the women he'd been with. His times with Sasha never resulted in sex, but they felt far more intimate.

Sasha indulged in the feeling throughout her body as he kissed only that one tiny part of her. It was new, but it was glorious. She didn't attempt to stop the moan that naturally escaped her.

James continued the movement, enjoying the scent of her as his tongue and lips danced over her skin. Feeling the subtle movements of her body, and hearing her soft moans, made his heart feel full. It was so little, but it was equally so much. When he felt her pull away, for a moment, he felt the emptiness of the movement. When he saw her face as she turned around to kneel, facing him, he thought she could turn any man to jelly with the look on her face. He didn't know her states of arousal, but he was pretty sure that was what was on her face. He wouldn't act on that thought, but there was no denying that she had his attention.

Sasha followed her desire, leaning forward and

kissing him with all the passion she felt. She wasn't ready for sex yet, but she knew she was getting closer. She finally understood what the term 'turned on' meant. She'd never believed it was a real thing, just as she'd never believed touch between a man and a woman could be enjoyable. She was sometimes overwhelmed that she could experience both with him.

Kissing him, her body wanted to move forward. So did her heart. She chose to not listen to either. Instead, she pulled away, looked into his eyes, and then turned around to settle back into his arms as she had been. She was close, but she wasn't there yet.

James wrapped his arms around her again. He understood her actions. Some guys would have thought she was being coy. He knew she was doing what was right for her, and *not* doing what wasn't.

Quietly, they stayed where they were as they watched the sun go down. When only the top of it could be seen on the horizon, James finally spoke.

"It's getting cold," he said. "Let's pack this up and go get in the car."

Sasha said nothing as she followed his lead. Her head was full of confusion. She knew she'd reached a point where she wanted them to go one step further. She fought the desire she naturally felt, but it wasn't easy doing so.

When they settled inside the car, James turned on the heater so they could watch the last bit of sun disappear. He was aware of time passing. The time was approaching when he'd be due to be at his family home for a planning meeting.

"I need to be at my Dad's in an hour," he said. "Do you want me to drop you home now, or do you want to come back to mine for a bit, and then I'll drop you home when I'm heading there?"

At the mention of him dropping her home, Sasha felt her anxiety increase again. She'd successfully managed to push her worries from her mind for a short time. The stark reality of it woke her up as if he'd taken a needle and popped a bubble that had been engulfing her.

"I … I can go home now," she said, the magic of the evening having disappeared and replaced with stark reality.

"You sure?" James asked. It wasn't like her to not try and seize every moment together that they could. When he looked closely at her, he could see the nervousness he'd learned to identify. He didn't ask what was going on again. She knew she could talk to him if she needed to. If she wasn't talking, she didn't want to, and that was very okay. He had no desire to tell her he'd later be planning a jewelry theft with his father and brothers. In his view, keeping quiet about the important family stuff was okay with him.

"Yeah," Sasha replied, attempting to smile at him.

James leaned over and kissed her. Once again, she seemed to take off and jump into passion with ease and speed. They kissed for a long time before he felt her take one of his hands and move it onto her breast. It was a bold move, and it was new. He pulled away only far enough so that he could look into her eyes.

"Touch me," Sasha whispered.

James held his lips back, continuing to watch her face as he lightly caressed her breast. Focusing on her nipple when it made itself known to him, he flicked one of his fingers back and forth across it, all the while shifting his gaze from her eyes to her lips and back again. He watched as her eyes took on the dazed of arousal and then closed. He continued to watch as her lips opened just a little, and a small moan escaped them.

He was mesmerized. Nothing had changed in his decision to not rush to anything more, but he knew that the second she wanted things to, he was going to be more than ready to as well. When he saw her eyes open again, he couldn't hold back from kissing her passionately again.

"I think I've changed my mind," Sasha said as she pulled back. "I don't know about this belief I had that I'll never want to have sex."

"Well, if that time does come, it's not happening in my car, Sassy," he said, chuckling before kissing her again.

"Do you want to?" Sasha asked, curious.

"If the time comes when you feel like you might be ready, don't you worry - I'll want to!" James said. "But there's no rush, Sasha. No rush, and no pressure."

"I know," Sasha replied as she nodded. "Thanks."

James grinned at her one more time before starting the engine. Before he moved the car, he reached over and took her hand in his.

"All of the time I spend with you is important to me," he said. "You know that, right?"

"Yeah," Sasha replied. Did she know it? She asked herself the question even after she'd given him her answer. Internal contemplation agreed. It was weird that he wanted to spend time with her, but she did accept that he did. "I know."

"Cool," James said as he began to veer the car away from the beach. "So, for the next couple of weeks, I'm helping my dad with some stuff on the nights that I'm not working at the bar, so I won't be able to see you much at nighttime, but it's only for a few weeks."

"Yeah, no worries," Sasha said, a little relieved. If he was that busy, there was less chance he'd see her or drop her off at her house, so less chance of seeing David's car.

James smiled. He hated lying to her by not saying what he was helping his dad with, but a smile covered that up. Since Max had been shot, their father hadn't approved as many jobs. It had evened out to one in maybe every two months, which was nothing compared to the level they'd done before that day.

They traveled in silence, each thinking about their own family issues. When they were close to Sasha's street, she felt nervous again. She kept quiet, ready to face whatever was to happen, but when her home appeared in their view, David's car was nowhere to be seen. She instantly felt her body relax. There was still a chance James would come face to face with David at some other time, but it wasn't going to happen at that moment.

James stopped outside the Leadbetter home, jumped out, and opened Sasha's door for her.

"Thanks," Sasha said as she moved close to him and wrapped her arms around his neck.

James kissed her while pulling her closer still. Whenever he left her, no matter where that was, he always felt like there was a chance he wouldn't see her again. He didn't know where that fear came from, and he didn't like it.

"Talk tomorrow?" he asked, regretful that he had to go and do family business planning when he'd rather spend the time with her.

"Yep," said Sasha as she pulled away. She was about to turn and head up the path when she found herself pulled into his arms once more, her face smothered with kisses that made her giggle. "Go away!"

James laughed softly at her and kissed her on the cheek once more before jumping into his car, waving, and then was on his way to his family home.

~~~~~

Walking into the lounge of the large Stonewarden home, James saw that he was the last to arrive. Already sitting around the coffee table in the center of the room were his father and brothers, Vic, Regan, Max, and Fitz. As always, it was Fitz who was pointing to things on the sheets of paper spread out over the table, explaining the way he thought was best for them to get in, get the jewels, and get out again.
~~~~~

James quietly acknowledged his father and then sat down among them, automatically switching his brain from boyfriend mode to thief mode. It had been a part of his life for so long that there was no longer any effort needed to make the transition. Life outside was just that - outside. Since he'd left home and moved into his apartment, most of the time he'd spent in the family home had been for planning. That made it even easier to segregate the two aspects of his life. As much as he loved spending time with Sasha, as soon as he'd left her to attend the planning meeting, she was forgotten, at least for the moment.

~~~~~

As Mitchell Stonewarden sat and listened to his sons, he made a point to stay back a bit and leave them to figure things out. In addition to having been their sole parent for a decade, he had also always been their leader when it came to the jobs that they did. The time for him to do that was coming to an end. Looking at his oldest son, Vic, he knew the time was right. It had been agreed that he'd start training Vic to be the full leader of it all. Mitchell and Vic were both looking forward to that.

Having started to spend more of his time at the ranch where his daughter, Charlie, lived, Mitchell had gained a better appreciation for taking more time to relax. The business wasn't continually high-stress, but even after jobs were completed, there was always that underlying knowledge that at any time, the cops could knock on their door. It wasn't a great way to live, but it was how the Stonewardens had survived for hundreds of years.

As he watched and listened, he could see that not only was Vic naturally comfortable in the role of leader, but his younger brothers were also regarding him as such. It was good to see. They'd all learned their roles well in the business, but Mitchell was aware that they could have just been doing what he said because they
~~~~~

feared him, or for any other reason. The upcoming job would be the first that Vic would primarily manage, with Mitchell there only for backup support.

He waited for something to be said that might demand he step in and rectify an error. Nothing like that happened. The planning by the five brothers was sound, even without his input. He knew he'd worry on the night, but the reality was that if he wasn't still alive, they'd be carrying on the business without him, so there was no reason why they wouldn't be just fine while he *was* still alive.

Looking around his boys, he felt pride, just as he always did. They were a good bunch of kids. Their mother would have been just as proud of who each of them had grown into.

Caroline. She was still the love of his life. A decade had passed since her death, but he still missed her terribly when he thought about her. Now there was a new Caroline, albeit a very young one. One of the joys he'd begun to indulge in was spending time with Charlie's daughter. It had been a long time since he'd felt needed. He'd never desired to be a grandfather, but he loved spending time with the new little love of his life.

"I think that's it for the night," Vic said a long time later. "We've still got plenty more planning sessions before the night, so if any of you think of anything that we haven't covered, make sure you remember it so we can talk about it."

Seeing his four younger brothers react to him the same way they usually did to their father pleased Vic. He was confident enough to take on the role. That didn't mean the others necessarily wanted to follow him. He was glad to see no resistance from anyone, particularly Fitz. Never one to take part in any kind of family activity other than job planning, nobody could ever be sure how Fitz was going to act or react to anything.

Mitchell watched as Fitz quickly left the house. It

was always the way, but it had been a long time since Mitchell had attempted to chastise Fitz for anything. All of his sons were adults. They all had to make their own choices in life. Something had always been different about Fitz. Mitchell briefly wondered if he would ever find out why.

"Does it all look sound to you?" Vic asked him.

"It does," Mitchell replied. "You've got this, Vic. This will be only the first success of many that you'll get to do from this point forwards."

"Thanks, Dad," Vic said. He'd known for a long time that he'd be stepping up to fill in his father's place as family head for the business. Now that the time had arrived, he was nervous, even though he knew he was ready. "I'm gonna head off unless there's something we need to go over?"

"No, everything's good as far as I'm concerned," Mitchell said. "Go and enjoy your night."

He watched as Vic smiled and said his goodbyes, leaving Mitchell with his three younger sons.

"Have you all been out to spend time with your sister and niece lately?" he asked, half in teasing.

"Dad, I see Charlie twice a week!" Max said, rolling his eyes and making his father chuckle and shift his gaze to James.

"Yes! I was out there last week," said James.

When Mitchell looked at Regan, there was no such happy teasing. In natures, Regan was far more like Vic than James or Max.

"I haven't been out there since the wedding," Regan admitted. "You know me and Charlie aren't that close. I'll be here for her however she ever needs me, but we just aren't chatty like you guys are."

His words were true, but his underlying reason for not liking being around Charlie was still the knowledge that he, his father, and his brothers had broken into Charlie's husband's parents' home and robbed them.

Every time he saw Ash, he was reminded of it.

"Fair enough," Mitchell said, nodding. He wouldn't pressure Regan. One of his sons - Max - was extremely close to their sister. Another - James - had grown closer since Max had been shot. That was reason for happiness enough. Charlie was out of the city, but she was happy, and she had a young man who adored her and their baby. Mitchell couldn't have been happier with how things had gone there. Charlie and Ash were young, but even he was sure that what they had was the real deal and not just some teenage infatuation.

"I'm heading to bed," Regan said as he removed himself. He rarely stayed at home, but it was always difficult for him in his relationship during the times leading up to a job. His girlfriend knew nothing about the life he lived away from her. Every job felt like a betrayal, and he hated that.

"Me, too," said Max, standing to follow.

"No date tonight, Max?" James teased him. The look and finger sign he got in return was hardly polite, making him chuckle at his younger brother.

When only Mitchell and James were left, Mitchell seized the moment of one-on-one time with his second-oldest son.

"Is all good with you?" Mitchell asked.

"Yeah, nothing's new in my world," said James.

"How's work?" Mitchell asked as he sat down and encouraged James to do the same.

"It's okay," James replied. "I still like it, but I don't enjoy it as much as I used to. Might be time for me to look for something else. I dunno."

"And your girl?" asked Mitchell, finally getting to the question he really wanted an answer to. When he saw the grin on James's face on hearing the question, he knew he was getting close to the boundary of what he could ask as a father.

"I'm enjoying the time I spend with Sasha," said

James. "She's cool. No drama there." He paused as he considered how little he shared with her. Would it always be that way? "She's the first woman I've been with, who I feel bad about keeping such a big aspect of my life from," he said and saw his father nod. "I haven't had to lie, but the whole lying by omission thing doesn't feel good." He looked at his father for a long while before he spoke again. "Do you think Charlie would have come clean about us to Ash if he hadn't happened to overhear everyone talking at the ranch that night?"

Mitchell considered the question. Generally, he avoided trying to guess what might have happened in a different situation. With the particular question that had been presented to him, he understood why it was a good question to ask.

"I don't know," he replied. "But Charlie's situation isn't the same as yours, James. Ash is just a guy from a normal family. Sasha is from a family involved in violent crime. And if they were at that gala night, they must have their eyes on the same stuff to steal as we do, at least some of the time. I don't know how the news would go down that you're a jewel thief too." He paused. "But you know her, and I don't. Do you think you *want* to tell her who you are?"

"No," said James, shaking his head. "I don't want to disclose anything about what we do. And that's not because of her family's stuff. It's more because I don't feel positive about what we do when I think about it in terms of how other people would see it. I know that Ash accepted us when he wanted to marry Charlie, but those two … they have a different level of connection. I don't know if I'll *ever* find that with anyone."

"It's not that serious with this girl, then?" Mitchell asked. He'd assumed it was serious. James usually slept with women now and then. As far as Mitchell knew, James had never kept any of them around for too long.

"Hmm, when I'm with her, I'm happy - I mean,

really happy," James replied in full honesty. "I don't want to spend time with anyone else, which is new for me. I dunno. I'm just taking each day as it comes. She's changed a lot since I first met her, so anything could happen as she continues to change."

Mitchell nodded but didn't ask James about his reference to Sasha changing. Mitchell had met her only the one time, when Charlie had been in the hospital giving birth to Caroline. The girl on James's arm had seemed quiet. That was all Mitchell had gathered about her then, and he hadn't seen her again since.

"Are you sure you're not wondering whether to tell her about us?" he asked, but saw James shake his head.

"No," said James. "I think we're in a good place, not telling each other anything about our families. I don't want to talk about us, but I also don't want to know about them. I mean, I'll go with her to family things like her brother's wedding if she wants me to, but I don't need to hear anything. It's better not to, right?"

"Only you know that," Mitchell replied. "But if she isn't asking, it sounds like you have nothing to worry about anyway."

"Yeah," James said as he stood. "Anyway, I'm gonna head home. Thanks, though, for being here to talk to."

Mitchell chuckled. "You hardly ever come and talk to me."

"Yeah, but I know that I can, and I know that you're here to listen and provide advice when I do need it," James replied as he walked toward the door. "Bye," he said, opening the door and walking out.

As Mitchell looked at the closed door, he felt emotional. It was rare for his kids to say they needed him. Even if it was only sometimes, it was enough to remind him that he had kids who weren't afraid to share their emotions from time to time. That made him smile.

CHAPTER 30

On his arrival back in the city, Rhett went straight to visit Mark. There was no obligation to do so, but he had missed the friend who'd been like a brother to him since they'd been teenagers.

Throughout the journey from the cabin, Rhett's mind had insisted he think about and confront his feelings and what had happened between him and Greg. At one level, he knew there was nothing wrong with it. The closer he got to the Leadbetter family home, the more he remembered just how much Mark's parents had talked badly about homosexuality. Rhett had been young enough to have believed their words. As he'd grown into his own person, he'd not seen any reason to discriminate against people who liked people of their own gender. Although he'd accepted everyone as an equal part of the human race, as he regarded himself as being kind of in the middle of such desire, the thoughts of Mark's parents conflicted with Rhett's own beliefs.

It had been hard enough to deal with just having kissed Greg. Over previous days, they'd moved through two more levels of intimacy. How did he truly feel about that? He'd wanted it, and he'd enjoyed it. In the moment, there had been nothing about it that had caused any negative feelings in him. As he replayed the scenes in his head, he grew aroused again. Not only weren't they a turn-off, but remembering them was an incredible turn-*on*. Surely, that meant that it was right.

He didn't need to do anything about it for the moment, and he was glad. Greg had said he'd be out of town for a while yet. Until he returned, Rhett didn't have to stress about anyone seeing the two of them together and reading that something had happened and changed between them. That was a relief. He wanted to believe that he and Greg would still get on just the same as they always had when around others. He wanted to believe it, but he wasn't sure how realistic that thought was.

Approaching the Leadbetter home, he attempted to discard any thoughts about his intimate moments with Greg. He expected Mark would ask how Greg was. Rhett just had to keep his head straight and answer truthfully while not focusing on the pleasure they'd shared.

Stopping outside, he saw Mark and Stacey on the swing seat on their porch.

"About time you got back," Mark called out as Rhett walked up the path. "Is Greg with you?"

"No, he's taking more time out, but said he'll probably be back in town in a week or two," Rhett replied, hopeful that would be the last mention of Greg for a while. "How are you guys going?" he asked to change the subject.

"Yeah, we're doing okay," said Mark before he kissed Stacey and stood. "Come and get a beer."

Rhett followed his friend inside, still not confident that he'd get away with hiding his feelings for Greg. When Mark got them a beer each and led him to his office, Rhett was relieved that the conversation went in an entirely different direction.

"Thanks again for going to find David," Mark said.

"Least I could do," said Rhett. "How's he doing?"

Mark shrugged. "It's hard to say. He's talked to Phillip and Sasha a bit, but hasn't said hardly anything to me or Stace."

"Sometimes parents are the hardest to open up to," said Rhett. "You know that."

"Yeah, I know," Mark replied. "It's just so hard, knowing he's going through something, and I can't seem to help him in any way."

"Well, I might be way off base with this..." Rhett

started to say.

"But?" asked Mark.

"But, knowing how David was when we found him, it wouldn't surprise me if Sasha's the best person for him to talk to," Rhett replied. "In some ways, they're actually alike."

Mark was surprised by the comment but didn't argue with it. He'd seen David and Sasha talking alone. It wasn't easy to understand, but Rhett's words fitted with what had actually been happening.

"As long as he's okay, or going to be okay," Mark said. "That's all I really care about."

"He'll get there," said Rhett. "Did he make contact with the girlfriend?"

Mark nodded. "Yeah, he did tell us that he's talked to her about a few things and told her he was the one who shot into the supermarket."

"How did she take that news?" asked Rhett.

"David said they were working through it," Mark said. "I guess as long as they're talking, it's good. She's having his baby. Did I tell you that already?"

"No," Rhett replied. "Wow. That's some news."

Mark chuckled. "Yeah, I'll say. I didn't see that one coming."

"Well, hopefully, they work it all out before the baby comes along," said Rhett. "You're gonna be a granddaddy," he added, grinning.

"Yeah, *twice*, maybe," Mark said. "Phillip and Daisy are trying too."

"I bet Stacey's loving that!"

Mark grinned and nodded. "She is, but I have to admit, I am too. Since Rex … well, it'll be nice having kids around again."

Rhett smiled. He'd never wanted kids in his youth. He still didn't feel like he wanted them, but he could concede that it must be nice for people to have offspring around now and then. Since his parents had tossed him out of their home, he'd known no family other than the Leadbetters who'd offered him a home way back then. He had no blood relatives that were in his life. Already 50, he never would have. There was sadness in that realization.

"Everyone's happy then," said Rhett. "Sasha too?"

"Seems it," Mark said. "She's got her pretty boy. She hasn't been seeing him as often, I think because she feels conflicted knowing that David was the one who shot that guy's brother."

"Huh?" Rhett asked, sure he'd missed some details somewhere.

"Sasha's guy," Mark said and saw Rhett nod. "His brother was the one that was shot in the supermarket ... by David."

"Fuck ... me," said Rhett. "How the fuck does that kind of coincidence even happen? Did she know that was who he was when she met him?"

Mark shook his head. "No, apparently they met a few times and hung out, and then he realized who she was and told her who *he* was. It's a mess, alright."

"Does he know it was David?" Rhett asked.

"Apparently."

"Does he know David's back in town?"

"Not sure," said Mark. "Sasha mentioned she was hesitant to tell him, but I don't know if she has told him since then."

"That wouldn't be an easy thing to look past," Rhett said. "If I was seeing someone and I found out their brother shot my brother ... fuck, I don't know if I could keep seeing that person. I mean, obviously, it wasn't Sasha who pulled the trigger, but still..."

"Yeah, I don't know if I could do it either," said Mark. "I guess it's an indication of how much he cares for her, though..."

"Or is using her, or purposely setting her up to hurt her..."

"I did consider that," said Mark. "But I've seen them together. You saw him at the wedding, didn't you?"

"Yeah, but only in passing," Rhett replied.

"He's stuck around and continued to be a support to her," said Mark. "I know he has reason to hate us, but I don't think he wants to hurt her."

"What about David, though? Will he want to hurt *him*?"

"That's the unknown," said Mark. "I hope not. I'm hoping that even if he learns that David's here, this guy will put his feelings for Sasha ahead of any resentment or need for revenge."

"Well, keep an eye on her," Rhett said. "She's tough, your daughter, but anyone can be fooled when it comes to the heart."

"I know," said Mark. "Don't worry - I'm keeping my eyes open."

Rhett briefly thought to himself that there seemed an odd level of romantic happiness in the family all of a sudden. Phillip had found and married his Daisy. Sasha had her man. Rhett had … he stopped himself from completing that thought. Did he have romantic happiness? It was difficult for him to align the word 'romantic' with two guys doing what he and Greg had. It was an illogical thought, but it was a natural one for him.

"Any jobs on?" he asked to divert his mind.

"Not that I've heard," said Mark. "I haven't even heard who's stepping up to lead. Since Pete's death, nobody else has put their hand up. Nobody's said *anything*."

"Well, that could be a good thing, right?" asked Rhett. "Maybe everyone's over all this formal criminal life. Is it time for everyone to break away and just live their own lives however they want to?"

"That's all well and good if people live well," Mark said. "You know as well as I do that when these guys are at their lowest point with no money to buy food for their families, they'll do anything, and their decisions aren't usually wise. Too many innocent people have been hurt because of the desperation felt by one Leadbetter or another."

"Yeah, but it's all our own choice how we live," said Rhett. "When I've done stupid things, I've had to then live with watching my back all the time, constantly thinking people are watching me. I've only done one stint in prison, but I survived. Been there, done that, but it's that paranoia that I hate."

Mark nodded. "True. Well, hopefully, either someone will step up and lead the family, or everyone will get on with living a quiet life however they can."

"You're not tempted to take the role on again?" Rhett asked. "You were a good leader. You laid down the no-violence law, and people respected that."

"I do think I led better than others have, but I made a promise to Stacey, and I don't want to go back on it," Mark replied. "Besides, I think I'm over this lifestyle as much as anyone else. I lost my son. I won't risk losing anyone else."

Rhett nodded but didn't reply. How anyone could enjoy being in a position where they were responsible for hundreds of family members and other people who'd joined them over the years, he didn't understand. It was too much. He'd always done as he'd been instructed to, but he'd never desired power. When that got into the wrong person's hands - as it had in Pete Leadbetter's case - too many things could go horribly wrong.

"I think Greg would be good at it," he heard Mark say, commanding his attention again.

"You think?" Rhett asked. Just the thought of Greg being put in such a vulnerable position was enough for Rhett to instantly be worried. "He seems to want to be away from everyone more and more."

"Yeah, it does seem that way," said Mark. "I hope he does come back soon. I worry about him. How did he seem when you were with him?"

"Fine," said Rhett, wanting to change the subject but not daring to. "He seemed happy."

"Do you know what's behind this sudden need to be away from us all?" Mark asked.

Rhett looked at him for a long while. The three of them were friends, but Rhett felt his loyalty had to lie more with Greg than Mark at that moment.

"I think he'll be back next week or the week after," he said. "Just ask him."

Mark heard the avoidance in Rhett's response. He didn't pull him up on it. Some things shouldn't be repeated. He understood that perfectly. It was an indicator of the level of trust that any of them could put in Rhett, that he didn't repeat things that it wasn't his place to.

"I hope he does come back," Mark said. "I miss him."

"He will," Rhett reassured him, hoping it was true. The sudden consideration that Greg might not return made his heart ache. He supposed it didn't matter. He knew where Greg was. He could go and see him anytime. Still, it would be nice if Greg returned to the city. If he continued to stay away, what would that mean for the two of them? "I've got a few things to do, so I'm gonna head off," he said as he stood. He'd only just arrived back in town. Already he felt claustrophobic.

"Are you okay, Rhett?" Mark asked, sensing something was off.

"Yeah, just tired," Rhett replied as they made their way out the front door.

"I'm always here for you," said Mark. "You know that, right?"

"Yep," Rhett said, smiling. "See you guys later."

As he walked down the path and jumped in his car, Mark sat down beside Stacey again.

"How's Rhett?" she asked.

"Don't know," Mark said, extending out his arm and pulling her close. "Something feels a bit off with him, but he said he was tired, so maybe that's it."

"Did he mention Greg? Where he is?"

"No," said Mark. "I didn't ask where he is. Rhett seems certain Greg'll be back in a week or so. I hope that's true."

"What are you worried about?" Stacey asked. She knew her husband's body well. It was easy for her to feel how tense he was.

"I dunno," Mark replied before kissing her softly. "Just a feeling. Might be nothing."

"You need me to help you with another feeling to distract you?" Stacey said, pulling out of his hold and turning to kiss him deeply. When she pulled back, the grin on her husband's face was much preferable to the tenseness of the moment earlier.

"You trying to seduce me?" Mark asked, chuckling before sinking one hand into her hair and easing her lips back to his. Kissing her was something that had never ceased to produce incredible feelings for him. When they pulled apart again, he smiled at her and kissed her cheek.

"Anya's due home soon," he reminded her.

Stacey grinned and nodded. "Maybe later then."

Mark laughed. "No 'maybe' about it, my sexy wife," he said and pulled her into the comfortable security of his arms once more. "You are the most incredible woman I've ever met. Have I told you that?" he asked before kissing the top of her head.

"Once or twice," replied Stacey, grinning to herself. "I'm so thankful that you pursued me like you did all those years ago."

"You've never wished you'd met a normal law-abiding guy who was clean-cut and nice?" Mark asked. It could have been a serious question, but he was only teasing her. One thing he'd never doubted in his life was her love for him.

Stacey pulled back and looked directly into his eyes.

"Not once," she answered honestly, even though she knew she didn't need to. "And besides, you might try and act tough, Mark Leadbetter, but I know the truth about you. You're a lot nicer than a lot of so-called 'nice guys' out there. You're the only one for me, and you know it."

Although it was a speech that was said in a lighthearted manner, it was also a speech full of passion and love. Mark couldn't help but pull her close again and kiss her with all the love that he felt for her.

CHAPTER 31

Max Stonewarden sat in his car outside the police station, waiting for Christy to finish work. The last time he'd seen her, they'd gone for a drive and had a meal together before he'd dropped her home. The time before that, she'd brought up the possibility of them having sex. While Max's body liked the idea - he only had to think about Christy for his body to jump to life - his mind wanted to hold back.

He didn't want to lie to her about anything, but he remained sure that he was going to hurt her in some way or other. In the evenings, he was involved in planning meetings with his brothers and their father. That had given him a reason to not get too close to Christy and give her what she'd asked for. He'd always been a player, just having fun with girls. He didn't want to see anyone else while he was spending time with Christy, but with her, he wanted to be sure he did want to have sex with *her* and didn't want to have sex with just anyone. He knew she had self-esteem issues. He suspected that his lack of blatant desire to get her into bed could feed that. It worried him, but he had to be happy knowing that he was holding back so that he didn't use her and hurt her, not because he didn't desire her.

As he saw her exit the police station doorway, he watched her slowly walk down the concrete steps before he jumped out and walked around to greet her.

"Hey, Max," Christy called out. As always, when she first glanced at him, she was happy and wary all at the same time. He was gorgeous. In her eyes, she wasn't. To her, the equation just didn't add up. Regardless, he kept wanting to see her. They kissed, but he didn't seem to want to do more than that. She was glad he wasn't using her for sex. She was also sad that he didn't want to. It was an ongoing source of confusion inside of her.

When she reached him, Max happily wrapped his arms around her and kissed her very kissable lips. He'd never been attracted to girls who weren't slender, but he loved who she was. He felt no embarrassment whatsoever about standing out in public with the young woman whose shape reminded him of an apple, and kissing her as much as he wanted to. He knew he shouldn't still be thinking about her shape so much. He put it down to him being only twenty-three. He'd been having fun with girls. It was scary to think he might have matured enough to want something more with a young woman who inspired him.

"Hey, yourself," he said when they broke apart. "What would you like to do today? I have to be at my dad's later, but I have four hours till I need to go."

"Would … would you like to come to my place? I'd like to cook for you," Christy said as she felt her face grow red. She didn't know why it kept happening, even with her having spent so much time with him already. It frustrated her, but she was thankful he only ever either ignored it or laughed it off.

"You sure?" Max asked. He'd been to her apartment a few times. It was still a new enough request for him to be surprised.

"Yeah, only if you want to," Christy said.

In response, she was greeted with the widest grin.

"Okay," Max replied, happy that she was always moving forward in her confidence. "Do you want to stop at the supermarket and pick anything up?"

"No," Christy replied. "I'm sorted."

"Cool," said Max as he opened the passenger door and waited for her to get inside. Once he was settled into his seat, he turned to her. "You're sure about this?"

Christy chuckled nervously. She and Max had prepared and eaten a meal at her house before. She just had to tell herself that it was nothing to be nervous about. He was the one who kept initiating their time together. He was the one who kept picking her up from work or visiting her in her lunch breaks. Everything that was happening between them was happening because he wanted it to.

"Yep," she said, reassuring him and herself.

Max grinned, leaned over, and kissed her kissable lips again before he edged the Mustang out and began the journey to her apartment. He was aware that the next job he was doing with his brothers was drawing nearer. The closer each job got, the more he found his mind on it. It had always been the way. The fortnight or so before a job, he'd always steered clear of spending time with women. In those weeks, he needed to be focused. Usually, it wasn't an issue. Women were around for a few hours, and then they were gone. He wasn't sure how he was going to go during the fortnight that he'd avoid Christy so he could focus only on his family duty.

"You're so quiet," Christy said as they pulled into the apartment carpark. "Is everything okay, Max?" she asked, her mind naturally taking her to a negative place.

Max turned off the engine and turned to face her.

"I've got some family stuff coming up, and it's on my mind a bit, but yeah, I'm okay," he said before jumping out and rushing around to open her door for her. "So what's on the menu?"

Christy heard and recognized the subject change. Little things like that were exactly what her mind wanted to use as fuel to make her believe she was being used, or she was being set up to be made a fool of. Before meeting Max, she'd accepted everything her mind told her. Since meeting him, she felt like she'd begun an all-out battle, fighting off every negative argument that entered her head.

"You'll have to wait and see, won't you," she said, teasing him.

Max grinned. He never liked seeing her in her negative mode, but he loved it when she was relaxed to the point where she was cheeky and teasing. Slowly, he was seeing the ratio of negative to positive changing. It was a slow process, but one he certainly enjoyed watching.

As soon as the apartment door was opened, the smell hit them.

"Wow, Christy, whatever that is, it smells amazing," Max said. "You've been at work, though. Do you have a magical chef hidden away here?"

Christy giggled. "Yeah, he's in the closet," she said as she walked into the kitchen.

Turning off the slow cooker, she opened the lid. Even with her naturally negative nature, she couldn't deny that she could cook decent meals.

"I'm just going to get changed out of these work clothes," she said.

"Yep. What can I do?" Max asked, his stomach growling in anticipation.

"Grab out some plates and plate up if you like," he heard Christy call from her bedroom. "It's ready to go."

For a moment, Max's mind wandered to the fact that she was in her bedroom, undressing before she'd get changed. With any other woman, he'd have seized that moment. Imagining her undressing was all it took to arouse him. It wasn't enough to make him move to put the thought into action. Instead of walking to where she was changing, he focused on what she'd suggested he do. By the time she walked out of her bedroom again, he'd arranged the casserole into two large bowls.

"Thanks," Christy said as he handed her one.

Sitting comfortably beside one another on the sofa, everything felt easy. She was relaxed. It was yet another day when she'd fought with her negative mind, and she'd won. Max wasn't using her. Max wasn't setting her up to humiliate her. Max was just Max - nice, kind, generous, and attentive.

Max didn't wait before taking his first bite. Whatever she'd added into the mix, it smelt far too divine. As he indulged in eating, all previous thoughts were forgotten.

"This is amazing," he said in full truth after a few mouthfuls. "Wow, you are an incredible cook."

Christy smiled. "Thanks," she managed to say. Accepting compliments was still a challenge, but she knew how to be gracious.

"For the next few weeks, I've got to do some things for my dad, but after that, I'd like to get you over to our place," Max said.

"Oh … to meet your … dad?" Christy asked.

Max laughed and nodded. "Well, not specifically, but yeah, he'd likely be there. He's at home a lot, unless he's out visiting my sister. Actually, I would like to introduce you to her. Charlie's cool, and she's been bugging me about you."

"Me?" asked Christy. "How … what … how does she know about me?"

"Because I talk to her about you," Max said, smiling. "Yeah, I can see your surprise, Christy! But, yeah, me and Charlie talk about stuff. I didn't say a lot, but she knows a bit about you. She knows I'm seeing you, and she teases me about how much I like you, so I'm guessing she's picked up on that when I've talked to her."

Christy felt dumbstruck. It wasn't the first time Max had said he liked her. It *was* the first time he'd indicated what they *were*.

"You look really surprised," Max said, enjoying the moment. "Did you think I'd be keeping you a secret?"

"Yeah," Christy began to say. "I mean … no … maybe. I guess I am surprised."

"Well, don't be," said Max. "You're the first woman I've wanted to get to know like this. Of course I'm telling everyone about you - well, not James, but that's because he hates not knowing stuff," he continued as he chuckled. "James can't stand not knowing what's going on in my love life. He's so funny in his attempts to find out."

As he looked at her face, he could see the degree to which he'd surprised her into a stunned silence. For a long time, they sat together, eating the rest of their meal while in their own thoughts.

"Yum, that was really good," Max said, standing and taking her bowl and heading into the kitchen to wash up. "Do you want me to wash this cooker thing, too?"

It took a moment for Christy to realize what he'd asked. Walking into the kitchen, she pulled her head back into the present moment.

"You don't have to wash anything," she said, moving to where he was. "This whole thing comes out, and I can put it in the fridge till I bag some up and freeze it."

Max watched her move to place the slow cooker interior bowl into the fridge. Watching her bend over to do so stirred him to a surprising amount. She was wearing some kind of peasant skirt, which didn't do much for her figure, but when she bent over, he could clearly see the outline of her butt. It was yet another view that he didn't think should turn him on but definitely did.

When Christy stood up and turned around, she was surprised by the look on his face. Walking right up to him, she stood up on her tiptoes to kiss him. It was a stretch, but she was relieved that he bent down to meet her halfway. She indulged in the kiss - even more so when she felt his arms move around her and his hands reach down and cup her butt. She figured it kind of gave her free reign to do the same to him. Tentatively, she moved her hands around and cupped his butt in return. To her further relief, he didn't react in any way, and he certainly didn't move away.

Max held her close. They'd built up plenty of kissing hours. He kept trying to do the right thing and not move forward physically until he was sure he was doing it for the right reason, and he wasn't going to hurt her. She might have turned him on an incredible amount, but he loved who she was as a person. He would do anything to stop himself from hurting her if he could help it. The problem was, it was getting harder and harder to ignore his body's obvious desire for her.

Christy had felt her boldness growing each time she saw Max Stonewarden. She'd never had sex, and she wanted to with him. The longer he kept pulling away and stopping it from happening, the more she wondered if he did intend to ever share that with her. Her logic told her it was nice he wasn't pressuring her. Her body told her it was time.

"Come with me," she said, feeling her face get hot. There was great potential for her to be rejected. She didn't care about that. She wanted to explore more with him.

Max looked at her, uncertain, but placed his hand in hers and let her lead him into her bedroom. Once in there, he let her lead him further.

As she lay back on the bed, Christy didn't know what would happen between them. She was a virgin, but of course she knew about sex. She just wasn't sure how much he *didn't* want to touch her. That was her internal question as she saw Max lie down on the bed beside her, encourage her to lie on her side and face him, and then kiss her.

For a long time, they lay still, facing one another and kissing. Eventually, Max pulled back.

"Christy..." he started to say. It was hard to get words out as he saw her facial expression. "You really want this?"

"Yes," Christy answered.

"You're not just trying to see if *I* want it?" Max asked. "Please don't say you want this, just as a way to please me."

"No, Max," said Christy. "I want to have sex … with you."

Max smiled. "Okay, but I have to go to my dad's place in a while, and I'll be doing that each night for the next couple of weeks," he said, tracing his finger over her lips - her very luscious lips. "If we're heading towards sex, I don't want it to be rushed, like it would have to be until this family thing is done." He kissed her, unable to stop himself as he studied her lips further. "Will you wait for me?" he asked, half teasing.

Christy grinned. "Yeah, I think you're worth waiting for," she said. "But, Max, I *am* ready. You'll be … I'm a virgin … you'll be my first."

"I know," Max said. "That's exactly why I don't want us to rush. If we're doing that, I want to be here with you afterward - preferably all night."

"Not a love 'em and leave 'em kind of guy?" Christy asked, curious.

"Actually, usually I have been, but I'm not going to be with you," he replied. "You deserve so much more than that."

His words touched Christy's heart. She still had that sliver of doubt, but it was lessening. She didn't hesitate before leaning in and indulging in kissing him passionately.

Max was enthralled. When he tried to coax her to move with him so he could lie on his back with her on top, he sensed her tense up.

"Roll on top of me," he whispered.

Christy pulled back, embarrassed. "I can't."

"Why?" Max asked. She'd changed from confident to nervous in seconds.

"I'll … I'll squash you," she finally said.

Max grinned at her. "Christy, you're not going to squash me!"

He watched her face as she appeared to process her options. He didn't mind if she moved onto him or not, but it was interesting for him to see her grow timid even though she was the one who had wanted them to move forward. It was even more interesting to see her change again, as if determined to overcome her fear.

Christy raised herself on all fours and saw him roll onto his back, reaching out with his hands as if to guide her. She felt humiliated, but she knew that came from her, not from him. She'd known she wanted sex. She hadn't thought through the reality of how he'd be feeling and seeing her body in the process.

After too much chit-chat in her head, she straddled him. It felt raw, looking at him and seeing him watching her face. It left her wondering if she was making a fool of herself. For a moment, she felt embarrassed and regretful about having been forward.

"Don't look away," Max said, seeing her start to do so. "I'm here. Look at me, relax, and just enjoy us being here like this." He reached up and stroked her cheek before moving his hand into her hair and guiding her mouth downwards.

As Christy's lips met his, she forced herself to let go of any concern about her weight. She hadn't killed him by putting her weight on him. As far as she could tell, he didn't even seem to notice her size at that moment. She pushed her fears aside and indulged in the feelings flowing through her body.

Max loved the way she lay on top of him. He couldn't deny to himself that he'd considered her body shape far too many times. He'd never been with someone like her, but having her lying along the length of him was no unpleasant thing at all. While he kept one hand in her hair, holding her lips to his, he moved the other to her butt again. That was nothing unpleasant either. In truth, he was looking forward to them getting naked too.

"You turn me on so much," he said. "It's hard for me to walk away from you sometimes."

"I doubt that…" Christy started to say. It was an automated response that left her mouth before she'd thought about it.

"Well, don't," said Max as he pushed back her hair from her face and looked into her eyes. "You must be able to tell how you affect me."

Christy felt herself blush. They weren't lying pelvis to pelvis, with him being so much taller than she was, but she had thought at different times that he might have had an erection.

"If you can't tell, touch me," Max said, a little in teasing but also wanting to gauge how much she really wanted them to move forward. When he'd been younger, he'd been with girls who'd thought they wanted sex but had only been doing it as a way to try and get him to like them, or love them, or whatever it was that they'd needed at the time. He didn't ever want to be with a woman for the wrong reasons again.

"What?" Christy asked for clarification. Her face felt like it was burning, but she wanted to keep pressing forward, fighting her embarrassment.

"Touch me," Max said again in a whisper. "If you doubt how much you turn me on, place your hand on me through my jeans. You won't be able to misread it," he said, encouraging her further. "I'm not ready for us to have sex, but do this if you need to know for sure how much you affect me."

Christy lifted herself off him and lay beside him. She knew he wouldn't pressure her into anything she didn't want to do, but he'd given her a green light to do *something*. Slowly, as he lay still and did nothing, she glanced down his body. It took great effort, but she reached out with her hand once, then pulled back. With still no response from Max, she tried again. It was difficult. She didn't know what unknown she was venturing into, but she finally reached her hand out further and placed it over the zip of his jeans.

"Pretty tight, huh?" Max asked, smiling at her as he coaxed her to look at his face. "That's *you*, Christy. I know you don't want to believe it, but you are an incredibly sexy woman. Trust me - I am not in any way turned off by the idea of you and I getting to know each other's bodies."

He looked at her, hoping for some kind of visual or audible confirmation that she believed him. When he got none, he nudged her onto her back and rolled onto her, resting between her legs. Once there, he began to kiss her gently, over and over. He was heavily aroused, but he didn't need anything sexual at that moment. What he wanted most of all was to help her in her own desire to have sex by getting her to simply relax.

Christy enjoyed the feeling of him lying on top of her, nestled between her thighs. As his kisses continued, she found it easy to reach both arms up and hold him close. Despite having thought she was ready for sex, she realized as he lay in her arms that she hadn't fully thought through everything about that scenario. She hadn't considered that she'd have to show her body, and they'd be moving around together, and she'd have to be completely vulnerable and open to him. For a moment, she considered whether that was all something she was ready for, after all. Her body said it wanted sex. Her head said that she couldn't bear him looking at her without clothes on.

"Are you okay?" Max asked, checking in with her comfort levels. "If you're not, that's okay, Christy," he reassured her.

"I know," she replied. "I ... please stay here, like you are. It feels nice."

Max grinned and kissed her. It was a start.

CHAPTER 32

Greg Leadbetter spent a further week alone in the cabin he'd inherited from his mother years earlier. The only person he'd shared even the knowledge of it with was Rhett. No other Leadbetter knew about it - not even his cousin, Mark.

As he sat in front of the fire each evening, Greg continued to enjoy and appreciate the peace. He had no electricity, no technological devices, and therefore no screens. During the daylight hours, he had plenty to keep him busy in and around the cabin. In the evenings, he'd found he could gaze at the flames in the fireplace for hours. That was something that helped him continue to prefer to be there rather than return to the city.

The city. He had a home there, and he suspected it was currently empty if Phillip had gotten married. Leaving it empty wasn't a wise choice for the long haul. He could have asked Rhett to look after it, but there were too many unknowns between them. Everything had been good when Rhett had been at the cabin. The day that he'd left, the two of them had crossed one more line of intimacy, and that had been great too. For Greg's part, he had no reason to feel anything negative about their friendship, regardless of how close they'd gotten. He wasn't so sure that Rhett would be as confident about it.

Glancing around the cabin interior, Greg tried to imagine returning to his other home. There was nothing wrong with living in the city. It had its advantages. In truth, he knew he didn't have to make a solid choice about living in one or the other. He owned both outright. For the rest of his life, he could spend some days in one and some days in the other. People did that all the time, owning a main home and visiting a holiday home only when they could get away from the daily stresses that held them in the busy city areas.

The other alternative was that he sell his other home and move to the cabin full-time. It wasn't a necessary move, but it was a tempting one.

He shifted his gaze back to the fire. Whatever lay ahead for him in whatever future he had left, he needed to make some kind of decision rather than sitting where he was, hiding away from everything and everyone. What had happened with Rhett had happened. There was no reason for anything to be uncomfortable when they saw each other again, but Greg knew that might be the case. It had been different when they'd been in a small bubble away from the world. Rhett might have shared something about it with Mark, but Greg suspected not.

Placing one more small log on the fire, he moved around and readied himself for the night of sleep before climbing into the bed, lying on his side while continuing to watch the flames. There were unknowns when it came to Rhett, but Greg knew he could at least be positive that Rhett had enjoyed their time together just as much as Greg had. Hindsight might have changed Rhett's view of it since he'd left the cabin, but Greg was positive that at least the happiness had been real at the time.

As he felt his eyelids begin to fight to stay open, he relaxed back and let his mind rest. As always, whatever was going to happen, would happen. He didn't know what fate had intended for him. All he could do every day was appreciate that he was alive, he was healthy, and he was safe. Anything beyond that was only static noise that pressed into his peacefulness.

Before he completely drifted off, one thought kept going through his mind…

'Tomorrow, I'll go home.'

CHAPTER 33

As he packed up everything that he didn't want to leave at the cabin, Greg's mind once again returned to Rhett. It had been over a week since they'd spoken. As much as he'd enjoyed their intimate moments together, what was more important to him was their friendship.

After securing the cabin, he jumped into his car, taking a long moment to pause and question again what he truly wanted to do. He'd followed the instruction of one senior Leadbetter or another for his entire life. He'd never questioned anything about the jobs he'd been assigned. He'd never questioned anything about why he had to keep stealing to contribute to the family ways. He'd lived half a century. It was time to live life however he wanted to live it. Figuring out how he wanted to go on for however much of the second half-century of life he had left wasn't easy.

Rousing himself to stop thinking so much, he started the engine and began his journey back to the city.

~~~~~

Pulling into the driveway of his home, he found himself unexpectedly happy to be there. There was no sign of anyone being around. No car sat in the driveway. No curtains were pulled. No windows were open.

Climbing out of the car and making his way into the house, it was silent. As always, in the distance, he could hear the traffic on the nearest busy road. It was a sound he'd never noticed that much before he'd started spending so much time in the quiet of the cabin.

He walked from room to room. His room was completely intact as if nothing had been touched. When he walked into the room that Phillip had occupied for a while, everything was gone except for the bed and the
~~~~~

furniture. However much that Phillip had kept there when he'd stayed, he'd cleared out since.

Greg walked back to the living room and sat on the sofa. He wanted to get on and unload the car, but there was something alluring about stretching out on the sofa he'd spent many days and nights relaxing on, partying on, sleeping on, and even shagging on. It was only a piece of furniture, but it held memories, just like everything in his home did. There was comfort in that.

It took some effort to rouse himself to move and begin shifting the contents of the car into the house. Once it was done, he sat down again. It was late afternoon. He wanted to see Mark but decided to put it off till the next day. For a moment, he considered calling Rhett and telling him he was back. He resisted the idea. He wanted to be in his normal, relaxed mindset for that. He wasn't there yet. Too much was playing through his thoughts - pleasant memories, worries about his friendship, doubt that he and Rhett could ever move on with anything intimate again if they were so close to people they knew were prejudiced against guys being sexual with guys. It was all stuff that he suspected he was wasting energy on. Maybe nobody would care if he was honest about his feelings for Rhett. Maybe nobody would care about the consideration of Rhett and Greg having kissed and touched each other. There were many considerations starting with 'maybe'. It was a waste of time even thinking about it all. He needed to have a good night's sleep and then just see what the next day would bring.

He smiled as he climbed into his bed that night. It was larger and more modern than the one in the cabin. After taking time to appreciate the bed's qualities, he felt lonely. It had been over a week since he'd seen Rhett. It had been well over a year since he'd spent time with a woman. It was a tempting thought to go out and find someone to share mutual pleasure with. That idea, he tossed aside. His long life of physical loving had taught him it was never truly satisfying being with a stranger. It had always filled a physical bodily need in his past, but he'd never felt fulfilled in the hours afterward. He knew it was always an option. He'd never had any trouble picking up women when he wanted to, but he didn't want to at that moment, no matter how lonely he felt. He needed to figure things out with Rhett first.

~~~~~

The next morning, he took time to appreciate the joy of electricity, hot running water, and the deliciousness of fresh coffee made in his high-quality espresso maker. Small joys they were, but joys all the same.

After a long hot shower, he began walking to Mark's house. It was a distance he'd always preferred to walk to rather than take a car. Walking gave him more thought time before and after he interacted with his cousin. The Leadbetter way had always been to steal whatever one could. Whoever was in the lead position for the family wanted to know that everyone was doing something and not sitting idle. Greg didn't know if Mark had stepped up to be leader again or not. Whoever it was, Greg hoped he wasn't going to be expected to do any more jobs for them. The last one he'd done had turned to horror, and he'd only been a driver that night.

At the Leadbetter house, he was greeted by Anya when he'd knocked.

"Oh, hi, Greg," she said in her seventeen-year-old voice that consistently made people smile. "Come in," she continued, adding a low-sweeping bow as he walked in. "The lord and lady of the house are in the backyard."

Greg grinned. Seeing Anya as her usual chirpy self reminded him that there was happiness to be had in the household that Mark occupied with his wife and kids.

As he walked through the kitchen, he could see
~~~~~

Mark and Stacey through the window. They looked happy. It was good to see. Following news of Rex's death, Greg had wondered how they could survive something like that having happened. The smiles he saw them exchange as they sat at the outdoor table in the sunshine was positive. Theirs was a love that he'd admired his entire adult life. They might not have had much as far as monetary richness or number of things they owned went, but they had an incredible connection that never seemed to falter, even when things were rough.

"Hey. I hope I'm not interrupting," he said, grinning as he walked out the back door.

Mark jumped up and wasted no time in wrapping his arms around the cousin who was also one of his two closest friends.

"I didn't know you were coming home," Mark said, curious. He'd never been one to ask where people were. All that ever mattered was that they were safe and well. People who wanted to share details always did. If they didn't share, they didn't want to, and that was perfectly fine. "Are you here to stay?"

Greg nodded as he walked to sit down beside Stacey. "Yeah, I think so."

Stacey turned to him and smiled. "We've missed you," she said. "I'm glad you're okay."

"Yeah, I'm all good," said Greg, smiling at her. "I've just felt like having time to myself lately. It's been nice, being in solitude, but it feels good to be home too." He shifted his focus to Mark. "What's new? Anything I need to know about?"

"Discussion's underway about who's going to be brave enough to step up and be head," Mark said.

"You're not tempted?" Greg asked. "With all due respect to your father when he reigned, you're the best leader the family's had in my lifetime."

"Thanks," Mark replied, grinning. "But no, I have

no desire to do it. There is a part of me that wishes I hadn't stepped aside when the only other candidate was Pete, but he was the worst of the worst. I think anyone who'll put their hand up now will be assessed a bit harder by everyone before they're secured in that position." He paused and studied his cousin's face. "More than one person has mentioned *your* name."

"Me?" Greg asked, surprised. "I doubt that."

"You don't believe me?" Mark asked, grinning. "Why the fuck would I lie about that?"

Greg chuckled. "I'm not saying you're lying. I'm saying it's unlikely that someone thought I'd be best for it. Maybe whoever told you that got their wires crossed or something."

"Maybe, but…"

"No! Before you even suggest it, I am not doing that job," said Greg. "I'm fifty years old…"

"So am I!" Mark said, laughing.

"Yeah, but you grew up being trained and primed for that position," Greg said. "This dog is too old to learn new tricks. I'm at the other end of the responsibility spectrum. I'm ready for retirement."

Stacey chuckled. "I think retirement implies you have a job or a career to leave," she said, teasing him.

Greg grinned and nodded. "Yep," he said. "I'm ready to lie back and chill for the rest of my days now. Time to give up my day job."

Mark threw back his head in laughter. "You've never had a day job in your life!"

"Yeah, well, enough about me," Greg said, smiling. "What's been happening with you guys? Everyone happy?"

"Phillip, Sasha, and Anya all seem happy enough," Stacey said. "David…"

"How's he doing?" asked Greg when her sentence tapered off.

"Well, he's back with Kasey, so we don't see him

much," Stacey replied. "It's good he's with her. They've talked about her being pregnant, and they're both set on keeping the baby. I'm hopeful that'll change David's view of things."

Greg thought about how David had been when they'd found him.

"Stace, the things in his head … they might need to be addressed by someone professional," he said quietly.

Stacey nodded. "I know," she said in agreement. "He wants to see someone, so he's said he'll find someone. Kasey knows now how he is, and she's told him he needs to be sorted before the baby arrives. I think he'll be okay. Whatever it is that haunts him in his mind, he seems intent on fixing it."

"Yeah, when we found him, he was pretty set on doing whatever it would take to not feel that way anymore," said Greg. "I never … I never even noticed anything like that about him. He's always seemed so quiet."

"It surprised us all," Mark said. "It's still hard to believe it was him that did that supermarket shoot up. Just goes to show how little we can know our kids."

"Well, at least he's aware of it and wants to get help. That's more than most who think thoughts like that, I'm guessing," said Greg. "And Phillip and Sasha? All good?"

Mark grinned. "Phillip's happy as a married man," he said. "They're trying to make a baby, so we don't see much of him at the moment," he added, chuckling. "Sasha's still seeing her pretty boy."

"Don't call him that!" Stacey said to Mark, pretending to scold him. "He seems to be a nice guy," she continued, turning to Greg.

"Didn't see that one coming either," Mark said, smiling.

"He's genuine, though?" Greg asked. He'd

watched Sasha grow up from birth. Her entire backlog of angry childhood, teenage-hood, and young adulthood had been on display for him to see as she'd grown. "Not using her or anything?"

"No," replied Stacey. "He sussed something out about her the moment he met her, I think. Sussed her out and proactively established trust with her. I don't think he's using her. Seeing them together, they look genuinely keen on each other."

"That's cool," said Greg, nodding. "I guess anything that's helped her find peace within has to be good."

"Well said," Stacey replied.

"Only one more baby to find true love then," Greg said, teasing her. As soon as he'd said it, he regretted it. Always, the unspoken truth about Rex not being alive anymore hung over everyone. He was relieved when Stacey and Mark didn't address his lack of thought before he'd spoken.

"Anya's only sixteen," said Stacey. "It'll be a while for her yet."

"Yeah?" Greg asked, grinning. "I seem to remember you hooking up with this one around that age," he said, inclining his head toward Mark. "Or was it when you were only *fifteen?*"

Stacey chuckled. "Maybe," she said, making Greg laugh. "My baby girl is younger at sixteen than I was."

"Maybe," Greg acknowledged. "Probably best to still be prepared," he went on, adding a wink.

"Nah, she doesn't even hang out with boys, as far as I know," Stacey said. "I don't think there's any upcoming trouble there."

Greg smiled at her and Mark but didn't respond. He was happy to be among them. Although happy around them and for them, he did often experience moments of regret as he watched Mark and Stacey's family grow. They'd had such an incredible lifetime of loving one another and raising their kids. It all added up to something that Greg had never desired. Now that he had the gift of hindsight, he increasingly wondered if he should have taken the leap at any time throughout his lifetime of being involved with women.

"Hey, stranger," he heard Rhett's voice say as the backdoor opened and he walked out. "I didn't know you were back."

Greg looked at Rhett. It was the first time they'd seen each other since Rhett had left the cabin the week earlier. Greg took in the sight. For a fleeting moment, he instantly felt like leaping up and placing his lips on Rhett's. Being in the company of Stacey and Mark kept him right where he was.

"Got back last night," he said, trying to show no emotion as he watched Rhett sit down next to Mark.

As the four of them resumed conversation, Greg was surprised by how natural it felt for them to all talk, and nothing to feel wrong. Whatever physical feelings he had for Rhett, they seemed to take a backseat as the four people who'd known each other for most of their lives talked and laughed together.

"We were talking earlier about the possibility of Greg stepping up and being leader," Mark said to Rhett after a long while.

"That's something you want?" Rhett asked, surprised.

"Fuck, no!" Greg replied, making Rhett smile. "I'm not cut out for that kind of responsibility, and even if I was, I'm not interested in leading everyone."

"*You* could do it," Mark said to Rhett.

Rhett grinned. He appreciated that his friend had seemed sincere in the suggestion, but it wasn't something Rhett would take seriously.

"I'm not even a Leadbetter," he said. "I don't think that would work very well at all."

"Fuck off," said Mark. "You're as much a

Leadbetter as any of us. Everyone looks at you like that, whether or not you have the same last name."

"Yeah, maybe," said Rhett as he looked directly across the table at Greg. It all felt good and normal to be sitting together with their friends and chatting. He suspected that normal feeling wouldn't hang around for too long once he and Greg were alone. "Not for me, though."

"Maybe, for once, the family doesn't need someone to lead them," Stacey suggested, prompting all three men to look at her. "They're all surviving well enough at the moment, without even a murmur that they need someone to step up. Maybe Pete's death has given everyone a jolt."

There was a moment of silence as they each considered that Pete wasn't the only one who'd died that night, but he would always be the one that people of the extended Leadbetter clan would remember far more easily than they'd remember Rex. It was sad, but it was true.

"Well, for now, I am keeping out of it," said Mark. "I'm content just being here with my kids and this beautiful woman of mine," he continued, smiling at Stacey. "If anyone needs me for anything, they're welcome to come and ask. I'm not chasing anyone anymore."

"Fair enough, too," said Greg. "You've done a lot for the family. I have no doubt there's someone else itching for the position. I'm surprised they haven't come forward yet."

"Time will tell what'll happen," said Mark. "I just want a quiet life now. My rebel years are behind me," he added, making Greg and Rhett both chuckle.

"As if," Greg said as he stood. "Right, I am going to head off and leave you lot in peace."

"Stay for lunch," Stacey said. "It won't be anything fancy, but you're welcome."

"Thanks, but I've been sitting too long," said Greg, grinning. "These old bones need to move. Catch you later," he continued as he started to move away.

"I should head off too," Rhett said, suddenly eager to catch up with Greg alone. "Wait up," he called out just as Greg reached the back door. Turning back, Rhett smiled at Mark and Stacey. "Enjoy the rest of your day."

"Yeah, you too," Mark and Stacey said in unison.

As Greg and Rhett passed through the house, they said nothing. Once they were outside the front of the Leadbetter home, Rhett turned to Greg.

"I can give you a ride home," he said, beginning to feel oddly nervous. "If your old bones aren't *that* eager to move," he teased.

Greg smiled. It was weird. They'd just been in the company of old friends, and everything had felt just like it always had. Suddenly alone with Rhett again, Greg felt his arousal automatically kick in. It was bittersweet with a feeling of being right and wrong all mixed into one.

"Yeah, okay," he replied. Once in the car and on the road, he turned to his friend. "How've you been since you got back?"

"I'm okay," Rhett replied. "I … it's just that it's so fucking odd, this whole situation with you and me. Don't take that as any kind of insult or anything, but I want to be with you - and *not* be with you - all at the same time."

"Mark doesn't know then?" Greg asked. He didn't think he needed to ask, but it didn't hurt to double-check.

"Hell, no," Rhett said. "Nobody knows except you and me. I … yeah, I'm not ready for that. I don't know if I'd ever be ready for that, to be completely honest."

Greg nodded. He couldn't argue with the conflicting feelings that his friend had. He'd experienced all of them himself at one moment or another.

No more words were said as they traveled the journey to Greg's home. Once there, Greg resolved to not push for anything, but it would have been strange if he hadn't invited Rhett in. It was something that had been normal forever.

"Coming in?" he asked before he got out of the car. With the engine still running, he thought Rhett had full intention of getting out of there as quickly as he could.

"Okay," Rhett said, turning off the engine. Whatever was to follow was unknown. That didn't stop him from wanting to further explore the possibilities.

When they got inside, Greg tried to force himself to keep back and not do anything to make his friend uncomfortable.

"Coffee?" he asked as they entered the kitchen.

The reply he received was Rhett moving close to him and tentatively leaning forward as if to kiss him. Greg watched his friend's lips move closer to his own. He gave Rhett the distance to pull back if he changed his mind. He was glad when Rhett's lips joined with his.

Both moaned as the natural passion they'd been feeling ignited again. It was a short time before they held each other tightly and kissed without thinking or worrying about anything.

Making their way into Greg's bedroom, Greg pulled away long enough to close the curtains. With a woman, he probably wouldn't have worried about it. He wasn't ready for anyone to learn about what he and Rhett were doing, even if there was nothing wrong with it.

When he turned back, Rhett was undressing. It was something Greg had seen many times over their lifetime as friends. At that moment, the act affected him far more than usual. By the time he'd started undressing himself, he was as erect as he could be. It hadn't felt wrong when they'd embraced naked at the cabin. Greg was glad to notice that it not only didn't feel wrong, but it felt incredible standing with Rhett, belly to belly each standing tall in their arousal.

No words were needed as they both reached down to touch the other while kissing and moving toward the bed. It was a long time before either spoke again, taking their time to explore and indulge.

Lying facing one another on the bed post-orgasm, they stared at one another.

"I feel like I want to hide this, but I also feel like I don't," Rhett said quietly.

"I know," Greg replied. "I'm happy for us to keep this to ourselves, at least for now. As right as it feels, I'm in the same place you are. We've been taught so strongly that this shouldn't be, that it's playing with my head."

"Mine too," said Rhett. "I guess while you're living alone, we can do this, and nobody'll know."

"Yeah, I don't anticipate Phillip will be back, given that he's now a married man," Greg said. "I've never been someone who needs to live with anyone, so I don't expect anyone to be wanting to move in here."

"You happy to keep this a secret, definitely?" Rhett asked and saw Greg nod in reply. "We can keep it to your bedroom?"

"Yeah, of course," Greg said, chuckling. "No PDA, and no raunchy backyard nude sunbathing."

Rhett burst out laughing. "Yeah, that would be a sight for your neighbors, alright."

As Greg saw Rhett grin, he felt a familiar stirring again. Although he hadn't been with anyone else for over a year, he'd always had a healthy libido. It was nice to see and feel his body react so easily in arousal. He suspected he was approaching an age when that side of things might not work so well. For the moment, it appeared to be working pretty well indeed.

"You know, that is a surprisingly big turn-on," Rhett said, glancing down.

"What?" asked Greg.

"Seeing you grow like that," Rhett replied as he reached out and began stroking Greg again. "Shit, all the years of women experiencing these things when they were with us, I never realized how invigorating it could be to feel or watch a guy get hard," he said, moving down in the bed. "Or to…" he added before taking Greg in his mouth. After that, he didn't say anything more for a very long time.

CHAPTER 34

Daisy's ex, Pete Brandon, had been following her constantly since her wedding day. He'd been following her for much longer than that, but that was the most recent date that had stuck in his mind. It had been one thing seeing her with that guy who looked like a loser when they'd been on a weekend getaway. It had been quite another to see her vow in front of their friends and families that she would always be with that freak.

Pete had spent time following her travels between her apartment and the office she'd worked in. He'd followed her to the supermarket or any other store she'd gone to. He'd even followed her when she'd attended the semi-regular dinners out with the friends that she'd known long before that guy had appeared. Those friends had once been Pete's friends too. That they now regarded Daisy's so-called husband to be someone to be friends with was just another level of what Pete considered unacceptable.

As he watched her jump into her car, he veered out into the traffic, always taking care to remain a few cars back. He'd purposely traded in the BMW that she would have recognized. That had been replaced with an older car that Daisy wouldn't probably ever suspect him of owning. It gave him no joy to own it or drive it. It served him no purpose whatsoever except to blend in with the thousands of other cars just like it, purely to follow Daisy around in.

His full-time job had taken a backseat while he was observing her. That hadn't been ideal, but it hadn't mattered. He'd made enough money to live off for the rest of his life without having to step inside another office again. Work had once been his full-on passion.

Now, monitoring every move of Daisy was.

He watched as she pulled into the supermarket carpark. He was glad she was alone. Those moments gave him joy. The moments when he saw her with the asshole in her life didn't make him feel anything but anger.

For a long time, he'd waited for the right moment to approach her. He'd waited for when a moment arose that she was alone, and he had the confidence to do what he wanted to do. He'd never been one to like women chasing him. He didn't concede that the degree to which he was stalking Daisy was much more serious than that.

Once he saw her enter the large sliding doors, he took some time to deal with the level of pounding he felt in his chest. The day had arrived when he would put a slow-burning plan into action. He'd wanted to get Daisy away from the man she reckoned she loved. The day had arrived when he would. He'd have loved if all he'd had to do was present himself to her. In a perfect world - in a perfect dream - it would have been that easy. He didn't live in a perfect world. Getting Daisy to listen to him and ultimately spend time with him was going to take much more than just talking to her.

CHAPTER 35

As Daisy walked into the supermarket, she felt happy. Since the night she'd met Phillip, her life had taken a few turns - some happy; some not so much. The one thing that had evened out had been her love for him growing, and her equally seeing his love grow for her.

Having been dedicated to working in the legal profession to get criminals off the street, meeting Phillip and knowing he was part of a criminal family had tested Daisy's thinking about many things. She'd gained joy from meeting him, anger from learning he was on the opposite side of the law to what she'd been, and intense sadness in learning that his brother had been killed by police. Since then, all they'd experienced together had been happiness.

They were setting up a life together. She truly believed it would be a long life. One thing she'd observed as being amazing about Phillip's life was the way that his mother and father loved one another. They were criminals, and they looked like criminals. From what she'd read about them in her job, Daisy had expected them to be rough to the point where she'd fear them. She'd been surprised to see how they related to one another, and had done for decades. It had surprised Daisy, but happily so. Phillip had role models for the recipe of how a successful marriage looked. That was amazing for her. She was hopeful that some of the recipe for love between his mother and father would have rubbed off on him, making the future easy for Phillip and Daisy both.

Since the wedding, they'd primarily indulged in baby-making. As she thought about just how much effort they'd been putting into that, she couldn't help but grin to herself. She didn't care who saw her like that in the middle of the supermarket. She was happy - blissfully so. Phillip wanted to be a parent as much as she did. That in itself was a wonderful thing. Her previous relationship had been with Pete Brandon - someone who had no intention of having any kids in the near future *or* the far-off future.

For a moment, she thought about Pete. He'd acted weird the time she'd seen him when she'd been away with Phillip on a mini vacation. Seeing Pete then had made it easy for her to know for sure that any feelings she'd had when he'd ended things had definitely disappeared. The contrast between the two men was immense. It was a reason why her friends had teased her so much when she'd first started talking about Phillip. Pete was rich and liked to *show* that he was rich. For him, no amount was ever enough. He'd been the type of person who constantly needed more. In contrast, Phillip had nothing but equally didn't need anything to be happy. He didn't care about material things, and Daisy loved that about him. He was relaxed and easy-going, except when it came to protecting those he loved. When there was a threat of any kind, Daisy knew Phillip's fighter instinct would show. It didn't bother her. She also knew he was just a really good person.

As her thoughts and memories continued, she moved around the aisles of the supermarket. Since she and Phillip had decided to move ahead with becoming parents, she'd taken more of an interest in what she ate. She wanted to be healthy, not just for her but also for any little one that might come along. It wasn't too much of a change, but she liked being more aware of what she was consuming than she had been before.

Seeing the trolley approaching the mid-full point, she stopped and considered what else she might need to buy. She was sure she'd gotten everything she'd need, and everything that Phillip needed. After a few minutes of consideration, she walked to the checkout area.

As the food items moved in front of her along the conveyor belt, she smiled to herself. She was cooking one of Phillip's favorite meals for dinner. It was only a little thing that she could do for him, but she knew he'd appreciate it. In truth, everything seemed to make Phillip pretty happy. He was probably the most easy-going man she'd ever been involved with.

After paying, she pushed the trolley out to her car. Glancing at her watch, she could see it was getting on in the afternoon. There was no rush. She'd have plenty of time to get the groceries unloaded and put away before she had to begin cooking. She knew Phillip would be hungry after his day of working on cars. She equally knew he'd want lots of replenishment of energy to offset how much he'd then go on to use up after they'd eaten.

Daisy softly chuckled to herself. She was hopeful she'd fall pregnant in the weeks or months ahead. In the meantime, there was definitely much fun to be had in trying to get that way.

After loading the car, she jumped in and started the engine. It was at that moment that she saw the shape in the backseat.

"Hello, Daisy," Pete's voice said as she viewed him in the rearview mirror. "I've missed you. Have you missed me?"

"Pete," Daisy said, her heart pounding in surprise. "What are you doing here? And how did you break into my car?"

Pete smiled at her reflection. "You didn't answer my question."

"And you didn't answer mine," Daisy said as she moved to open the door. At that moment, she realized something was wrong. "Why can't I open this..." she started to say. "What have you done to my car?"

"Don't worry. You'll get to go home ... maybe," Pete said. "First, we're going to have a little chat."

CHAPTER 36

As Phillip Leadbetter finished up his day's work on a black Camaro that made him envious of its owner, he felt his daily end-of-day eagerness flow over him. His initial months of seeing Daisy had been enjoyable enough. Living with her and getting to go home to her every evening was a form of happiness he'd never experienced before.

Despite the moral differences between Phillip's family and Daisy, Phillip had stayed on the path that had pulled him completely into her heart. He didn't doubt how strongly she loved him or how much he loved her. They were going to make it, and they were going to be together for as long as his parents had been together. When he'd married her, he'd taken her last name so that there'd be no possible risk about her being a Leadbetter. The name was behind both of them. With that gone, there was no threat to either of them, or the life that they were embarking upon.

"You rushing home again to that woman who's far too good for you?" Phillip's boss, Enrique, asked with a mock look of disbelief on his face.

Phillip grinned and nodded. "Absolutely!"

"She's gonna *sooo* wear you out one of these days," Enrique said as he shook his head, smiling. "Just remember - too much sex is not a valid reason for a sick day!"

"Yes, boss," Phillip said. He was happy in his marriage. He was happy in his job. He didn't need anything more than that.

Eagerly, he packed up his gear and walked out. The sun was already descending, but it was fine enough for him to walk home.

Home. The word used to stand for something else. It used to be the large structure of many rooms that he'd grown up in. Now he had a new home in Daisy's apartment. Eventually, they'd have to move out of there, especially when little ones began arriving. For the moment, both were happy to stay right where they were, so they could save money and concentrate just on each other.

As always, when he reached the street-level outer door to Daisy's apartment, Phillip bounded up the stairs to the next entry door. It was a moment that he cherished every day when he'd finished work. Unless she had something else that she needed to do, Daisy was always home when he got there. She was always there, looking beautiful and welcoming him into her arms. It was the most amazing end to any day of work.

"Daisy?" he called out when she didn't immediately appear. He walked through the apartment, wondering where she was. He had no reason to worry. She had a life with family and friends, and he had no issue with her visiting and spending as much time with all of them that she needed or wanted to. Regardless, it was a first that she wasn't home and hadn't mentioned anything.

He pushed the concern aside in his mind. Daisy was an independent woman. That was one of the many things that had attracted Phillip to her in the first place. Wherever she was, he had no reason to worry.

Taking his time in the shower to get rid of the day's grease from his work, he indulged in the heat of the water. He loved his job, but a clean job it was not.

When he got out, he thought she might be home. She wasn't. Seizing it as an opportunity to cook something for her, he walked into the kitchen and scoured the refrigerator for anything within his skill set for cooking. There was little there. His mind moved to a comment Daisy had made that morning. She'd said she was going to do grocery shopping that day. She'd asked him what he needed and wanted, and she'd appeared pretty set in that plan.

Phillip subconsciously opened the fridge again. He then opened cupboards. If she'd done any grocery shopping, she'd hidden the items well. As much as he didn't think there was reason to worry, a small niggle began in the depth of his mind.

When he picked up his phone, he took a moment to contemplate whether he should call or message her. If she was out with friends, he didn't want to interrupt them. Another moment later, he sent a message. It wasn't wrong if she was out doing things. There wasn't any requirement for her to tell him where she was going or what she was doing. It was a small thing, but because she was such a creature of habit, it felt like a big thing.

'Hey, I'm at home, thinking I'll cook. Will you be home for dinner?'

He glanced at the message before pressing the send button. He didn't want her to feel like he was checking up on her or anything. He did want to know that she was okay, no matter what was happening.

After sending the message, he got to work. There wasn't a lot to work with, but he didn't want to leave in case she returned. As he started to throw ingredients together, he kept looking at his phone. Thirty minutes later, no reply had arrived. An hour later, no reply had arrived. Two hours later, Phillip's concern grew.

Scouring the list of numbers on the refrigerator, he messaged a couple of her close friends. Neither had seen or heard from Daisy. The last friend on the list, he called.

"Hi, this is Phillip," he said. "Have you seen Daisy?"

"No, not today," replied Daisy's closest friend, Emma. "What's up?"

"Oh, she isn't here, which I wouldn't normally

worry about, but..."

"But that girl loves routine," Emma said. "Umm, have you contacted Vinnie or Nicola?"

"Yeah, but neither have seen or heard from her," Phillip said. "You know her better than anyone. Should we be worried?"

"She's usually home when you get home from work?" Emma asked. When Phillip replied, she began to be worried too. "Hmm. Right now, I can't think of any place she'd go, Phillip, but can I call you back? I'll talk to the others. With enough drilling, they might know more than they think they know."

"Okay, thanks," Phillip said before the call disconnected.

Trying to turn his focus to finishing preparing the meal, it was hopeless. He got through it and prepared two plates of food but found his focus returning to his phone. Daisy had taken time out from him before they'd gotten married, but even then, there had been words that told him she was going to take space from him.

He called his family home. It seemed unlikely that Daisy would have gone there, but it was a consideration. His parents knowing someone he was involved with was new. He didn't know what his mother might try and drag his wife into.

When his mother answered the landline, he was relieved.

"Hi, Ma, is Daisy there, or have you seen or heard from her today?" he asked, not bothering with small talk.

"No," Stacey replied. "What's going on?"

"I don't know," said Phillip. "She's not home, and she isn't responding to my messages or calls. It's just not like her."

"You've checked with her friends?" Stacey asked.

"Yeah, so far, nobody's heard from her," said Phillip. "Okay, well, thanks..."

"Call us again if you have news or you need

anything, Phillip," Stacey said.

Phillip had just hung up the call when his phone rang. Answering it, he heard Emma's voice.

"Hey," she said. "Nobody knows anything about where she is, or was going, but Vinnie's gonna try and figure out where her phone is through an app he's got. He said it'll take a little while, but we'll call you as soon as we have a result."

"Can you let me know if it doesn't work, too?" Phillip asked, feeling a blend of hope and despair.

"Yep, hold tight, and I'll get back to you soon," Emma said.

Phillip grabbed his meal and sat in front of the TV. He might be worrying over nothing. A meal and some mindless television show could be just what he needed to chill and not be so concerned.

As hard as he tried, he couldn't turn off his worrying. Whatever Daisy was doing, her lack of communication with him or any of her friends was out of character. His thoughts shifted to the possibility of something having happened to her. He suspected it was too early to dwell on that. It was only a few hours past when she'd normally be home. She could have just gone for a walk. She'd been saying for ages that she wanted to start going to the gym. Maybe she finally had. If she was there, it made sense that she wouldn't have her phone on her, so wouldn't know he and the others had tried to contact her.

He relaxed back. He was worried, but he'd wait till Vinnie had at least tried to find her phone before he'd decide if he needed to take any action to find her.

CHAPTER 37

Daisy woke up feeling giddy. The giddiness didn't hide the pain in her head. She hardly ever got headaches. The one she was currently experiencing was the worst that she could remember.

"You're awake," a voice said. The tone was quiet and soft, but Daisy recognized it. She'd had plenty of experience not only hearing it but also waking up to it.

When she turned her head, her suspicion was confirmed. Her ex, Pete, was sitting in front of her, studying her.

"What … ?" Daisy began to ask in her confusion. "Where am I?"

"You're at my place," Pete said as if it were a perfectly acceptable and obvious answer. "Oh, you haven't seen my new place. Well, this is it."

Daisy watched his face as he spoke. He'd always been handsome, in an obviously-rich kind of way. Regardless, she didn't like the vibe emanating from him.

"My head feels like it's splitting open," she muttered as she raised her hand.

"Yeah, sorry, that'll be from the chloroform," Pete said in a matter-of-fact voice. "It should clear soon."

"You … you *drugged* me?" Daisy asked in disbelief. "What the *fuck* is going on, Pete?"

Pete was surprised by her tone and her words. She'd never been one to swear. Hearing her do so provided him with further belief that she wasn't meant to be with the lowlife she'd married.

"I was hurt when I heard you were marrying that … that … *loser*, Daisy," Pete said. "If you did it to get my attention, you succeeded."

"Get your attention?" Daisy asked. "Are you

insane? I married Phillip because I *love* him."

Pete stood up and began walking while shaking his head.

"No, I don't think so," he said. "You can't love someone like that. You're too good for him."

Daisy sneered at him. "Too good for him? As opposed to being not good enough for you, I assume?" she asked. When he looked surprised, she continued. "That was the reason you broke up with me, wasn't it? Because you didn't think I was good enough for you."

"No. Why would you think that?" asked Pete as he sat down in front of her again. "I always wanted you."

"You threw me away…"

"And I regret that," said Pete. "You and I are meant to be together, Daisy. You know that as well as I do."

"No!" she replied. "No, we are most definitely *not* meant to be together. You're cold-hearted and manipulative. Why would I, or any other woman, want someone like that?"

"You're saying these things to annoy me," Pete said, not wanting to believe what she was saying.

"Am I? Do you doubt that you're cold-hearted?" Daisy asked.

"Yes! If I was that, why would I love you so much after all this time of watching you with that lowlife…"

"You've been … *watching* me?" Daisy asked.

"Of course," Pete said. "How else would I know when was the right time for us to be back together?"

"The right time for you to *manipulate* us being back together, you mean?" Daisy said. "You decided that I need to be with you, and that's the end of that decision-making process. Once again, what I want is of little relevance or importance to you."

"Daisy, when you've been here with me for a while, you'll forget the person you've been using to make me jealous..."

Daisy scoffed in disbelief. Before saying anything more, she took some time to look around. She had no idea where she was, and she suspected that if she tried to bolt, Pete would have anticipated that. She wouldn't rush to try and get away. She'd have to be far more subtle than that.

"I love Phillip, Pete," she said, maintaining calm in her voice. "No matter what you think of him, he is caring, generous, and loving."

"He looks like a criminal who just got out of prison," Pete said.

"You think I care what he looks like?" Daisy asked.

"You should!" said Pete. "You are worth so much more than that."

"I'm worth ... enough ... to be with someone like you?" she asked.

"Yes!" Pete said.

"But if that was the case, why did you throw me away? Why did you tell me you never wanted to see me again?"

"I ... I ... I didn't know then just how valuable you were to me," said Pete.

"Valuable?" Daisy asked. "How could I possibly be valuable? What exactly do you think I have? Money? Property?"

Pete chuckled. "I don't need money or property from you or anyone else," he said. "I have plenty."

"Then what do you *want* from me?" Daisy asked.

"You," said Pete. "Just you. You loved me for who I am and not what you could get out of me. Nobody else is like that."

"That can't be true," said Daisy, continuing to scan the room for exit points while she worked to keep him calm and talking. "Any woman could love you and not want all of *this*," she said, pointing around. "Plenty of women want to be loved. They don't need the glitz and glamour. They don't need or even want lots of money. They just want to be loved by a good man."

"And I want to give that love," said Pete. "To you."

"I don't love you, Pete," Daisy said. "Maybe I did way back then, but you threw that love away. Now I love someone else, and I intend to stay with him for the rest of my life."

"He's nothing," said Pete.

"He's *everything* … to me," Daisy said.

She watched Pete's face. They'd only spent a few years together, but she could read his expressions well enough. She could see his frustration growing.

"Well, it's time he wasn't," said Pete. "He's had his time with you. Now it's *my* time."

"I'm not some … *thing* … to be passed around," Daisy said, horrified. "Is that what you think of me? You can have a turn, then discard me, then take me back for another *turn?*"

Pete was disgusted by his choice of words being interpreted as they had been, and the result they'd had.

"No, I didn't mean …" he started to say. "But you aren't meant to be with him. You're meant to be with *me*."

"No," replied Daisy, shaking her head. "No, Pete. I won't ever be with you again. I have found the man that I love. I'll always be with him."

"And if he isn't in the picture?" Pete asked, standing. "If your precious *Phillip* is no longer around? *Then* you'll come back to me."

Daisy watched him as he readied to leave.

"What are you doing? Where are you going?"

"I'm going to remove him from your life," Pete said as if it was an easy, obvious, and satisfactory answer. "Oh, and don't bother trying to leave. This house has the highest security, including guards at every possible exit point. Only the best for me, as you know," he said, grinning. "You can move between the rooms, but stepping outside is something I'd advise against. My men have instructions to do whatever it takes to prevent you from leaving."

Daisy remained where she was as she watched him deliver her one last sickening smile before walking out. She sat still, her mind working. She remembered seeing many movies where she'd seen someone in her situation run around like they were crazy, desperate to get out. She saw no point in that. She was highly analytical. She fully intended to use that to her advantage and not act rashly.

He'd said that there were armed men outside the house, watching for her. That was her first thing to check. Walking from one window to the next, she could see he'd been telling the truth. They were there, and they looked ready to take her down with the weapons slung over their shoulders.

Still feeling the effects of what he'd done to her to get her there, she walked into the kitchen. She wanted to be alert. It probably wouldn't have made any sense to anyone else that she'd stop and make herself a strong coffee in her predicament, but she wanted thought clarity. Caffeine was perfect for that.

She took her time, finding her way around the kitchen and preparing something to eat and drink. The one thing she was sure of was that Pete didn't want to hurt her. She focused on that to maintain hope that she could be the one in power *if* she played her cards right.

He'd said he was going to remove Phillip from her life. Daisy worried about that. Her only relief in that was that she suspected if the two of them were to fight, Phillip would easily pummel Pete. The unknowing was whether Pete was intending to take a weapon with him - or an armed man. Phillip was strong, and a fighter. He wouldn't be able to fight against bullets.

After eating and getting caffeine into her, Daisy started to look around. Her purse and phone weren't in sight. She suspected Pete would have made sure they weren't in the house if he was letting her move around freely. Regardless, she had time to explore, so she did.

Walking from room to room, she silently wondered why the world had changed from having cabled phones in homes to only having mobiles. There was no landline in Pete's home. If there had been - even one that was forgotten - she could have at least called the police. Instead, he'd have his phone on him, and her phone was either hidden or had been disposed of.

Thinking about the absence of her belongings, she realized he must have done something with her car, too. Was it in a garage on the property? She walked further around the home interior, peering out each window to get a feel for the home's layout and placement. One door that she reached, she couldn't open. The nearest window showed that it was likely the garage. Through the window, she could also see two guards standing outside. It was an exit point they thought she might get to. There was no getting outside there or into the garage either.

She wanted to contact someone - anyone. Most of all, she wanted to warn Phillip, but alerting anyone at all would have been a start.

Wondering how much time she'd have to explore the structure she was a prisoner in, she began to move faster. If she was stuck there, she may as well begin delving into every cupboard, wardrobe, and set of drawers. If there was anything that might prove handy to her in her dilemma, she might have the time to find it.

CHAPTER 38

As Greg and Rhett were enjoying spending time together in Greg's home, word reached them that something was amiss in one part of their family.

"Missing?" Greg asked Stacey when she'd called him and explained how worried Phillip had sounded. "What's he doing to find out where she is?"

Stacey relayed everything she knew from the second phone call Phillip had made to her. There was still so little being done, but it was also only a short time that Daisy had been regarded as missing. While Phillip had sounded concerned, he'd also ensured that everyone understood that Daisy was an independent woman, and there was a chance that she was just doing something that she'd left her phone off for. It wasn't normal for her. That didn't mean it was impossible.

"Where's he at now?" Greg asked. Phillip was his cousin's son. If he needed help with anything, Greg was there.

"I think he's staying put at their place just in case she returns," Stacey said. "I don't know whether to encourage him to call the cops or not."

Greg pondered the option. Calling the cops at any time was something that made every Leadbetter nervous. Still, if it was with regards to someone being missing, it had to be considered.

"I'll call him and see if he wants me over there," Greg said. "Maybe we can look for her before we drag the cops into it."

Stacey thanked him, hung up, and called the next person she thought might be able to help. It might all turn out to be for nothing, but she was still pleased that everyone she contacted was willing to do something to help find Daisy if she was missing.

"What's going on?" Rhett asked when Greg had hung up the call.

"That was Stacey," Greg said. "Phillip's worried that his wife hasn't returned home yet, when she would normally be there by now, or at least have made contact. She's not answering calls from him or any of her friends."

Rhett stood without hesitation. "Let's go then," he said. "You got his address?"

"Give me a minute," Greg said before dialing Phillip's number and getting the details from him. "Yep, let's go. If that little lass is out there and in trouble somewhere, we'll find her."

A short time later, Phillip let them into the apartment.

"Tell us what's going on, Phillip," said Greg. "Your mother only gave us a brief summary."

"I don't know whether to be so worried or not, but I can't get hold of Daisy," Phillip said.

"And she's usually home by now?" Rhett asked.

"Yeah, but even on nights when she isn't, she'd still be contactable or would message me or *something*," said Phillip. "None of her friends know where she is either."

"You two have a fight? Any chance she's just avoiding you and cooling down somewhere?" asked Greg.

Phillip shook his head. "No, everything was fine when I left this morning, and even if it wasn't, she'd still talk to her friends. Even if she told them she didn't want to talk to me, I don't think they'd let me keep worrying about her if they knew she was safe somewhere. No, something's not right."

"Okay, what are our options?" Greg asked. The only response he got was a shrug of shoulders from Phillip. "Alright, we'll wait here to see if anything happens in the next hour or so. If you need us, we're here."

"Thanks," said Phillip. He didn't know if there was anything that anyone could do, but he appreciated that calling the cops could be put off till a decent number of hours had passed, at the very least.

When his phone buzzed, he read the incoming message from Emma.

'Vinnie didn't find anything on the phone app, but we'll keep asking around.'

~~~~~

In the Leadbetter household, Stacey and Mark sat their daughters down and explained how worried Phillip was about Daisy.

"Have either of you seen or heard from her?" Stacey asked. It was doubtful they had, but it didn't hurt to ask. She wasn't surprised to see Sasha and Anya both shake their heads.

"How long has she been missing?" Sasha asked.

"Only a few hours, I think," her mother replied. "Still, Phillip says it's not like her, and he's worried."

"I'm seeing James soon," said Sasha. "He met her at the wedding. Maybe he's seen her around."

Stacey nodded. "Ask him. It's not likely he has, but we've just got to keep spreading the word, I guess."

"Will Phillip tell the police she's missing?" Anya asked.

"Contacting the police is always something we avoid where possible, little one," Stacey said. "But yes, I hope that if too many more hours pass and he hasn't heard from her, Phillip will do that."

Sasha's mobile vibrating in her pocket prompted her to pull it out.

"James is out front," she said. "Do you want me to cancel?"

"No," said Stacey. "Go and enjoy your time with him, Sasha, but maybe keep an eye out when you're out
~~~~~

in the car?"

"Sure," said Sasha before walking out. When she reached James's car, he was already standing at the passenger door, waiting to open it for her. "Hey you," she said, smiling.

James kissed her before assisting her into the car. When he was behind the wheel, he noticed the serious look on her face.

"What's up?" he asked.

"My sister-in-law is missing," Sasha said. "You haven't noticed her around the streets anywhere as you've been driving today, have you?"

"This is the bride from the wedding?" James asked and saw Sasha nod. "No, although I haven't been looking. Do you want to drive around a bit and see if she's about anywhere?"

"Do you mind?" Sasha asked.

"No, not at all," said James as he started the engine. "Let's cruise around for a bit. What's being done to find her, though?"

"I don't know," Sasha replied. "What can anyone do in cases like this?"

"My kid brother is good at finding anything and anyone," said James. "I can ask him to help if you want."

"Yeah, if you think he can," said Sasha. "What could he do, though?"

"I don't know, but he's real good with hacking into systems - probably best not to ask me about that too much," he said, smiling sadly at her and seeing her nod. "He's hopeless at contact, but let's call in at my dad's home. Maybe we'll get lucky, and my brother will be there."

Sasha nodded. She'd met some of James's family when his sister had given birth. She'd hardly known James then. Since she'd gotten closer to him, she hadn't seen any of his relations. She wasn't fully open about her family, but he was even more closed off about his.

As they pulled up to a large home, she felt intimidated. The idea of entering the place he'd grown up in and meeting any of his family in their home played on her insecurity.

"Don't worry," James said, holding out his hand to her. "None of them might be home, and if they are, they won't bite. You've met my dad and my younger brother, Max, before. Fitz is the one we need to find. It's impossible to know where he is at any given time. He used to play hide and seek all the time when he was a kid. Sometimes it seems like he's still playing it when any of us want to contact him."

As they approached the front door, Sasha smiled at him, appreciating his effort to help her relax.

On entering, James's father, Mitchell, walked out of the kitchen.

"James," he said before noticing the young woman beside him. "Hi, Sasha," he said, holding out his hand to her. He wouldn't have remembered her name from the hospital, so was glad that James had talked about her enough since then to make him able to address her.

Sasha shook the older man's hand. She felt nervous but was thankful James continued to hold her other hand.

"Is Fitz home?" James asked. He and Sasha were both relieved to see Mitchell nod.

"You're in luck," he said. "First day I've seen him at home for ages. He's up in his room."

"Thanks," James said before turning to walk up the sweeping staircase, still holding onto Sasha's hand to help her feel comfortable.

"Yeah," they heard Fitz reply after James had knocked on the bedroom door.

On opening it, they saw Fitz quickly reduce down whatever he'd had on his computer screen. The move didn't surprise James. Fitz was the technological genius for their jobs. Whatever he'd been doing on his computer was probably best not shown to anyone else.

"Can you find someone, Fitz?" James asked, not bothering with any pleasantries. Fitz wasn't the kind to chat for the sake of it. He liked to have something to do and prove his skills in.

"Maybe," Fitz replied, not particularly liking someone from outside his family standing in his room. "Who're you looking for?"

"Sasha's sister-in-law," said James. "She's been missing for a fair few hours, and people are worried about her. Is there anything you can do?"

"Yep," Fitz said, turning back to his computer and pulling up a new window. "What's her phone number, first of all?"

"Um," said Sasha, suddenly aware that she didn't know that much about Phillip's wife. "Hang on."

She quickly messaged Phillip. A few seconds later, she received a reply and passed the details onto Fitz.

With his know-how, Fitz was able to figure out in a relatively short time where the phone was. Whether that meant its owner was with it, he couldn't tell.

"I've got the phone here," he said as he delved into transferring the GPS coordinates into a map. "It's turned on, and it looks like it's in this building..." he continued, changing the street map to a satellite view. "Actually, that might be a house, although a really big one. Looks swanky as."

"What's the address?" James asked.

As Fitz read out the details, James watched Sasha type into her phone.

"Don't go there, James," Fitz said before the two walked out again.

"Why not?" James asked. He knew his brother well. If he said don't go somewhere, James listened.

"Because..." Fitz said, hacking into one street

cam after another around the home. "There are ... look ... they're security guards, and they're armed. What the fuck is going on *there?*"

"That's not normal?" Sasha asked.

Fitz replied without shifting his gaze from the screen. "Nope. Whatever's happening there, it's serious. I'd highly recommend you avoid it."

"But if Daisy's there..." Sasha began to say to James.

"Call the cops," said Fitz, finally turning to look at her. "That's not something I'd usually suggest, but if someone bolts in *there* with all those guns hanging around, it ain't gonna be pretty."

Sasha nodded. There was little it seemed they could do.

"Can you see *inside* the house, Fitz?" James asked as an afterthought.

"I can try," Fitz replied, always happy to be given a challenge. It took a few minutes before he smiled to himself as he successfully hacked into the house security system. "Yep, there's the interior. Is that who you're looking for?"

Sasha and James both moved forward to look over Fitz's shoulder.

"Yes!" Sasha said, looking at Daisy on the screen. It was easy to see that she was looking through things and doing so under some kind of time pressure. "Is there anyone else there?"

Fitz coaxed the screen from one security camera inside the home to another until he'd done a full loop and was looking at the first one again.

"No, but that's a lot of guards outside," he replied. "Whoever owns that house is either rich beyond belief, or they have something serious to hide."

"Or some*one*," James said. "Can you find out who owns it?"

"Yep," Fitz said before doing his thing with the

keyboard and mouse again. "Dude's name is Peter Brandon."

"Ring a bell with you?" James asked Sasha.

"No, but I don't know Daisy well enough to know who she's friends with," Sasha replied.

"Okay, thanks, man," James said before encouraging Sasha out the bedroom door. When they were alone in the hallway, he hugged her. "I trust my brother," he said as he pulled back. "If he says it's not safe to go there, I believe him."

Sasha nodded. "Okay."

"Do you want to go to your brother's place and see if we can do anything there?" James asked. He didn't want to invite himself to any home of the Leadbetters, but the thought of someone being held against their will was something he'd overlook discomfort for.

"Yeah," Sasha replied. Her mind was full of concern for her brother. It had taken time for their mother and father to accept Daisy, but she'd proven to be pretty amazing, and Phillip loved her. Sasha couldn't imagine how he was feeling.

She pulled out her phone and messaged Phillip to let him know she and James were on their way with some information. Having heard the suggestion of James's brother to stay away, she added that she didn't think Phillip should leave the apartment yet.

When they arrived, Phillip let them in.

"Hey," Sasha said to him before she saw Greg and Rhett and greeted them. "Have you guys met James?" she asked the older men. "James, this is Greg and Rhett."

James greeted the men before him. There was no denying he was in the company of three rough-looking men. Two of them he'd met previously. The third looked even tougher. For a fleeting moment, James wondered what Sasha could possibly see in him when he was such strong contrast to the men she'd grown up around.

"What info did you have?" Phillip asked.

"Oh, yeah, so James's brother searched for Daisy's phone," Sasha began to say.

"Yeah, a friend of Daisy's did, too, but didn't find it," said Phillip.

"Well, this guy did," said Sasha. "I've got the address…"

"Let's go," Greg said, standing abruptly.

"No!" Sasha and James said at the same time.

"She's there," Sasha said. "James's brother showed us security camera views inside the house, and we could see Daisy. She looks like she's okay, but outside the house are … armed guards."

"Lots of them," James added.

Phillip, Greg, and Rhett all took a moment to process what they'd just heard.

"Daisy's in a house that's being guarded?" Phillip asked. "Why would she … that makes no sense."

"She looked like she was rifling through drawers and stuff," James said. "She didn't look like she was there … because she was a guest or for fun."

"Where is this house?" Rhett asked.

Sasha relayed the address.

"And it's a *house*, not an apartment or something?" Greg asked.

"It's a house, but it looks more like a mansion," said James. "Apparently belongs to a guy called Peter Brandon."

On hearing the name, Phillip's attention was fully grabbed. It was visible to everyone in the room with him.

"You know who that is?" Rhett asked.

"That's … that's Daisy's ex," Phillip said.

CHAPTER 39

As Pete made his way across town, he felt some confusion inside. He still believed that once Phillip was out of the way, Daisy would remember how happy she and Pete had been together. He chose to forget that it had been him who'd pulled the plug on their relationship. When he'd listened to her say that it was his doing, he'd fought to remember why he'd ended things with her. She was beautiful, and she'd been on her way up the legal ladder as a lawyer. She'd be perfect for any high-quality man to have on his arm. Although he'd never admit to being stupid, he knew he'd been an idiot to cast her aside. He'd assumed someone even better would want to be in the place she'd left empty. Nobody of any value had. Sure, he got women easily enough. None of them were good enough for him.

He considered what he'd do when he came face to face with Daisy's husband. He could have taken someone armed with him. He'd chosen not to. He wanted to fight for her himself. When he'd done that, she'd see that he was true in the feelings he'd expressed to her. Surely that would secure her heart.

Finding her apartment was no problem at all. He'd been following her since he'd seen her that weekend. He knew where she lived, where she shopped - in truth, he knew everything about her movements. She'd always been a schedule person. She did certain things at certain times on certain days of the week. Since they'd split up, she'd changed a lot, but she hadn't changed that about herself. She was a creature of habit. He smiled as he rejoiced in that. It had made it all that much easier for him to know where she was at any given time on any given day.

When he reached his destination, he sat in his car for a long while. He'd built up his business empire through making good decisions. He wanted to be sure he was making a good one when it came to Daisy. He had no idea if Phillip was at the apartment. He had no idea if Phillip even knew that Daisy was missing. In hindsight, Pete knew he could have hired someone to keep an eye on the lowlife while he was taking care of Daisy. He hadn't done that. There was time to go home and engage one of his guards to find Phillip and take care of him, or at least figure out where he was. There was time, but it was time that Pete didn't want to waste. He wanted to be rid of Daisy's husband. The sooner she was a widow, the sooner she could be happy again and marry Pete. In his mind, it was that easy.

He took a moment to think about how much force he was going to have to use to take Phillip down. The guy was a thug. There was no doubt he'd be a good fighter. Pete could only hope that his recent martial arts training would be enough to counteract whatever Phillip could throw at him. Pete had excelled in his learning with his personal trainer in that area. He was good. His trainer told him that, and Pete believed him. He was hopeful that as soon as he came face to face with Phillip, he could deliver the right move to get the lowlife down on the ground. Once that was done, he'd do whatever he had to next to make sure Phillip wasn't in Daisy's life anymore.

After another few minutes of deliberation, he finally climbed out of his car and made his way to the apartment.

Looking at the buzzer panel used to grant entry to visitors by whoever was inside, he smiled. As soon as he'd learned where Daisy's apartment was, he'd learned how to get past the security. It took only minutes before he was inside the external door to the street. From there, he made his way up the staircase until he stood outside the internal security door. He was confident getting through that lock, too. The unknown was whether Phillip was inside.

Instead of trying to break in, he did what he believed was the bravest thing he could to prove to Daisy how much he loved her. He knocked.

~~~~~

On hearing it, Phillip glanced around the faces of the other people in the room before moving to the door. Nobody was expected, but it was easy to think that any or all of Daisy's friends might turn up. He had no expectation of who exactly might be at the door. When he opened it, he didn't need to wonder any longer.

It was only a couple of seconds that he looked at Pete before Phillip put all his might into his right arm and extended it out. It was only seconds from when Pete saw the door open until he was on the ground, unconscious.

"Whoa," James said as he saw the movement. He'd thought the Leadbetter family might be used to fighting rough. The speed at which Phillip had taken someone down was impressive, to say the least.

"Fucking freak, coming to my door when he's done what he's done to my wife," Phillip said. "Help me get this guy inside," he called out to the others.

Rhett and Greg didn't hesitate to get Pete in the door and secured in a chair. He was unconscious, but he was the key to getting Daisy out of the house that had armed security around it.

"You might want to not see anything more here," Phillip said to James.

James glanced at Sasha before nodding.

"Yeah, you might be right," he replied. Whatever was going to go down, it was already criminal to a degree. One thing he never wanted was to give the cops a reason to drag him into the cop shop.

"Take Sasha with you," Phillip went on to say.
~~~~~

"But..." Sasha began to object.

"Go!" Phillip said. "I'll message you if you can help in any way, Sasha, but get out of here," he continued before turning to James. "Keep her safe. We don't know what backup directions this guy has in place for me or anyone else in my family if we're his target for some reason."

James nodded and guided Sasha out of the apartment, neither of them speaking until they were in James's car.

"What are they going to do to him?" Sasha wondered out loud.

James started the engine and turned to her. "I think you might be best not to ponder that. Whatever's gonna happen, I'm guessing you'll know about it soon enough."

Sasha looked out the window, feeling nervous and confused. Should she tell her mother and father that Phillip had Daisy's ex in their apartment? Was it her place to? She guessed not. Her oldest brother was a grown man. He was a good judge of character and always seemed to know best. She placed her hope in that.

"What do you want to do?" James asked, veering the car into the traffic. "Do you want to go home?"

"Can I stay with you?" Sasha asked.

"Yeah, of course you can," James replied. He didn't know if she meant for a short while or overnight. It didn't matter which she meant. He wanted to be there for her, whatever was about to happen. He was just glad that what was happening was doing so on the only night he had to himself before the upcoming robbery he was going to be doing with his brothers. It was one of the many ways fate had seemed to look after him.

Glancing at her as he drove, he reached over and placed a hand on her knee.

"Phillip looks like someone who can take care of

himself," James said. "Don't worry. He'll be okay."

Sasha nodded. "I know, but will Daisy?"

~~~~~

"You're sure this is the guy who owns the house she's in?" Greg asked, a little freaked out by the very person they'd wanted to find having knocked on the door.

"Yep," Phillip replied. "He appeared when Daisy and I went away for a weekend ages ago. Told me then that he intended to get her back. I haven't seen him since, so didn't think about it again."

"She hasn't mentioned him being around or contacting her?" asked Rhett.

"Nope," said Phillip.

"I wonder if he's been stalking her," Greg said.

Phillip groaned at the thought. He and Daisy had been living in a pretty happy bubble since that time they'd gone away together. That had been the time that their feelings and relationship had been solidified. Even seeing Pete that weekend hadn't been enough to break them apart. In some ways, it had strengthened them.

"Hopefully, we'll get some answers when he wakes up," Phillip said, checking the tape wrapped around Pete's feet and hands. "In the meantime, what do we do about Daisy?" he asked Rhett and Greg. They had a couple of decades more of life experience than he did. He was ready to put full faith in any suggestions they made.

"Phillip, if it was just a few guards to take down, we could do it," said Rhett. "Going up against as many guards as Sasha said were there, and with them being armed - it's not a great idea. If things went wrong, we could all be killed, including your wife."

Phillip nodded. He agreed.

"What a fuckwit, putting a woman in a house and surrounding her with armed guards," he said. "What kind of man does that to anyone, let alone a woman?"
~~~~~

"Not someone that's sane, that's for sure," Greg said.

"You've met him before," said Rhett. "Just how much fight do you think is actually in this guy? You think he's the kind who'll stand up to some heated questioning?"

"I'm hoping he's a pussy who'll give the simple command to his security to stand down so that Daisy can get out of there," Phillip said.

"What…?" they heard Pete say. "Why am I tied up?"

"What have you done with Daisy?" Phillip asked as he moved up to Pete. "Why are you holding her against her will?"

"Against her will?" Pete asked, smirking. "You think she loves you? She doesn't love you. She wants to be with me. She's *meant* to be with me."

"Yeah? She wants to be with you? Is that why you've got her held captive in your house, with no freedom to leave if she wants to?"

"She's too good for you," said Pete. "Did you really believe she wanted a lowlife like *you* in her life?"

"Yep," Phillip replied. "And you know it. She doesn't want you and your flashy clothes and your money. If you truly think she's that kind of person, you don't even *know* her."

"I'll have you arrested for kidnapping me," Pete said as he analyzed the situation he was in.

Phillip laughed. "Yeah? You came here. Your car is probably parked right outside. How did I kidnap you if you came here willingly?"

"I didn't consent to being tied up like this," Pete said.

"No, but perhaps you can tell us why you *did* come here," said Phillip. "Daisy's at your house, so you knew she wasn't here. I can only guess that you were hoping to talk to me. Well, here I am. Talk."

Pete looked at the solid, tattooed man before him. He had an overpowering presence, that was for sure. When Pete had gone to the apartment, he'd expected he'd be able to take Phillip down easily with the martial arts training he'd been doing. It had been a fruitless plan. Pete felt regret as he sat in the chair. Behind Phillip, he could see two other men, and they looked even more threatening. It had been a bad move on Pete's part. He began to wonder how he could get out of it.

"When will you let me go?" he asked. "Daisy will be worried…"

"Daisy is trying to find a way out of there that won't result in her getting shot by your goons," Phillip said.

"How…"

"How do I know that?" asked Phillip. "That isn't relevant. The important thing is that she is trying to find a way to get free from the prison you've put her in. Is that your entire plan, Pete? To keep her locked up like a caged animal until she pretends to love you?"

"She does love me!"

"If that's the case, why do you need all those guards to keep her there? How about you call your goons now and dismiss them. Then let's see what Daisy does. If she feels like you say she does, she'll stay put," Phillip said as he leaned forward until he was almost nose to nose with Pete. "On the other hand, if she loves *me*, she'll come straight home, won't she."

Phillip waited for an answer.

"Where's Daisy's car?" he asked when none came. "Where is it?!"

"Parked in the next block down from the house," Pete finally said. He felt exhausted. He'd done nothing physically, but he could feel the stress in his body.

"She'll see it if she can get out?" asked Phillip. In response, he saw Pete shake his head.

"I'll go," Rhett said, prompting Phillip to face

him. "I've got the address of the house. I'll go and drive around the area to find it. What street's it on?" he asked Pete. He was relieved to see Pete answer without hesitation. "I'll message you when I've found it," he said to Phillip on receipt of Daisy's spare car key.

As Greg watched Rhett leave, he felt a sliver of concern. The look Rhett gave him before walking out the door told him not to worry. It also told him how much Rhett cared for him. Greg could have gone with him. It was more important that Phillip had support in case the psycho ex got out of that chair.

"Call off your security," Phillip said, holding up the phone they'd retrieved from Pete's pocket.

"You'll have to let my hands go free," Pete said.

"I don't think so," said Phillip as he opened up the phone screen. "Not even password protected. That's not very wise for someone like you. Now, which contact is it?" he asked. "You're confident that Daisy wants to stay there, so she will, even when your goons are gone. That's what you believe, isn't it, Pete? Let's put that theory to the test."

Pete sat still, not answering. He could convince the authorities that he'd been kidnapped, and Phillip was the one who'd done it. If he held out long enough, things could still go his way.

"Not keen to try that experiment?" Phillip asked. "Okay. You sure?" he checked one more time. Seeing the stubbornness on Pete's face, he decided to not devote any more time to the attempt to change Pete's mind.

Phillip stepped backward before pulling out his phone and calling the police. It was a risky move, given who he was, but there was no way that Pete would be able to deny something going on at his house with the armed security around it.

A short time later, Phillip turned back to Pete.

"I don't know what your ultimate plan really was, but the cops are on their way to your place to have a chat with the guards there," Phillip said. "If things go well, I guess Daisy will walk out of there a free woman. If she's worried about you, she'll ask the cops to find you and make sure you're okay. If she doesn't care, she's more likely to tell the cops you abducted her. Which do you really think she'll do?"

For the first time, Pete felt panicked. He couldn't move. His heart pounded as he imagined Daisy telling the police about what he'd done. He tried to devote his thoughts to any story he could tell the cops if they found him, that would make Phillip look like the person who'd done it all. There was little that could be said to make it look that way. Pete had screwed up in the sick plan he'd developed. It had seemed easy, and the outcome obvious. He hung his head low in the realization that he'd gotten things very, very wrong.

~~~~~

As Rhett approached the small car he knew was Daisy's, he saw five cop cars drive past. He hated cops with a passion, but he hoped they would find Phillip's wife alive and well. Wanting her to see her car if she got out of there, he jumped into the driver seat and slowly drove up towards the house.

Stopping in view of the house, but far enough back to not look suspicious, he watched what was happening. He could see several police officers approach the armed guards, guns raised. Rhett wondered if the guards were from a business, legitimately hired as security, or people from the criminal side of life. Looking at them, he suspected the first option. They weren't criminals. They were hired security, simply doing a job. When the police approached them, they lowered their guns and raised their hands while explaining their situation and the simple job they were on. It was a short time before the guards were led away from the house.

After that, he saw two officers knock on the front
~~~~~

door. He was relieved to see Daisy open it and then fling her arms around the first officer she saw.

Rhett gave them a few minutes before he climbed out of the car and began walking toward the house. It was a brave thing to do. He knew he could be viewed as a criminal to be taken down if Daisy didn't recognize him from their introduction on the night of her wedding. He didn't care about that. He just wanted to see she was safe and then tell the cops where her abductor was.

When he approached the front door, he was immediately stopped.

"Wait," he heard Daisy call out. "I know him. He's a friend of my husband's."

"Let him in," the cop near her said.

"Is Phillip okay?" Daisy asked, dreading the news she was going to hear.

"Yep, your ex didn't get to hurt him, like I think he'd planned to," Rhett said before turning to the cop questioning her. "He's at their apartment."

"Pete?" Daisy asked.

"Yeah, he's there with Phillip and Greg," Rhett said to her before turning to the cop. "He's bound up to stop his effort to hurt Daisy's husband, but it'd be good if you guys could go and get him so that he can't hurt Phillip or Daisy. He's not sane."

After further questions, the cop radioed for help to go to the apartment.

"We've got your statement, but we're going to need to talk to you again, Mrs. Leefton," the officer said.

"Yes, of course," said Daisy. "I'll … I'll head home shortly, after Pete's gone. I don't want to see him."

"Of course," the officer said before walking out.

"I've got your car outside," Rhett said. He was surprised when Daisy moved close to him and encouraged him to hug her. They'd only met once. It was nothing much, but it reminded him how much he did still enjoy the softness and curves of a woman's body.

"Thank you," Daisy said, pulling away. "You don't even know me…"

"You're part of the family now," said Rhett, smiling. "We look after our own. Let's give the cops a while to do whatever they're going to do at the apartment. Phillip or Greg'll message me when they've been and taken Pete away, I'm guessing."

Daisy nodded but didn't move. She wanted to see Phillip. She wanted his arms around her and the feeling of security she always felt when she was close to him. She didn't know the guy she was standing with, but knowing he was entwined with Phillip's family was enough to help her feel safe. She'd been glad to not have the Leadbetter name. At that moment, she was glad that Phillip was a part of a family who looked out for one another as well as they did. It changed her entire perspective on them.

A long time later, Rhett felt his phone vibrate.

"They've taken Pete away," he said. "Sounds like Phillip's been questioned at the apartment. Doesn't need to go to the station yet. Ready to go home?"

Daisy nodded and began to walk out.

"Are you coming with me?" she asked.

"My car's only a block away…"

"I'll drop you off at it then," said Daisy. "I'd rather you were right behind me as we drive back if you don't mind."

Rhett smiled and nodded. Daisy's outward appearance made her look like she was one cool woman. Underneath the cool exterior, he could see she was shaken up and still fearful.

In their journey back to the apartment, Daisy was thankful that Rhett was close by. She didn't know him, but he emanated the same kind of strength that Phillip did - the Leadbetter strength, she guessed. She'd seen it in Phillip, his parents, and especially his sister, Sasha. It was yet another level of discovery for her about the family who she'd learned so many negative things about when she'd been in law. So many negative things that were bad, but in so many ways, also amazing.

~~~~~~

After Phillip received Rhett's messaging saying he and Daisy were on their way back, he felt a new eagerness to see his wife. He'd experienced moments throughout his life when he'd been nervous about his own safety. The fear he'd felt for Daisy had been at a whole new level for him.

As soon as the door opened, he ran to it and pulled her into his arms.

"Thank God," he said before kissing her passionately. "I've been so worried about you."

Seeing them kissing more, Rhett looked at Greg and smiled.

"Time for us to leave, I'm thinking," he said, prompting Greg to grin and start walking toward him.

"Yeah, I don't think these two need us here," Greg said.

Before they walked out, Phillip finally spoke again.

"Thanks ... both of you," he said, not stopping the tears that were flowing.

"You might have changed your name, Phillip, but you're still one of us," Greg said, reaching out to shake Phillip's hand and then walking out.

When they were out on the street, Greg turned to Rhett.

"Fuck, how do we keep ending up being part of these frigging dramas?" he asked, smiling but relieved it was over with.

"I have no idea," said Rhett. "Just the beauty of being a Leadbetter, I guess. Come on. I'll take you home."

Greg followed the instruction. Climbing into the car, he saw the smile on Rhett's face. It was enough to
~~~~~~

stir him. They weren't anywhere near ready to let the world know how they felt about one another. They weren't anywhere near ready to express their feelings even there in the car. They had no desire to show their affection in public. For the moment, they'd keep getting to know each other intimately, and they'd keep it a secret. Both were perfectly happy with that.

~~~~~

The End
~~~~~

When Mitchell Stonewarden lost his wife to cancer more than a decade ago, he vowed to never give his heart to anyone else. With all of his children now adults, and a new generation having already begun, he's finally started to wonder - does he really want to be alone for the rest of his life?

OTHER BOOKS
BY
ANN M PRATLEY

POWER MOORE INVESTIGATION TALES
~~ Crime Solving ~ Action ~ Adventure ~~

HOONIGAN

Tristan Clarkson has woken up, over and over, bound to a chair, and unable to see. He has no idea where he is, or why he is in the situation he's woken to. His memory is vague, protecting him from recent events that will eventually haunt him for the rest of his life. He wants to remember, but at the same time, his mind acts as though he really, really doesn't. Initially, he's confused. With each waking, his memory clears that little bit more, as do his senses. He soon becomes aware that the very person who has abducted him, is in the room with him, determined to make Tristan pay for something he cannot even remember.

Meanwhile, in a hospital nearby a patient has been taken. With the help of Special Agents Ashley Power and Tim Moore, an investigation begins into where the man has been taken, and who would have reason to remove him. With the patient having already been weak from time in a coma, time is of the essence in finding him alive.

Hoonigan is a blend of crime and suspense, intermingled with the strength of friendship, and the awakening of one father's realization of just how much his son really means to him.

RESOLUTION OF HAPPINESS

Fiona Thompson - better known as Flo to everyone who knew her - took a plunge and stepped out of her comfort zone and into the world of online dating. With persistence, she found her prince. He ticked all the boxes. He was handsome. He was financially secure. He loved her. He married her.

She was warned by friends and family that there was something off about him. She didn't listen.

Then she woke up cold, inside the darkness of a wooden box.

Join Special Agents Ashley Power and Tim Moore as they investigate the disappearance of Flo, going on a surprising journey that nobody in Flo's world could possibly anticipate.

TIGER IN OUR HOUSE

The first time a tiger escapes from a local wildlife park and makes its way to a family home, it's considered a simple matter of bad luck. The second time ... not so much.

Join Special Agents Ashley Power and Tim Moore as they delve into an elaborate and rather unconventional scheme to hurt someone through an act of revenge.

HOME BY THE SEA

A decade ago, homeless people began disappearing from four neighboring towns. Day to day, the commuters making their way to and from work never took notice of the less fortunate they passed. They didn't notice as the number of homeless reduced. They didn't even notice when entire groups of homeless people vanished.

A young woman, eager to find out where her grandfather disappeared to, began trying to find him. When four police departments dismissed her, telling her that her grandfather would no doubt turn up when he wanted to, she was too young to realize she should pursue the matter further.

Now, ten years on, she's stepped up and pushed harder for something to be done to find not only her grandfather but also the countless other people who seemed to have disappeared around the same time.

Called in to investigate the disappearances, Special Agents Ashley Power and Tim Moore find themselves searching for - and finding - so much more than they thought they would.

CHISHOLM MANOR SERIES
~~ Historical Romance ~~

ALESSANDRA

After receiving news from her parents of a possible
betrothal, Alessandra, an 18 year old with an ingrained
belief that no-one would ever wish to marry her, finds
herself in a love so great that at times she cannot breathe.
Married to someone as inexperienced as herself, she
finds herself on a sexual journey of learning and
exploration.

The combination of their mutual inexperience
contributes to Alessandra discovering a degree of
emotional and physical love that she has
never before realized could exist.

That love will be tested by someone from her past with
sinister intentions. Jealous of the physical love
Alessandra shares with her husband,
he is set on doing whatever it takes
to have the woman he desires,
no matter the cost.

CHRISTIAN
(FREEDOM OF FLIGHT SERIES - BOOK #1)

Twenty four year old Christian Shaw has a good life.
He's had a rocky ride with being charged for a crime he
didn't commit, but he's come out on the other side, older
and wiser. He has good friends who've stood by him. He
has a family who loves him. However, there's something
about Christian that he's never understood. There's
something about him that sets him apart. It has made him
not want to get close to anyone.

Now someone's appeared unexpectedly. To his surprise,
she's just like him. Even more importantly, she has the
knowledge to help him understand more about the
strange existence he lives. But is she as nice as she
appears, or could she have a darker reason for seeking
him out and devoting time to him?

Providing an insight into one man's strange journey of
coming to grips with who he really is, 'Christian' tells a
story of courage, friendship, and crime solving intrigue.

BRANDON
(FREEDOM OF FLIGHT SERIES - BOOK #2)

For fifteen years, Brandon McStevens has held himself away from everyone he knew prior to the day he turned fourteen. That day changed his life forever. Something happened to him that he can't explain to anyone. He feels ashamed and embarrassed. The only way he's ever been able to move past that and live has been to find somewhere else to reside.

Since leaving his family home, he has continued to live in a small cave. Nestled high above a small coastal community, he has come to spend most of his time enjoying the ocean … oh, and up in the sky. He doesn't know how it happened. He doesn't know *why* it happened. All he knows is that despite understanding how much hurt he must have caused when he left home all those years ago, he now lives the only existence he can imagine.

He's never met anyone like him. He's never *seen* anyone like him. Until that day when that woman and her dog saw him change, no-one had ever seen or heard of him doing that. To this day he regrets having shown himself like he did. But time passed and it has all been forgotten … or has it?

Certain he's the only one like himself, he's surprised when two people come looking for him … and have much to tell him. Finally, the time will come when he no longer has to feel like a freak of nature … or so alone.

PAINFUL DELIVERANCE SERIES
~~ Obsession ~ Romance ~ Psychological Trauma ~~

PAINFUL DELIVERANCE
(PAINFUL DELIVERANCE SERIES - BOOK #1)

She just wasn't made for inflicting pain.

She knows it's nothing abnormal. She knows others enjoy it. But with every new level of pain he directs her to deliver to him, Alexis feels another piece of her soul die. He has wealth and he has power, and she knows he won't easily let her go.

But she has to leave. Escape. Move on. Forget. She has reached her limit of what she can do. The plans are in place to get away. She just has to hope that wherever she goes - whoever she meets - she won't find herself in exactly the same situation again.

REVIEWERS SAY:
"Something captivated me right off the bat...plot was intriguing and the pacing spot on, while the transitions between past (flashbacks) and present were easy to follow....I would recommend this to readers looking for a captivating plot, dynamic characters...great erotic passages."

"First, let me start off saying that this is a book that is unlike any other that I have ever read. Plainly stated, it is believable and raw in a way that is captivating ... Will I read the next one? YES!!!... I would say that you would really have to read this to understand... to get how believable it is."

"From the opening few pages, this book draws you into the story...I found the book hard to put down. The author does a great job interlacing the flashbacks with the present to form a tight story line."

DARKNESS OF HEART
(PAINFUL DELIVERANCE SERIES - BOOK #2)

She thought he'd stopped looking. He hadn't.

She got away from him to start a new life. She moved
on. But in his mind, he still loves her and needs her. He
still believes that she loves him. That she is meant to be
his. That he is meant to be hers.

He will not give up searching for her. He will not give
up *fighting* for her. He will pursue her and stop at
nothing to get her back. But it will come at a cost … a
sacrifice much greater than he will see coming. A
sacrifice that will finally wake him up and bring him
back to stark reality.

REVIEWERS SAY:
*"… author did a great job of making brief references
from the first book. Lincoln, Lexi and Alexis are back,
though perhaps the most complex character is Diana …
very easy for me to recommend this book with 5 of 5
stars."*

*"This story continued the journey of Alexis, Anthony and
Lincoln while giving us a new perspective into the
repercussions of Lincoln and Alexis's relationship: from
the POV of Lincoln's wife Diana! I loved her addition to
the story … kept the tension of the story just right,
balancing the calm new life Alexis has been building and
keeping the reader engaged."*

*"It is a book of courage, the courage to leave everything
you know behind, the courage to change, the courage to
face your fears, and the courage to face the unknown."*

FRIENDSHIP OF DESIRE
(PAINFUL DELIVERANCE SERIES - BOOK #3)

Tom and Samantha. Feisty friends from childhood who feel like they know each other inside out until the day comes when one of them suggests they go to a BDSM club together, and become formal play partners. Pushing the limits of what each of them can individually stand in their lifelong friendship, they attract and repel like magnets, until the time comes when they must choose how they will relate to one another - and what kind of relationship they will go on to have in the future.

While on this journey of discovery, the two of them meet and make a new friend - Alexis. A young woman with a hidden and secretive past, and a mystery surrounding the relationship she has - or has had - with a renowned business entrepreneur who begins to integrate himself into Samantha's life, unknown to any of them whether he has done it for him, or for her … or for Alexis, being the mysterious link from his past.

REVIEWERS SAY:
"While this book is billed as the third in a series, I would classify it more as a spin-off … I enjoyed this book. Samantha and Tom's relationship was sweet. Their exploration and experimentation, and how it stressed the boundaries of their (frustratingly) platonic friendship was fun to read about. Fans of Ms. Pratley's first books in the Painful Deliverance series will surely enjoy this more intimate peek into Samantha and Tom's relationship."

THANK YOU!

Thank you so much for reading my book, 'Sapphire of Prejudice' (Book #4 in the Forbidden Conflicts Series)'. I greatly enjoyed writing this story and I appreciate your enthusiasm for reading it.

~~~~

If you would like to make contact with me, please:
Visit My Website
http://authorannmpratley.wixsite.com/writingisbliss

Visit my Goodreads Author Page
goodreads.com/author/show/14777236.Ann_M_Pratley

Thank you,
Ann M Pratley
~~~~